snake eyes

masks #3

MELISSA PEARL

love ultimately wins ... as you can *imagine*

Snake Eyes, Book III, The Masks Series by Melissa Pearl
1st Edition published by Evatopia Press
2nd Edition published by Melissa Pearl Author 2018

www.melissapearlauthor.com

ISBN: 1721536507
ISBN-13: 978-1721536504

For Nana and Granddad, Grannie and Poppa

I was lucky enough to have all four of you in my life for such a long time. What a privilege it was. Thank you for everything you poured into my life over the years and thank you for cheering me on no matter what I was up to.

one

caitlyn

The coffees arrived at our table smelling like everything we needed them to be. I picked mine up and sniffed the scent with a happy sigh. Taking a tentative sip, I licked the foam off my upper lip and let out a satisfied moan.

Eric glanced over his laptop and chuckled. "Needed a kick, huh?"

"Oh, yeah." I cradled the mug in my hands and grinned at the waitress as she passed our table.

My laptop sat open in front of me, my class schedule all mapped out. Lectures for my sophomore year started on Monday and I so wasn't ready.

It had been the perfect summer, flitting between my place in L.A. to Eric's grandfather's place in San Diego. We even popped over to Hawaii with the rest of my family to see my sister, Holly, and her fiancé, Max, get married. Eric came, too, which was a total treat. It had been ten days of sun, surf, and luxury. And my parents had paid, so that was a bonus.

Since getting back, the prospect of school had been looming, but I put it off for as long as I could. I wasn't ready. After the disastrous start I had last year, getting caught up in Professor Hoffman's drug/gambling ring, nearly losing my life and my boyfriend for that matter, I was a little dubious about kicking off another year. Eric assured me everything would be fine. The rest of my freshman year had gone smoothly.

It helped that I'd basically stopped reading people. It was intentional. I just couldn't handle it anymore and decided I needed some time off, so every time people's masks began to slip and I saw something even vaguely sinister, I'd shove them back in place and turn the other way.

The homeless man I'd met two years ago never should have trusted me with the power to see what everyone was feeling. I'd nearly gotten myself killed twice and I wasn't ready to throw myself into the fray again. Instead, I pretended I was just like any other normal human being and tried to ignore the guilt that lived permanently on my shoulders.

I took another sip of coffee, briefly reliving my final encounter with the man who changed my life.

He smiled at me. "This is your path now, you must accept it."

"I don't—I don't want to! How am I supposed to help people? Everyone has something to hide! Everyone has problems!"

"Focus on the ones who touch your heart. It may be one, it may be five. Spend time with them, peel back the layers. As you learn to control your vision, you'll know what to do." He pointed at my heart. "Ignoring this will only make you miserable. Trust me, I know."

The deep shame and failure on his face made me want to cry.

"Help those around you, one person at a time, and you will have a full and happy life. You can do what I never did."

Well, I'd tried to do what he never did and it was awful. Sure, I'd helped people, possibly even saved lives, but I'd never signed up for this and the break was doing me good.

I frowned into my coffee cup.

"Hey, it's not going to be that bad. Our course

schedules aren't that different. We'll still get to see each other." Eric rubbed my knee with a tender smile, totally misinterpreting my expression. I went with it. We hadn't talked about my special eyesight in months and we both seemed happy to keep it that way.

I grinned back at him, placing my mug down and leaning back toward my computer.

"So on Monday, you have Human Neuropsychology at nine a.m. and I have Human Memory at the same time. Those classes are really close to each other; maybe you could swing past my dorm on your way in. We could walk there together."

"Sounds good to me." He wiggled his eyebrows. "Or you could just spend the night and we could drive there together."

I blushed.

Since Eric had moved out of the dorms and about two miles from the UCLA campus, he'd been using any excuse he could to get me to stay. I wasn't complaining or anything. Eric and Scott finding a 3-bedroom house to rent was everything my roommate, Piper, and I wanted. Now both our boyfriends lived in an off-campus house. It was freaking awesome.

It had happened just before the summer break. A contact of Scott's, Matt Houston, had two friends moving out and they snatched the spots up immediately.

Eric moved in as soon as school let out. Scott had moved in, too, but he was still in Palm Springs hanging out with his parents for the rest of the break. According to Piper, they were driving back on Sunday morning. I couldn't wait to see them. We'd spent the first half of this year hanging out together. After surviving the drama of exposing Professor Hoffman's underground gambling ring and organic drug operation, we became really tight. Piper had become a close friend and the four of us got along really well now.

I glanced back at Eric. His eyes were still on me. The edge of his mask began to slip and I pulled it away, his smile changing from a look of innocent sweetness to outright hunger. Oh yeah, he wanted me...bad. I bit my lower lip, igniting the expression even more. Man, I loved that he let me read him now. It made our relationship so open and free. Eric was often closed off from the world, protecting himself from anything that might hurt him, but with me, he was exactly himself and I loved it.

Gently closing my laptop, I ran my fingers up his arm and leaned toward him.

"Come on," I whispered. "Let's go do something about those hungry eyes of yours."

His eyebrows rose as he realized I had been reading him and then his lips broke into that killer-watt smile of his, the one that turned my legs to putty.

Snapping his laptop shut, he shoved it into his bag and, coffees forgotten, we headed for his jeep.

It didn't take long to get to his place; the coffee shop was only a couple of blocks away. We pulled into his driveway and grinned at each other. Matt's car wasn't in its usual spot, which meant there was a chance we had the place to ourselves.

We jumped out of the vehicle. A giggle bubbled inside me as I skipped up the stairs and stopped outside the wooden door. Eric let us in, slipping his backpack off his shoulder and placing it on the floor in the entryway.

"Matt, you home?"

The answer was a long beat of silence. Eric grinned at me, his eyebrows wiggling as he snatched me into his arms. I lifted my feet off the ground and let him swing me around, clinging to his shoulders as he carried me down the hallway.

When we neared his door, he placed me down, his lips finding mine and sending them into overdrive with his warm, coffee-tasting tongue. I grappled with his shirt, pulling it over his head as we stepped into his room. I ran my fingers down his hard body, savoring the feel of his rigid muscles. He had a surfer's body to die for. I knew, because I watched him out on the water most days and saw the way the beach bunnies eyed him as he jogged up the sand toward me.

He was the sexiest guy on this planet...and he was mine.

A thrill raced through me as the thought hit me once again. I still didn't get it. I didn't know what he saw in me, but I'd take it.

He lifted my shirt off, throwing it over his shoulder

before pulling me against him. Our skin smacked together and I let out a luxurious sigh. I was in paradise.

We stumbled toward the bed. The back of Eric's knees hit the edge of the mattress and we tumbled onto it, both laughing. The sound was cut off quickly as our mouths fused together. Eric held my head, brushing the loose strands of hair off my face with his thumb as our tongues danced.

I closed my eyes, getting lost in his touch. In a flash of movement he spun us over, his weight pressing down on me and filling me with that sense of security it always did.

I was so in love with him and the longer we were together, the more the feeling grew. I couldn't imagine ever being with someone else. He'd promised me that I'd be his girl forever and I knew down to my core that it was true.

We were meant to be, and nothing could break us apart.

two

eric

I nestled Caity against my chest and kissed her forehead, loving the feel of her naked body lounging beside mine. An afternoon of making love to this beautiful woman made me a happy man. My muscles felt like cooked spaghetti and I couldn't wipe the stupid grin off my face as I gazed up at the ceiling.

Caity let out that cute sigh of hers, adjusting her

head on my shoulder and drawing patterns on my chest with her finger. It tickled a little, but not enough for me to stop her.

Her trailing fingers stilled on my abs, her soft hand splaying over my skin before she went still. I wondered if she was drifting to sleep and I smiled. It was only four-thirty in the afternoon. Yes, it was definitely the life.

"You should hang some stuff in here. It's really bland."

Her soft voice startled me. I squeezed her shoulder and gazed at the walls of my room. I'd never really thought about it. Whenever I was in here I was either sleeping, getting dressed or distracted by the very sexy girl in my arms.

"I'm not really into artwork." I shrugged.

"It doesn't have to be artwork. It could be pictures of your family or the ocean or something."

I grunted, not loving the idea, but not opposed to it either.

"Like, you know that gorgeous one hanging in your grandpa's place? That would look great in here."

"No way," I snapped.

Her head swiveled on my shoulder, her eyes narrowing at the edges as she read me.

"What does that picture have to do with your dad?"

I gave her a dry look, wondering how she always knew to bring it back to my absent father. I really didn't enjoy talking about the guy.

Why had I snapped? I should have just kept it casual

and she never would have looked up at me. I wished I could control my temper better. It was such a curse sometimes.

Her permeating gaze wouldn't let up, so I eventually gave in with a sigh. "He shot that picture, okay? The guy was really into photography apparently, and for some reason Gramps likes to keep it up on the wall."

"The picture was taken by his son; you can't really blame him."

"A useless son who disappeared and never contacted him again."

Caity pressed her lips together before nestling her head onto my shoulder and looking back at the wall.

"Well, he was a good photographer."

I humphed, resting my cheek against her head and hoping like hell she'd drop it.

"Do you think you'll ever forgive him?"

I went still, hating the question.

How could I?

The guy had let me down in so many ways, chipped at the heart of a child until there was nothing except a lumpy piece of rock left...and then he'd just vanished.

I cleared my throat. "Look, it's done, okay. Yes, I really hate the guy for dropping off the face of the earth, but there's nothing I can do about it. He could be dead for all I know and I've had to move on. Talking about it is not going to solve anything and it definitely won't make him the father I want him to be."

"I guess we can't choose family."

"Nope. At least I've got Gramps."

"Yeah. It makes me realize how lucky I am. As much as I'm the tail-end, after-thought in my family, at least I know they love me and still remember to call and invite me..." Caity's voice trailed off, her head snapping off my chest. "Shit! What day is it?" She grabbed my wrist to look at my watch and check the date. "We're late!"

Flinging back the covers, she jumped out of bed, giving me a decent view of her tanned skin. I leaned up on my elbow, admiring her flurry of movements as she scrambled for her clothes.

"Get up!" She threw my board shorts at me. "Get dressed!"

"I'm just admiring the view."

"You can look at it later; get your ass out of bed! Mom hates it when we're late. Come on!"

With a groan, I threw off the rest of the rumpled sheet and moved to the edge of the bed. Caity paused while buttoning her little denim shorts, her eyes lighting with a smile as I stood tall. I threw her a droll look, which made her blush and giggle.

Her eyes traveled slowly from my chest to my pelvis as her tongue skimmed the edge of her lips.

"If you keep looking at me like that, these will not be going on." I shook the shorts in my hand. "And those will be coming off." I pointed at her shorts.

She whined in her throat before throwing on her shirt and mussing up her golden curls. "Let's go."

I quickly threw on my pants and collected my shirt

from the hallway, sliding it on as Caity snatched my keys off the entranceway table and opened the front door.

Although we were running late, I wasn't willing to risk a ticket, so I kept to the speed limit. Nerves got Caity's fingers twitching. She really hated letting people down, and her mother was always a stickler for time. Caity and I had been late on more than one occasion over the summer break and it hadn't gone over too well. It didn't help that we often walked in looking radiant and scruffy. I'm sure her parents knew exactly why we were late every time. I was grateful they hadn't said anything.

Leaning forward, Caity flicked on the radio, tapping her fingers on her knees as we caught the beginning of the five o'clock news.

"…eight kidnappings in the last three weeks. No one knows what's become of these missing girls or if the cases are even connected, but there is speculation that a serial killer may be on the loose. Police are struggling to find a solid lead and people are calling for FBI involvement—"

Caity flicked it off, her nose wrinkling. "I hate hearing about that kind of thing. It breaks my heart. I can't even imagine what those poor parents must be going through." She shook her head.

"The idea of a serial killer lurking around isn't much fun either. I don't understand people sometimes."

"Me neither and being able to read behind a mask doesn't always help. Some people are just sick and twisted, and there's nothing you can do about it."

I nodded, hating that she was right...and glad we were nearly there so the conversation could come to an end. The Davis's driveway was full of cars, so I parked on the curb, taking a quick peek at my mother's house, which sat right next door. I noticed her car parked outside the garage, along with a black Ford Mustang. It looked old school, like it'd been lovingly restored...a real American muscle car.

I smiled. That was good. It meant Mom was still dating that mechanic guy, and I kind of liked him. I made a mental note to pop over before we left.

Racing after Caity, I caught up to her just as she burst through the door.

"Hey, everyone! Sorry we're late!" She threw a wink over my shoulder and headed for the sunken lounge where everyone was gathered around Max and Holly who were over from Hawaii for a surprise visit. That was why the family was getting together. Even Toby had driven up from San Diego.

"What's going on?" Caity stood at the top of the stairs and looked down into the lounge.

Brody's head popped out from the fray. "Aunt Holly's pregnant and they're moving back to L.A. because Uncle Max doesn't have any family and he doesn't think they can raise a baby all by themselves without Grandma's help."

I kept a close eye on Caity's face as she absorbed the news. A smile bloomed across her lips, but I couldn't help wondering if she was a touch disappointed. Not in a mean jealousy kind of way, just in a *now I feel even more separated from them* kind of way. Everyone was so much further through their lives than us.

Caity already felt like the alien of the family and now that Holly, the young free spirit, was settling down, she'd feel like she'd have no one she could relate to.

Pillow talk had told me a lot in the last nine months.

I reached for Caity's hand and gave it a little squeeze.

"Wow. Holly! That's so great." Caity put on her best sunshine smile and descended into the living area with her arms outstretched.

Holly laughed as she hugged her kid sister. "I was actually pregnant at the wedding, but I didn't realize it. We had it confirmed three weeks ago. That's why we wanted to come over for this trip, so we could tell everyone in person."

"So how far along are you?"

"Ten weeks." She squealed. "Isn't it the best news?"

I walked into the living room and shook Max's hand, murmuring my congratulations. He gave me a nervous smile then chuckled as Mr. Davis slapped him on the back.

"So when are you guys moving over?" Caity stepped away from her sister, shifting to my side and giving Max a smile.

"Well, I'm going to stay from this point on and Max will go back and pack up our place." Holly's loved-up expression was radiant. Caity's mom looked ready to fly, her eyes brimming with tears, her lips stretched into a broad smile.

"You're going to live here?" I swung my arm across Caity's shoulders.

"Uh-huh, until Max finds a job."

"That's awesome. Congratulations."

"It's going to be so nice to have you home." Mrs. Davis rubbed her daughter's arms, a fresh batch of happy-tears brewing in her eyes. Holly turned and gave her mother another hug which Layla, the older sister, dove into as well.

Caity hung back beside me, suddenly jerking in my arms when her brother Toby jumped down the stairs and gave her butt a hard slap.

"Ow! Toby!" She whacked his arm and I curbed the urge to deck him.

I really hated how he treated his kid sister sometimes. He was the baby of the family before she came along shortly after his fourteenth birthday. Everyone else had swooned; Toby had made it his life's mission to tease Caity senseless. He claimed it was a rite of passage, having to put up with teasing from his three older siblings for so long, but I wished he'd drop it. The guy was in his early thirties, yet he still acted like an imbecile.

"Looks like the world's moving on without ya, little sis. More babies for you to look after." He chuckled, taking a swig of his beer. "See, I told these guys when

Mom got pregnant with you, you'd be good for something...plus, your old room's gonna come in handy, too. Hello nursery, right?"

"What?" Caity jerked again, but this was out of pure surprise.

"Toby, shut your mouth." Layla, now free from the hug, shot her brother a glare and rolled her eyes at Caity.

"You're turning my room into the nursery?" Caity looked at her mother, forcing a smile when the older woman glanced at her.

"Yeah, that's okay, right?" Holly waved her hand.

"Sorry, honey, I haven't had a chance to tell you. It's not like you've been around much lately." Her gaze ran over me before landing back on Caity. I swallowed, trying not to let the look bother me. Her parents approved of us together, but maybe they didn't approve of the pace we were setting.

Holly tucked a lock of dark hair behind her ear. "Mom figured yours is the best location. It's warm and dry and the perfect size. Max and I will be just next to it in my old room... and when you're home for the holidays, you can sleep in Toby's room."

"Where will Toby sleep when he stays?"

"I've graduated to the guest room." His smug smile was damn irritating. The guest room was the best room in the house, not counting the downstairs suite that belonged to Caity's parents. It looked out over the ocean, had a huge bay window and a skylight where you could see the stars at night. It was the biggest upstairs room by far and it was lush.

I pressed my lips together, squeezing Caity's shoulder as I remembered the weekend we spent in there when Caity's parents were away.

"What's the big deal, sis?" Toby nudged her with his elbow. "It's not like you're entitled to the guest room. You're the after-thought this family never meant to have. When it comes to the pecking order around here, you, little girl, are at the bottom of the food chain."

"Toby, shut up. You're such dick." Holly punched him in the arm and shot Caity a sympathetic smile.

"No big deal. I know he's only kidding." Caity's laugh was hard and plastic.

Seth jumped up behind his younger brother, throwing him into a headlock. I pulled Caity away from the action before our toes got trampled.

She looked up at me with a smile I saw straight through. I kissed her nose and let her read me. She blinked a couple of times and looked away, staying pretty quiet for the rest of the evening.

Thankfully, dinner was served soon after Toby's brainless comment and conversation rose around different areas of the living space. Caity and I went out on the deck with Layla and the kids. It was funny watching them eat and tell their cute little stories. Jake was nine and told jokes like a pro, with his little six-year-old brother butting in at frequent intervals. Layla kept rolling her eyes at her sons while encouraging her daughter to finish just a third of her meal.

"Come on, honey, just a few more mouthfuls."

I was so enrapt by it all it took me a few minutes to realize Caity had returned inside. Jumping up, I collected my plate and walked it into the kitchen, scanning the room for my girlfriend. With a little frown, I rinsed my plate and stacked it in the dishwasher before walking to the main hallway. I spotted the tail end of her slender legs disappearing up the stairs.

No one had seemed to notice her departure, and I was pretty sure no one would notice mine either. Running a hand through my hair, I made my way down the hallway, guessing Caity had returned to a room that would soon become a nursery.

three

caitlyn

I walked up to my room and nudged the door open with my toe. My desk and the surrounding floor were covered with empty boxes, ready to pack up all my stuff and store it away. I plopped onto my bed and scowled at the blank walls. I'd spent the night here less than a week ago and they hadn't said a word. Admittedly, Holly must have arrived and told them yesterday and they'd sat on the news while scrambling to empty out my room. I couldn't believe they'd made this big decision without consulting me and had already gotten to work.

Holly was only ten weeks pregnant for crying out loud. It felt a little extreme to be moving over so soon, and how long did they think it would take Max to find a job? They obviously planned on mooching off Mom and Dad for as long as they could.

I scowled, deep-down knowing the expression was brought on by hurt more than anything.

Toby was right...I was the after-thought no one meant to have.

I bit the inside of my cheek and looked across the room. The door gently swung open and I glanced back to see Eric leaning against the doorframe. His empathetic smile was totally going to break me.

I looked to the floor, digging my big toe into the carpet. "They've taken down my posters already."

With a soft sigh, he entered the room and sat down beside me.

"I used to watch you from that window, you know." I squashed my sheepish smile. "I used to live for the days you mowed the lawn."

He chuckled, running his finger down my forearm and threading our hands together.

"I always got the sense someone was watching me." Leaning his head against mine, he kissed my ear and tears sprang out of nowhere, lining my lashes.

"Why my room, Eric?" I drew in a ragged breath.

He squeezed my fingers. "Best location?"

I huffed. "Toby's old room would have worked."

"Yeah, but it probably smells like farts and stale sweat."

I giggled. "It totally does." I bit the corner of my lip, cutting off my laughter. "I don't get why this bugs me so much. It's immature and silly to feel this way. I don't think I'm moving back home after I graduate, so what's the big deal?"

"Maybe it's the fact they went ahead and did it without even discussing it with you."

I nodded. That was totally what it was. They hadn't counted me into the decision. My opinion was worthless. Yet again, it made me feel like the invisible alien of the family.

"I guess I am always the after-thought." I sighed.

Eric let go of my hand, his fingers moving to my neck and tenderly kneading the muscles. "Toby's a jerk. He shouldn't have said that."

"He's just thoughtless; he always has been."

Eric's massaging fingers shifted, making way for his soft lips; they nuzzled and tickled the sweet patch in the crook of my neck until I couldn't help a smile. Eric sat back and grinned at me, running his fingers lightly behind my ear. "You may be *his* after-thought, but you're always the first thought on my mind."

My smile grew and I leaned forward to peck him on the lips.

Pulling back, I rested my hand on his face and drank

him in. "Not to get way somber on this already melancholy conversation, but..." I bit the corner of my mouth. "I seriously feel like you're the only person on this planet who couldn't live without me."

"I couldn't." His look was so earnest I didn't need to peel away anything. There was no mask, just genuine honesty. Eric loved me, more than anything else.

"I couldn't live without you either." I smiled. "Never break up with me, okay?"

"I'm not planning on it."

"Good." I breathed in through my nose, my eyes once again stinging with unshed tears.

"You're my girl forever." He grinned before kissing me soundly and murmuring, "My sexy girl-next-door."

"My Hercules." I chuckled against his lips, swinging my leg over his thighs. He pulled me onto his lap, running his hands up my back and pressing me against him. I sighed into his mouth, grabbing two handfuls of his luscious hair and diving into another magical kiss.

"Want to go back to your place again?" I panted. "There's this view I really want to admire."

He pulled back with a laugh, running his eyes down my body and squeezing my hips. "I just need to go check on Mom first. I'll be back in about half an hour and then we can get out of here, okay?"

"Do you want me to come with you?"

"You're already having a challenging day. I won't unleash my mother on you as well."

I grinned, about to say it was no trouble, but then his

mask slipped and I could tell he wanted to go on his own.

"You want to check that the mechanic's still treating her good?"

He nodded.

"And you don't want me to be a distraction."

He nodded again, his cheeks heating with a blush.

"Okay." I reluctantly shuffled off his lap and pulled my shirt straight. "I'll take that as a compliment."

"You should; my mother adores you. I won't get anything but gushy sentiment out of her if I take you over there." He stood from the bed and winked at me.

We stepped out the door, threading our fingers together as we made our way down the long hallway and into the living area.

The ladies were congregated in the lounge, huddled on the couches chatting. I noticed Holly's hand on her stomach and guessed the conversation was all about babies. I cringed.

"Back soon." Eric kissed my forehead and called out to everyone that he was popping next door.

The front door clicked shut and I crossed my arms, slowly turning to survey the room.

"Way to skip clean-up duty, sis." I rolled my eyes at Toby who was pulling out a chair at the dining table. He slapped a deck of cards down as Dad opened the black box of chips. Max and Seth handed him a twenty-dollar bill each and he started counting out chips.

I glanced back into the lounge then listened carefully

and heard the strains of a Disney movie coming from the den. Weighing my options with a wrinkled nose, I finally headed for the table.

Leaning against one of the free chairs, I watched Toby shuffle the cards. "What are you playing?"

"The men are sitting down to a game of poker, Peanut." Dad grinned at me.

"Can I play?"

"Men only, sis." Toby tapped the deck on the table, ready to start dealing.

"Why? You afraid of being beaten by a girl?"

He paused, his eyebrow arching. "Do you even know how to play?"

I smiled. "Are you going with Five Card Draw or Texas Hold 'Em?"

"Does it make a difference?"

"Nope." I shrugged, pulling out the chair and sitting down.

Toby sighed, running a hand through his hair and throwing Dad a desperate look.

Dad glared back at him, his silent warning clear.

"Okay, fine. We'll go with Five Card Draw, because that's easier to explain. Now the way you play—"

"Toby," I stopped him. "I know how to play both. Eric's grandfather's been teaching me. I don't mind what we play, just deal me in." I leaned on the table and pulled a few rumpled notes from my back pocket. With a smile, I handed over my two tens and got back twenty dollars' worth of chips. "Thanks, Dad."

"You sure about this, honey?"

I ripped off Dad's mask and saw his uncertainty was actually worry. He thought I was going to lose, big time. I gave him a gentle smile.

"I'll be okay." I clicked my chips together and looked across the table.

The little smirk Seth was wearing made me puff with pride. Behind his mask was a very impressed older brother. He didn't think I had any chance of winning, but he was proud of me for trying. Max, always a little jittery anyway, seemed more nervous about playing his own game, and Toby...Toby looked smug. I whipped his mask off and saw he was actually way more than smug. He thought he was going to trounce me and he was looking forward to doing it.

I gathered my five cards and splayed them out in my hand. Usually when I played Eric's Gramps, Clayton, I made a special note to keep the masks in place. It was cheating to read the other players, but after glimpsing Toby's arrogance, I was so ready to cross that line.

Gazing at my hand, I noticed I had two fours, a king, a five and a two.

Hmmm. Slightly challenging to know what to do with. Did I risk trying to win on a low pair or did I go for the straight?

I glanced over my cards and skimmed each face, making sure they were all mask-less. Dad had his lower lip out and was nodding; he obviously had an okay hand. Max was frowning, shaking his head with a scowl, so he'd no doubt be folding unless he scored some decent cards in the exchange. Seth was grinning ear to ear and Toby had a deep frown.

I pulled every mask back up to compare what I'd seen and all of them were sitting like neutral dummies, their emotions tucked into hiding. I pressed my lips together, concealing my own smile as I peeled back each mask again.

"Max, you're first." Toby nodded at him.

Max chewed on his lip, scowling again before throwing one chip on the table.

"It's a two dollar ante, dude." Toby gave him a pitiful look.

With a sigh, Max picked up another chip and threw it in the pot. Seth threw in his two with a confident grin and then raised another two. Dad followed suit and so did I, throwing in my four chips. Toby considered the pot for a minute before throwing in four chips and turning to Max.

"I fold." He sighed, running a hand through his thick, black hair.

"You haven't even done the swap yet," Toby scoffed.

"I want to play more than three rounds. I'm not wasting my money on a bad hand. Know when to fold 'em." Max nodded, wincing at his no doubt late decision. His indecisiveness, and probably Seth raising the stakes, had already cost him two bucks.

I grinned at Max and saw the relief wash over his

face as he put his cards down.

Toby looked to Seth.

"One." Seth threw his card onto the table as Toby set the top card aside and threw him a new one. I watched Seth's face as he slipped it into his hand. His lips pursed to the side, a slight frown marring his features. I pulled his mask back up and noticed he was smiling. That little trickster.

Dad asked for two cards and his expression rose with confidence. The exchange obviously improved his hand.

I held my breath and threw in my four of hearts and king of spades and got back a five of clubs and a two of spades.

Well, not quite the straight I was looking for, but at least I had two pair. Admittedly they were pretty low pairs, but they were something.

Toby exchanged three cards and his frown deepened. Oh man, he had nothing.

A second round of betting ensued. Seth sat confident in his position, raising the bet by three dollars. Dad twitched a little then folded while Toby and I met the bet and then Toby went on to raise again. What an idiot! He had nothing.

I put his mask back in place and noticed his confident smirk. From the worry shimmering on Seth's face, he was obviously buying into Toby's bluff. Man, I wanted to say something so bad, but I couldn't.

Seth's lips twitched as he gazed down at his chips. Toby had brought the bet up to nine dollars, which was nearly half his chips. If he lost the round, he'd be out of the game pretty damn quickly. Being the sensible man he was, Seth quietly folded against Toby's smirk.

I narrowed my eyes and picked up two more chips.

"Call." I threw them into the pot and looked at Toby. My brother's head tipped to the side, uncertainty whistling over his expression as he stuck his chin out.

"You sure about that, sis?" His eyes narrowed.

"Oh, I'm sure." I grinned.

Clearing his throat, he laid his cards down with a sigh and I whooped with laughter as I laid down my two pair.

"What!" Seth looked at Toby's nothing hand then glanced at mine. "Aw, man! I had two pair, as well. Nines high. I would have won."

With a giggle, I pulled the chips toward me and neatly started stacking them. "You've got to have faith in your hand, Seth."

"If it wasn't for Toby's stupid smirking over there, I would have."

I laughed. "You should know better than to believe your little brother."

Toby gave me a glare and mumbled, "Beginner's luck," throwing his cards at Max. I pushed my cards toward Max, who collected them and began to shuffle the deck.

Sitting back with a grin, I rubbed two chips together and waited for round two to begin. The game was definitely improving my mood. I was going to relish cleaning Toby out of every last penny.

four

eric

Mom's house was quiet as I approached. I knocked on the door and let myself in, praying they weren't in bed or something gross. Thankfully they were sitting on the couch, watching TV. Cliff's legs were perched on the coffee table and Mom was draped against him, her head resting on his shoulder.

"Oh, hey." Mom grinned at me. "What are you

doing here?"

"Family thing at Caity's place." I pointed over my shoulder, inching into the room and flopping onto the one-seater adjacent to the television.

Cliff smiled at me then turned back to the screen, obviously not that interested in striking up a conversation. I eyed him carefully. I did like the guy; he seemed nice. I just really hated how much he reminded me of my father.

Why did Mom always go for men like that—long and lean with shaggy hair like mine?

I resisted the urge to openly scowl and turned back to Mom. Her eyes were bright, her dark hair shiny. Her fine features and high cheekbones made her beautiful. She always looked young for her age. It helped that, lately, there were no bags under her eyes and she actually looked happy and relaxed. I felt my shoulders loosen.

"Where are the girls?" I listened out for my little half-sisters, surprised they were in bed so early on a Friday night.

"They've moved in permanently with their father now." Mom's voice was tight, her lips pinching into a line.

I suddenly regretted my decision to leave Caity behind. I could have done with a read on my mom right then. She obviously didn't love the fact she'd lost the girls, but I couldn't help wondering if there was more to it. Maybe she felt like she'd failed them or something.

"When did that happen?"

"Just last week."

"I'm sorry," I murmured.

She shrugged, a tight tense one. "Their daddy's a strong man and he really wanted them full-time. His new wife is all nice and sweet so, you know, it's probably for the best. You don't come by hardly at all, so they had no reason to stick around."

I frowned at her snarky tone, but chose not to say anything about it. "When do you have them next?"

"This weekend. Their father's dropping them off tomorrow morning."

"Make sure you tell 'em I said hi. Give me a call if you like. Caity and I can take them to the beach."

"Don't trouble yourself." She turned back to the TV, resting her head on Cliff's shoulder.

I swallowed, not enjoying the guilt trip. I used to pop home all the time when I first started college, and if I was honest it was purely for the girls. After their dad moved back to town, I didn't feel the same sense of responsibility. They had started spending way more time with him and I wasn't really needed anymore. I hadn't realized Mom was feeling it so badly. To be honest, I thought she'd barely noticed. But now that the girls were gone too...

I pressed my lips together, swallowing down my sigh. Looked like I needed to start making more of an effort again.

"How's work?" I decided to go for a neutral topic.

"Oh, you know. Nails are nails."

"Still enjoying it, though?"

"For now." She shrugged.

Mom didn't have to worry about money. Her job was just to stop her from getting bored, and she'd always been into beauty stuff. She worked at a pretty nice place and had even done Caity's nails a couple of times.

She'd had a trust fund set up years ago, when her parents died, and she basically lived off the interest, gifting a portion to me every year, which I stuck in a bank account and only used when I had to. The fund also paid for my college education and it'd meant I hadn't had to work and study, which I was grateful for. I had no idea how long that money would keep coming to me, though. I guessed once I graduated and got myself a job, I'd be looking after myself.

I was running out of polite conversation. The main purpose of my visit was to check Mom wasn't being beaten or downtrodden, and that the girls were safe. Looked like that was the case. It was a huge relief.

"Well." I stood from the chair. "I better get back. I just wanted to check you were okay."

"Thanks." She forced a small smile and part of me wanted to tell her I loved her, just to get a proper grin, but it felt false.

I mean, yes, I did love my mother, but we definitely didn't have the kind of relationship where you said that stuff out loud. She knew I didn't agree with many of her relationship choices and when I started challenging her on them a few years back, something between us kind of died. She pulled back and I didn't feel like I should apologize for speaking the truth. So we settled for nice talk with an underlying knowledge that we may not see eye-to-eye, but we'd always be mother and son.

I bent down and kissed her cheek. "Have a good night, Mom."

"You too." Her gaze softened with a real smile.

I squeezed her shoulder and headed back out the door. Breathing in a lungful of air, I shook the awkward nerves off my shoulders and headed back to my girl.

Caity was right. Of all the people in my life, her and Gramps were the only ones I couldn't do without. It made me sad to honestly admit that, but it was true. Mom and I would never be close.

I knocked and let myself back into Caity's house. Closing the door behind me, I heard murmurs from different areas of the house and then a loud, "You've got to be kidding me!"

Turning for the dining room, I spotted Caity laughing as she pulled a pile of chips toward her.

Toby groaned, dropping his head into his hands. "I don't want to play with you anymore! No one ever calls my bluff!"

Caity shrugged. "Maybe if you didn't play it so often, it wouldn't be so easy to call."

His glare was dark with irritation. Collecting the one chip left in front of him, he tapped it on the table with a low growl.

Caity's father burst with laughter and squeezed his daughter's shoulder. "Nice going, Peanut. You've taken us all by surprise." He glanced up and noticed me. "How much poker have you three been playing down in San Diego?"

I chuckled, approaching the table and kissing her cheek. "My Gramps loves the game."

"Are you here to pick her up?" Toby snatched up the cards, tapping them on the table before breaking them apart to shuffle them. "Can you take her, please?"

"You don't want me to keep playing?" Caity gave Toby a cheeky smile while the rest of the men at the table laughed.

Sliding the chips towards her father, she waited for him to add it up and hand her eighty dollars.

I raised my eyebrows. "Impressive."

"This girl is a poker magician. I don't know how, but she plays like a pro. Your grandfather must be a pretty good teacher."

I swallowed back my chuckle, knowing exactly what made my girl so amazing. "He is." I cleared my throat and grinned.

Caity stood, folding the notes and sliding them into her back pocket before bending down to give her father a kiss.

"See you guys later!" she called into the living room.

"Good luck on Monday, sweetie. I hope it goes well," Caity's mother called back.

"And stay out of trouble!" Layla added. "No more

involvement with the police this year."

Caity rolled her eyes at me, her cheeks heating with color.

"I'll make sure of it," I called back, squeezing Caity's hand and pulling her out the door.

The night air felt great against my skin. Being outside always did my soul good. Wiggling my fingers out of Caity's grasp, I patted her back pocket. "Putting your powers to good use, I see."

Her grin was sheepish as she tucked a lock of hair behind her ear.

"I know I shouldn't cheat, but I just really wanted to put Toby in his place."

"Don't feel bad." I unlocked the jeep and held the door for her. "The look on Toby's face when I walked in was so worth it."

She chuckled. "I think it'll be permanently burned in my memory. Cleaning him out was the best feeling ever, babe."

I closed her door with a grin and ran around to my side.

"I probably should have rigged it so the others were left with some cash, too." She bit her lip.

"Maybe next time." I winked and gave her knee a little squeeze. "Fancy a detour on the way back to my place?"

"Sure. Where are we going?"

I wiggled my eyebrows. "Let's make love in the moonlight tonight."

The look in her eyes made my insides simmer. Without another word, I started the engine and spun the car around, heading for the private little cove we discovered over the summer. The perfect spot to show Caity how much I loved her, in the purest place I knew.

five

caitlyn

I shouldered the door open and slumped into my dorm room. It was Monday and I was already tired. We'd only been back at UCLA for one full week. Although I was determined to start the year off better than the one before, it didn't look like the workload would be any easier. I dumped my binder onto my desk, slid the bag off my shoulder and fell face-first onto the bed.

There was no hurry for me to shower or anything. Eric had a late lecture on Mondays and tended to head home straight after that. I'd see him Tuesday night.

I twirled a curl around my finger, wondering how I would spend my evening. I really needed to get on with my readings. If I got behind in the first couple of weeks it'd be a mad catch-up around exam time, and I wasn't sure I could cope with the pressure. I grimaced; the thought of study didn't thrill me. I sometimes wondered if I was cut out for college life, because I certainly wasn't inspired by it.

The door burst open, making me jolt.

"Caitlyn, this is huge." Piper, my gorgeous roommate, swung the door shut behind her, throwing her bag on the bed and spinning in a circle before perching on the edge of my bed. "This is epic. This is epically huge." Her petite hands spread wide.

Perching up on my elbows, I looked at her dancing green eyes. "I take it you have some good news."

"Yes!" She lightly slapped my leg.

My eyebrows rose in expectation and she did a little happy jiggle. "Matt's decided to quit college and move back to Utah. I have no idea why, BUT..."

And pause for effect.

"But...?" I pushed my chin forward, waiting for more.

"Hello! Caitlyn!" She slapped my leg again. "There's now a room available at the guys' house. A room we can have!"

My head shot back into position, my pulse accelerating as the news sunk in. "You want to move in with Scott and Eric?"

"Ya-huh!" She jumped from the bed and moved to her side of the room, unzipping her bag and pulling out her textbooks. "This is going to be so amazing. I can't wait!"

Piper got distracted by her makeup kit, pulling out her gloss and running it over her lips. It was like a habit she couldn't break. The girl had the world's shiniest lips, I swear.

I sat up, swinging my legs over the bed. "That's kind of huge, isn't it? Moving in with our boyfriends?"

"Why?" She popped the stick back into the tube and twisted it before turning to face me. "I'm going to be living with Scott eventually anyway."

"You seem pretty certain."

She shrugged. "After all the crap I went through in high school and then the whole near rape thing my junior year, Scott and I took things real slow. In fact he said he wouldn't sleep with me until I was sure I wanted to marry him."

My mouth dropped open. "He knew he wanted to marry you in high school?"

Piper shrugged. "Apparently he's been in love with me since moving to Palm Springs, but I was just too stupid to notice. That night he busted in and saved me from that mondo creep..." She shuddered. "It was like destiny or something. It seriously did not take me long to work out we're meant to be together. We've already talked about it. I know we're not officially engaged yet, but we will be one day." She dropped the gloss back in her makeup purse and zipped it closed.

She glanced back at me, her glowing smile faltering. "Caitlyn, I can't believe you're not all over this."

"It's just, you guys are so young."

Perching on her bed, she leaned forward, her expression taking on a quality I hadn't seen before. I was tempted to peel her mask away and see what was behind it, but it was too beautiful. I didn't want to ruin it.

She gave me a soft smile. "I may not have decided my major yet. I might have seven different careers before I finally retire, but I *know* no matter what my future holds, I'll be with Scott Ferguson. He's my constant and the only thing I am completely certain of. Why should I hold off moving in with him because of what other people might think? I don't care. They can say whatever they want." Her smile grew, her eyes matching Christmas lights as she gazed at me. "I just...I know, Caity. I know with every fiber of my being that I'm supposed to be with him." She shrugged. "Scott's my one. Don't you feel that way about Eric?" Her head tipped to the side, confusion wiping that pure, love-struck look off her face.

I sat back and thought for a second, not wanting to be flippant with my answer. Nibbling my lip, I looked to the ceiling, picturing my boyfriend and unable to stop a smile forming. "I can't imagine being with anyone else, *ever*... but it does seem really soon to move in with him."

"You're not moving in with him. You're moving in with me." Piper winked. "He'll just be around." She waved her hand in the air.

I chuckled at her cheeky grin.

"Oh, come on!" She squeezed my knee. "You have to come with me. Besides, it's not like you'll be sharing a room with him."

I tipped my head, giving her a dry look. "You've seen Eric, right?"

She bit her lip with a grin.

"I'd get nothing done. Like study would never happen." I paused, actually loving the sound of that, but knowing better. I pressed my lips together. Oh, man, the proposal was so damn tempting. Move in with Eric. Live with a great bunch of people, off campus. It would be epic! But...

"Look, you'll be fine." She flicked her hands in the air. "You can study in the library."

I frowned, still not sure why I wasn't buying into this.

Would Eric be cool with me moving in?

Would my parents?

I couldn't imagine it. That conversation would no doubt end up being a big talk about my future and if I was really old enough to settle down with someone.

"I'll be your sex police." Piper's comment snapped me out of my thoughts.

"Excuse me?"

"You know, like, you can't do it until your homework is done." Piper laughed then jumped up with a squeal. "Caitlyn, this is going to be so awesome! We can move in next weekend! I'm so excited I can barely stand it." Spinning around, she reached for her purse, checking her wallet and phone were inside. "I'm heading to Student Services now to let them know my change of plans. Do you want to come?"

"Actually, I just need a minute to think about it."

Her shoulders drooped, confusion marring her pretty features.

"I want to." I raised my hands. "Like, it sounds amazing. I just want to check with Eric first."

"Okay, I get it." She shrugged and reached for the door handle. "But trust me when I tell you, it's going to be great. Eric's in love with you. There's no way Scott would have asked us to move in if Eric hadn't been cool with it."

"Then why hasn't he said anything?"

"Maybe he's waiting for Taco Tuesday."

Taco Tuesday—I grinned—my favorite night of the week. The little Mexican place Eric and I discovered over the summer basically knew us by name. We'd walk in and I could say, "The usual, please," and they'd totally know what I was talking about. I'd always wanted to go to a place like that. Our discovery back in early June had been a little nugget of gold. We went as many Tuesday nights as we could and I was glad Eric wanted to keep the tradition going, even after college started.

"Think about it, Caity. This could be the start of our best year ever." Piper winked and swept out the door, her enthusiastic flurry of movements a testament to her pure excitement.

I fell back onto the mattress, running my fingers into my hair.

Did I like the idea of living with Eric?

YES!

Did I feel too young for something so monumental?

Kind of.

But was that really a big deal? I'd practically been living with Eric all summer anyway.

So what was I so afraid of?

I had no idea, but I did need to have an honest answer ready before I spoke to Eric.

six

eric

As per usual, the tacos had been delicious. I couldn't get enough of those things. Rubbing my over-stuffed belly, I hid my grimace. I really needed to control myself better. I felt near sick from stuffing my face so full, but I'd been a little edgy. Caity had been quiet since I picked her up and I could only guess why.

Because my guess was no doubt spot-on, I'd

chickened out and not raised it, instead filling meal conversation with talk of school and the idea of a night surf on Thursday.

Caity nodded sweetly at my chatter and filled me in on her own, but we'd danced around the big topic of conversation like two idiots. The worst thing was, we both knew we were doing it.

The restaurant door eased shut behind us and we stepped into the night air. I gathered her fingers within mine and gave them a little squeeze, a chuckle escaping my lips before I could stop it.

"What?" Caity glanced up at me, her blue eyes luminous under the street lamp.

"We're being idiots." I stopped, pulling her against me and grinning down at that perfect face.

"I know." Her nose wrinkled. "I'm sorry. I guess I was waiting for you to bring it up. To be honest, I was kind of surprised Piper told me before you did."

"Yeah, well, Piper wasn't supposed to say anything." I sighed, letting her go and capturing her hand again. I gently pulled her along and we ambled toward my jeep. "I hadn't told her not to; I just assumed she would leave it up to me."

"You assumed? With Piper?"

"Yeah, yeah, I know." I rolled my eyes with a snicker.

"So, you like the idea then?"

"Of you guys moving in? Of course." I nodded.

Caity's eyes narrowed at the corners and she stopped me under the next street lamp, holding my face and peering into it. My eyebrows rose and I stayed still as she read me, her expression melting to putty then washing with uncertainty.

"Wow, you're way cooler with this than I thought you'd be." She bit the edge of her lip and let me go, stepping back and shoving her hands into the back pockets of her jeans.

I frowned, assessing her and trying not to let my fears hinder the steadiness of my voice. "You don't seem certain at all."

"I'm not." She shrugged.

Ouch. Okay, that hurt.

I thought she'd be as excited as Piper. *Damn, I wished that didn't sting so bad.*

I lifted my chin and nodded, trying to be stoic.

Scott and I had chatted about it after I got home last night, imagining how it would all play out. I'd been so pumped by the idea that by the time I went to bed, I couldn't sleep. It took all my willpower not to text Caity at two in the morning and ask her if she was in. When I'd found out that Piper had already told her and Caity hadn't even contacted me about it, deflated was the best word to describe my mood.

Determined not to let my buried wounds trample over my common sense, I drew in a breath and stood strong. All I could do was trust she felt the same way about me as I did about her...which meant her deciding to move in or not had nothing to do with me.

"Caity, just say it. Why don't you want to move in?"

Her sigh was short. "The thing is, I do. I *really* do, but I'm..." Her nose crinkled as she pursed her lips, fighting for the right words. "The truth is...I love this." She pulled a hand from her pocket and pointed back and forth between us. "Like, a whole lotta love it, and I don't want to ruin anything." Her fingers ran into her hair and she grabbed two handfuls, looking at me with worried eyes. "What if you get sick of me? What if being together all the time makes us fight?"

My lips broke into a grin. "We practically lived in each other's pockets all summer and we had one small fight over where to eat dinner that night, remember? You weren't feeling well and I was shitty about...something."

"It was your dad's birthday," she mumbled.

I nodded, looking to the ground with a sheepish grin. "Maybe I should worry about you getting sick of *me*."

"That's not possible." She stepped into my space, running her hand up my chest and resting it on my collarbone.

"Then how would it ever be possible for me to get sick of you?"

Her face turned crimson, her big eyes looking adorable as she swallowed and shook her head with a shrug.

I caressed her cheek with my thumb, lightly running the tips of my fingers over her soft skin. "I understand your reservations, but this could be really cool."

"I just don't want anything to ruin what we have." She shrugged. "I feel really young to be moving in with my boyfriend and even though you are the only guy I ever want to be with, it just...it feels huge and I can't even explain why I'm hesitating."

"It's okay to be nervous. I am, too, but I just know...you know?"

She grinned.

"I love you, Caity, and nothing is going to come between us. I won't let it. "

Her smile was golden as she stretched up toward me. I met her lips with a soft kiss of promise.

"I love you, too." She pressed her forehead against mine.

"Then move in. I promise we'll keep the lines of communication open and you can totally read me, so I really don't know what you're worried about."

She giggled, closing her eyes and looking embarrassed by her fears.

I kissed her nose, lightly squeezing her waist.

"Okay," she finally whispered.

"Okay?" I held her back from me so I could see her face.

"Yeah." She nodded. "It's gonna be great."

I snatched her into my arms and lifted her off the ground, spinning her in a circle. "It's going to be more than great." I kissed her neck. "It's going to be epic."

Her body shook with laughter as she launched into the story of Piper's big announcement. I placed her on the ground and wrapped my arms around her shoulders, leading her to the jeep.

The tension between us had been decimated and we strode to the car with easy, relaxed steps, our free conversation leading into logistics for the weekend move.

I couldn't believe how excited I was. It was so not my style, but Caity...she was the one. I had absolutely nothing to doubt or fear. I was certain we'd be together forever and couldn't imagine anything getting in the way of that.

seven

caitlyn

Since opening up to Eric, I felt free. My nerves scuttled into hiding and the idea of moving in with him and my friends had me soaring. Piper and I started packing on Wednesday, which gave us plenty of time to get organized before the boys turned up on Saturday morning to help us.

I decided to let my parents know about the move

after I'd moved in. I figured the money they put toward my dorm room could just as easily be transferred to rent. Piper had already checked it out and because we were leaving so early in the school year, we were entitled to a refund. With the rent being split amongst the four of us, it was actually going to be quite doable. The plan was falling into place perfectly, and Saturday morning couldn't have come fast enough.

Heading up the stairs, I walked toward my room, planning on fitting in an hour of concentrated study before Piper showed up and we could get on with a little more packing.

Although I didn't feel like studying, I was determined; I wanted the weekend to be schoolwork-free and that meant a little sacrifice now. I could do it.

Swinging my door open, I dumped my books on the desk, unzipped my bag, looked at my bed and screamed.

"What the hell!" I placed my hand on my chest, my heart ready to explode.

The long, lean woman sitting on my bed snickered, tucking a lock of short, straight hair behind her ear before raising her sharp eyebrow at me. Everything about her was pointy and mean...just like I remembered.

"Agent Kaplan, how did you get in here?" I sucked in another lungful of air, my heart rate toying with the idea of returning to normal.

She uncrossed her long legs and leaned forward, gazing at me with those steely eyes of hers.

"I can pick locks, sweetheart. Now sit down." She flicked her head at my desk chair.

I hesitated, running my fingers over the wood until her eyebrows rose and I couldn't shrink away from her emphatic look fast enough. I lifted my bag off the chair, perching on the edge of it and trying not to be put off by the powerful woman.

Wrenching off her mask didn't help at all. This woman had no vulnerabilities. She was cold like steel, all the way through. I shoved her mask back into place, preferring the slightly milder version of what I was seeing.

Kaplan gave a short nod, happy with my compliance before her eyes scanned the room. She lifted her chin at the box of books behind me. "You going somewhere?"

"I'm moving in with some friends of mine." I scratched my cheek, not wanting to say too much. "They live a few blocks from campus. A room's just opened up, so..." I shrugged.

Kaplan cleared her throat and leaned back, her eyes narrowing. "Yeah, that's not going to happen."

"Excuse me?"

"I need you living in the dorms." She pointed to Piper's bed. "Quite convenient that your feisty little roommate's moving out, though."

My heart jerked to a stop, a tight anger pulling at my muscles. I gripped the seat of my chair. "You can't tell me where to live. I'm going in two days."

"Caitlyn." She sighed. "I need you for a job and in

order for you to do that job well, I need you to stay in the dorms."

Clenching my jaw, I forced air in through my nose, worried I'd pass out if I didn't. This could not be happening again.

"I don't work for the FBI," I finally managed between locked teeth.

"You will for this project. You're the best fit for the job."

Damn it. She couldn't assume I'd just jump at her beck and call. So I'd done one sting operation; that didn't make me her employee!

"I'm not staying here." I swallowed, meeting her iron gaze.

"Yes, you are and here's why..." She reached behind her and grabbed a stack of manila folders. With a little flick, they landed on the desk beside me.

Not wanting to look but knowing she wouldn't leave unless I did, I flipped the top file open. Gazing back at me was the headshot of a beautiful girl with fine brown hair and a mousy grin, her big hazel eyes dancing. She looked in her mid-teens.

"Who is this?"

"Her name is Angela Redding, and she's been missing for fourteen days."

I went still.

Kaplan edged down my bed so she was sitting closer to me. "Look at the next file."

I pulled out the next one and flipped it open. A girl

who looked slightly younger than Angela with light mocha skin and big brown eyes gazed at me. A luscious waterfall of ebony hair cascaded over her shoulder and the soft smile on her lips told me she was as sweet as pie.

"That's Rowena Murphy. She's only thirteen years old and she went missing three weeks ago." She reached across me and pointed to the rest of the files. "Natasha Burns, aged 12; Felicity Newman, 15; Serena Townsend, 13; Melanie Harper—"

"Okay, stop." I ran my finger down the stack, estimating at least ten files.

I shuddered, closing my eyes and squeezing my temples.

"They're all missing, Caitlyn. All snatched away within the last three weeks, and I need to find them."

"Where do you think they are?"

"We're not sure, but I have a lead I want to follow. That's where you fit in."

My head snapped up, bile surging in my throat. "Does your boss know about this?"

"He's given me permission to follow this lead, and I need an undercover girl who can get access to the man I want."

Fear coiled up my spine, wrapping invisible tentacles around each vertebrae. What the hell was she expecting me to do?

"Who is he?" I managed.

"His name is Diego Mendez. We're pretty certain he

has ties to the Mexican Cartel. We tried to pin him for drug trafficking a couple of years ago, but nothing stuck. Every time we go after this guy, he comes away clean. I need enough to get me a search warrant. If I can just get into his place, I know I'll find something."

I swallowed at the venom in Kaplan's voice. Pulling her mask free, I finally glimpsed something different. Her eyes were dark with unspoken agony... an old wound buried deep, maybe? Pure hatred for this guy was driving her on this one. She wanted him, bad...and this time around, the case had nothing to do with her one hundred percent success rate and everything to do with this man. I wondered what he'd done to her.

"And how am I supposed to help you do that?"

"His daughter starts UCLA this year. I need you to befriend her. That's our in."

"I don't—"

"You have a special ability, Caitlyn," she interrupted. "Don't waste it. With your gift of sight, you could be the best damn undercover agent we've ever had."

I gave her an incredulous look. "I nearly screwed up your last operation."

"Your boyfriend nearly screwed it up. We got our guys thanks to you, and I need your help again."

"I'm only nineteen. I have absolutely no training. I can't do an undercover operation for the FBI."

"Think of this as a one-off, 'under the table' type case. The only people who know you're working it are me and my team. They've been sworn to secrecy. And as for training, your ability—"

"I can't do it!"

"Caitlyn." She sighed, her voice taking on a soft quality I wasn't used to. "These girls..."

"Are probably already dead. The news said it was a serial killer."

Kaplan pursed her lips, lifting her eyebrows with a nod. "The news is wrong. I don't think they're dead. I think they're being sold."

My insides tried to lurch out of my throat. I clenched my jaw, swallowing the lump restricting my airwaves. "Human trafficking doesn't exist in the States. That's an Asia thing, isn't it?"

"Are you really that naive?"

My face crumpled and I could feel the tears brewing.

"They're beautiful girls, Caitlyn, and there are a bunch of sick men out there who want them."

I glanced up, catching that look again, that raging agony.

"They need someone to follow this lead. They need someone to find them before they're sold across the border and we've lost them for good." She stood from my bed, straightening her jacket. "Right now, you're the best chance they've got." She placed a business card on my desk. "I'll leave the files with you for twenty-four hours. Don't show them to anyone. This is a private matter." Clearing her throat, she walked to the door. "You have my number. I need your answer by tomorrow night."

With that, she flicked back the door and left.

Shock immobilized me for a long time. It wasn't until my phone dinged with a text that I finally jerked out of my stupor.

It was Piper.

Running late. Will be there in thirty to keep packing. Squee!

I threw the phone on my bed, unable to reply. My eyes traveled back to the files. I'd have to hide them before Piper got back. Running my finger down the stack, I randomly pulled one free and flipped it open.

My breath evaporated as I stared at the image of a stunning girl who looked similar to Eric's little sister, Lacey. The very idea of her being taken and sold to some vile creature made me want to wail. Tears burned my eyes as I placed it on the top and pulled the stack into my arms. Hugging the files against me, I sniffed at my tears.

What the hell was I supposed to do now?

eight

caitlyn

Sleep was impossible. I tossed and turned until well after midnight, begging for sleep to capture me, but it didn't play fair.

I knew the right answer. I knew what I had to do and it seemed insane that I was fighting the decision, but I was, because I didn't want to.

Going along with Kaplan would hurt my friends. I'd

have to lie, pretend, make up one excuse after another, not to mention be on full alert the whole time around this girl I was supposed to befriend.

It would mean reading people again and having to keep pulling back layers even when I saw the bad stuff.

Plus, Kaplan would make me lie to Eric; that was a certainty, and I'd promised him I'd never do that again. He was the kind of guy who needed the truth.

The assignment would be horrendous on so many levels. Any logical, normal person would tell Kaplan she was crossing way too many lines involving me in this and she could take a long walk off a short pier.

But not me.

Because I wasn't normal.

I'd hidden the files in my backpack. They were heavy, but easily mistaken for textbooks when Piper moved the bag to get beneath my bed.

We'd pottered around most of the evening, pulling pictures off the walls and gathering up the last of our things. I moved like a snail, something Piper noticed rapidly and tired of just as fast. In the end, she gave up and went to take a shower. I sat on the bed like a dummy until she returned, then I pasted on a breezy smile and blamed tiredness for my behavior. She bought it and we'd both headed to bed early.

I was grateful Eric had been out surfing. He'd have taken one look at me and known straight off that I was lying. It was going to be damn hard to hide this from him.

I cringed. Would it be the end of the world if I let him in? Would Kaplan let me do that?

Covering my face, I dug my fingers into my forehead, wanting to unleash a scream, but I couldn't. Piper was asleep and I'd rather die than wake her. Softly flinging back the covers, I inched out of bed, pulling a pair of loose sweats over my boxer shorts, snatching up my backpack and easing out of the room.

The air outside was warm and thanks to my flat chest, I could easily get away with walking around campus in my pajama tank top. Thankfully it was plain black. If I did bump into anyone at this late hour, they probably wouldn't even notice.

I headed to the 24-hour McDonald's down the street, knowing their Wi-Fi was pretty good. I bought myself a coffee and headed for a booth in the back corner.

Flipping my laptop open, I selected my favorite search engine and typed in: Angela Redding.

Because of her recent disappearance, it wasn't hard to find the right news article. I read through it then followed several more links, my eyes watering as I took in her parents' desperate pleas. The short, local news clip I watched showed the girl's mother and younger brother crying at the camera, their wobbly voices pleading for someone to find their bubbly ray of sunshine.

As much as it killed me, I then went on to look up Rowena Murphy. I stumbled across a Facebook campaign begging for information on the girl. She was a straight-A student and had just started her freshman year at Arcadia High School in Phoenix, Arizona. I didn't have complete access to her Facebook page, but her profile shot and cover photo were gorgeous. I could immediately tell she was a quiet, thoughtful girl with a passion for nature.

I gulped down another mouthful of coffee, trying not to choke as I imagined what was being done to her.

My fingers were shaking as I opened the next file and took in the picture of the Lacey look-a-like, Janey Templeton. She was from Southern California, had been born and raised in San Diego, not far from where Eric's grandfather lived. She'd been snatched on her way to school, and her disappearance hadn't even been noted until third period due to a glitch in the system. The school's apologies were falling on deaf ears as her parents tried to come to terms with the fact that their only child was missing.

Reports and speculation varied across the board. The serial killer story seemed to be sticking, but the disappearances spanned across four states - California, Arizona, New Mexico and Nevada. To me, it seemed unlikely a serial killer would travel that far—not that I knew anything about that kind of thing. Who knew how accurate those cop shows were, because they were my only experience with this kind of crime.

I wished they were my only experience with *any* kind of crime.

My shoulders twitched as I relived the gun being pointed at me by Professor Hoffman last year. If the FBI hadn't busted in the door when they did...

I pinched my bottom lip and gazed at the screen. Janey's open smile was so innocent and sweet.

If Kaplan was right, the girl would never smile that way again, because she'd be sold and hurt and her innocence would be ripped from her. Even if we did find these girls, they'd still be damaged. How did you recover from being snatched against your will and locked away somewhere?

My breaths grew short as my imagination took off again, picturing one horrifying scenario after another, hearing the girls' terrified screams as they were dragged into a darkened room.

Slamming my laptop shut, I spread my fingers over my computer, fighting for air. Leaning my forehead against my hands, I felt the scream work up my body, desperate to break free.

"Miss, are you okay?"

I sat up with a jerk, scaring the McDonald's attendant.

"Yes." I forced a shaky smile. "Sorry."

Snatching up my things, I shoved them into my bag and threw it onto my shoulder, keeping my eyes on the floor as I left the fast food eatery.

I burst out the glass doors and sucked in two big lungfuls of air.

A trashcan stood five feet away. I was tempted to

shove my bag, with all the information I didn't want to know, straight into that thing.

But I couldn't.

The truth was, I could run as hard and as fast as I wanted. I could walk, I could drive, I could fly out of the city, but I would never be able to escape what I knew...unless I did something to stop it.

nine

eric

"Okay, so you guys will get there at eight, and we really don't have that much stuff. Between Caity's Mini, your jeep and Scott's car, we'll easily be able to fit everything in." Piper grinned at me.

I nodded, kind of done with hearing the logistics for the next morning.

Scott dipped a French fry in ketchup and popped it

in his mouth. "We bought Matt's bed off him, so that third room is all set to go. Caity, we weren't sure if you wanted to move your stuff straight in there or into Eric's room."

I glanced across at her, but she wasn't listening. She was staring at her soda, spinning the straw around in circles and then, yet again, peering over her shoulder at the table of tweens who hadn't stopped giggling since they arrived. Their squeals and loud antics were borderline irritating...although they did remind me of my kid sisters and I couldn't help finding them just a little cute.

"Um..." Scott cleared his throat. "Caity?"

I gently nudged her arm with my elbow.

"Huh?" She spun around to face us.

"What is your problem tonight?" Piper threw a balled-up napkin at her.

Caity bashed it away with a half-hearted laugh before scratching the side of her neck and glancing over her shoulder again. Scott gave me a quizzical frown, which I shrugged at. I ran my hand lightly up Caity's back.

"Babe, are you okay?"

Pulling on her earlobe, she twitched beneath my touch then sat up straight.

"Would you guys hate me if I changed my mind about the whole moving-in thing?"

There was a long, silent beat while we all absorbed her words.

My initial reaction was a perplexed frowned.

She winced and looked down at her plate.

"What?" Piper snapped, having finally found her voice.

Caity drew in a shaky breath. "I just, um...the thing is, I'm nervous. This feels like a really massive step, and I'm not sure if I should take it yet. I've been trying really hard not to feel this way, because it's totally insane. I should want to say yes more than anything, but I just..." Her eyes flicked up to me, begging for forgiveness.

That look always turned my insides to mush. I gave her a soft smile.

"What the hell is wrong with you?" Piper wiped her mouth with Scott's napkin and dropped it on her plate, her pouty lips in a sharp line. She looked like a snake, ready to bite.

I gave her a warning glare, which she promptly ignored.

"I thought we'd agreed on this. You can't just change your mind at the last minute."

"Yes, she can." I softly stood up for my girl. Not that I wanted to, but like hell would I let Piper make her feel bad. Caity was already tortured over this; anyone could see that.

"I'm sorry. I don't want to let you guys down, I really don't, but I...I need some more time. I don't know if my parents would approve of me moving in."

"You haven't told them yet?" Piper looked incredulous. "I don't get why you're stalling on this. It's going to be awesome." Her hand flicked in the air. "And besides, who cares what your parents think? You don't need their permission. You're a grown woman; you can make your own decisions."

"Pip," Scott said quietly. I could tell he was rubbing her leg beneath the table, his gentle way of telling her to take it easy.

Piper gave him a sharp scowl and huffed, crossing her arms and flopping back against the booth seat.

Caity blinked rapidly, running her finger beneath her nose. "I knew you guys wouldn't get it, so I've been trying to pretend and go along, but...now it's crunch time and I'm not...I'm not ready," she squeaked, tears winning the battle and sliding down her cheeks.

"Hey." My heart pinched as I brushed the first few away. "It's okay. You're not letting anyone down. If you're not ready, you shouldn't be moving in. It's an open invitation; you can change your mind at any time."

"Not if she wants a refund from student housing," Piper grumbled.

I threw her a dark look. She caught it this time and made a face at me.

Caity swiped at her tears. "Piper, I'm sorry I'm backing out. I just need a little more time in the dorms."

"Why? That's insane?"

"Just because you're ready doesn't mean I have to be." Caity's eyes bunched at the corners, her face crumpling as she took in Piper's real expression. I wished I could see it, too. "It's not you...any of you."

She looked at each of us. "I love you guys and that's why I didn't want to say anything before, but I have to be honest with myself. I'm scared that living together will screw up what we have. There's a big difference between hanging out a lot and actually living together."

"We've been living together for the last year. It's been fine." Piper's forehead creased and I was starting to see the hurt buried beneath the anger; not the way Caity could, but there was a glimmer. Maybe I saw it because Piper and I were alike in more ways than I wanted to admit. We were happy to let the anger show, that part was easy, but getting down to the raw vulnerability scared us senseless.

"It wasn't fine the whole time," Caity mumbled, another tear breaking free.

Piper opened her mouth to say more, but I raised my hand before she could. "Ease up, okay? So she's not ready; big deal. I can cover the extra rent so money's not an issue, and Caity can move in when she's ready."

"That'll be fine." Scott gave us a closed-mouth smile and I guessed he was squeezing Piper's leg, telling her to shut up and let it out later when they were alone.

I mouthed, "Thank you" at him and he gave me a quick wink.

Caity sniffed, grabbing the paper napkin off the table and blowing her nose.

I rubbed my hand up her back, gently squeezing her neck and kissing the side of her head.

She gave me a watery smile. "Maybe I can sleep

over a few times a week and we can work our way into this."

"It's not a problem. No pressure, Caity, honestly."

She studied me for a moment and I let her peel back as many masks as she needed to. I felt surprisingly calm about it all. Maybe it was seeing her cry that did it. I wanted my girl to be happy and if she wasn't ready, I refused to take it personally. Living together was a big deal, and I actually liked that Caity was taking the decision seriously.

"Thank you for understanding." She smiled.

Piper scoffed in disgust, robbing that beautiful look from Caity's face. I thought more tears were about to form, but then the table of tweens erupted with giggles. We all turned to watch them as they snorted and choked on their drinks.

Caity turned back to look at me and sniffed out a chuckle. Her eyes were once again dry and her expression, although still sad, seemed peaceful. Obviously telling us the truth had been a huge burden off her shoulders.

I couldn't say I wasn't disappointed with her answer, but like hell I was going to make her feel worse.

Above all else, I wanted Caity to be happy and I'd do anything to make that happen...even if it meant sacrificing what I wanted. If I truly believed we were meant to be together forever, then what was a few months of waiting? She'd come around eventually, I could feel it in her...she just needed a little time.

ten

caitlyn

Although it felt good to finally accept my decision to help these girls, it still didn't take away the sting of letting my friends down. Eric was being really good about it. I could see underneath it all that he was disappointed, but he was hiding it well and doing everything to make sure I didn't cry again.

My tears had actually been quite genuine, unlike my

reasoning for moving in with everyone. In some ways, it was a blessing I had initially hesitated. It made the whole *I'm not ready* pitch so much easier to sell.

Piper always took time to adjust to things she didn't like. It was a compliment that she was so annoyed with me. She really did want me to move in with them, and I hated hurting her.

The next few weeks were going to suck, big time. I already couldn't wait for it to be over. I was determined to work as quickly and efficiently as I could. I needed to get as much information from this Mendez girl as possible...not just for those poor girls, but also for myself.

I let out a heavy sigh as Eric drove us back to UCLA.

"Hey, don't worry about it. Piper will get over it."

"Yeah." I rubbed my aching head. "I just really hate it when she goes all ice queen on me."

"That's just who she is. She's not really one to hide her emotions."

"She can when she wants to," I muttered.

"What was she feeling tonight?"

"Hurt," my voice wobbled.

"I thought so."

I huffed, wishing I could just drop the charade, but feeling like I needed to sell it just a little more. "I really wish I could explain to everybody that it's nothing personal."

"Hey, we know that." Eric squeezed my knee. "She just needs time to process her disappointment."

"And you?"

Nerves skittered through me as I gazed across at him. His jaw clenched for a second before an easy smile drew his lips north.

"You already read me at the table. You know I'm disappointed, but I care enough about you to want what makes you happy. If you're not ready, you're not ready. I know you still love me."

He braked at the traffic light and gave me his full attention.

I could have drowned in that soft smile and was tempted to say, "*Screw Kaplan; I want to move in with you!*"

I pressed my lips together and looked out the window. "I'm sorry I made you sad."

"Maybe just a little." He winked at me. "But I am happy you're being honest with me. I would hate you to move in if you didn't want to."

I swallowed, the word *honest* ringing in my ears.

When this was all over I'd have to tell him the truth. Would he hate me? Forgive me?

Why did I have to take this risk?

"I'm so torn," I muttered.

The light turned green and Eric accelerated through the intersection. "It's better to take your time and feel confident about a huge decision like this."

I flashed him a smile. "You're so good to me."

"That's 'cause I love ya."

My insides did that giddy dance they always do

whenever he said that to me. I shuffled in my seat, drinking him in as I leaned against the window.

We paused at the next intersection. Eric's fingers hovered next to the indicator. Right would take us to the UCLA campus, left to his place.

"Want to sleep over?" His voice was a little husky, and I couldn't resist it.

"Yeah," I whispered, not caring that there was a chance I'd bump into Piper the next morning. I just wanted to spend the night with my man.

With a broad grin, Eric flicked the indicator left and we headed to his place.

Scott's car wasn't in the drive, which meant we had the house to ourselves for a bit.

Eric walked through the door and stripped off his shirt as we headed down to his room.

"I'm going to have a quick shower. Want to join me?" He grinned.

I wanted to say yes, but there was something I needed to do.

"Actually, I might just hide out in your room if that's okay." I trailed my fingers along his bare torso.

He snatched them up and kissed my knuckles. "Back in a minute."

I waited until I could hear the shower running before grabbing my phone and Kaplan's business card. I dialed her number and held the phone to my ear with quivering fingers.

"Kaplan," she answered.

"Okay, I'm in."

She paused for a beat and I could almost see the smile forming on her sharp face.

"Good. Meet me tomorrow morning at nine for a briefing. I'll text you the address."

With that, she hung up. I pulled the phone away from my ear and switched it to silent, not wanting Eric to hear any kind of text alert. Sliding the phone into my back pocket, I unbuttoned my jeans and took off my shirt, sliding between Eric's sheets in nothing but my underwear. I'd need to get up early in order to get back to my room and collect the files hidden in my backpack.

Pulling a pillow toward me, I scrunched it beneath my chin and gazed at Eric's headboard. Although I knew I'd made the right decision, it didn't take away the sense of dread simmering in my belly. I had no idea what this meeting would entail, but I knew I'd have my work cut out for me.

No part of this assignment was going to be easy.

I closed my eyes and drew in a slow breath.

The girls.

I just had to think about the girls.

eleven

caitlyn

Kaplan chose a dinky little diner up in Santa Clarita. It took me about forty minutes to get there, but I didn't mind. I wanted the drive after a stony conversation with Piper that morning, which in retrospect had been the perfect excuse to leave as quickly as possible.

Eric understood that I didn't want to hang around and help her move. Although the truth was, I actually did want to be there, except I wanted to be putting my own boxes in the back of Eric's jeep, not taking off to have a clandestine meeting with a woman I didn't even like!

I pulled my Mini into the small diner parking lot and stopped next to a black SUV which I assumed was Kaplan's. Didn't the FBI have any other kinds of vehicles? Black SUV, tinted windows—it basically screamed law enforcement.

Flicking open the door, I spotted Kaplan immediately. She was in a corner booth, away from the windows. I nodded and smiled to the waitress who told me she'd bring me a menu.

Dropping into the booth seat, I forced a tight smile. "Parked next to your SUV."

"Not mine." Her thin lips smirked. "This is an undercover operation; you seriously think I'd bring a black SUV? It practically screams FBI."

I hid the scowl I wanted to throw at her snarky tone by looking at the tabletop.

"The less people who know about this, the better. So far it's just you, me and my two guys — Rex and Eddy."

"That's it?"

"My superiors know I'm trying to go after Mendez, they just don't exactly know how."

I frowned.

"Don't worry, I'll write a full report when this is over—dot every i, cross every t—but I need to keep things under wraps until then."

I could tell she was lying. Her report wouldn't include every single detail. If we succeeded in this case, she was going to fudge the facts, probably like she did on the last one, playing down my involvement to a bare minimum in order to cover her own ass. All those freaking interviews I'd sat through with the FBI and the police, they'd probably been for nothing. I could see the guilt scorching the edges of Kaplan's expression and wondered how she'd gotten away with it. She was not shy about admitting she played dirty sometimes. She did whatever it took to catch the bad guys and she never failed. I bet her bosses even turned a blind eye as long as she got the job done...

Rubbing my thumb over my knuckles, I squeezed my fingers, suddenly doubting myself. This could potentially be the world's worst decision. I thought about Piper and Scott setting up home together while Eric helped out then went for his surf. I should have been there with him. Eric should have been helping me unpack my stuff, but...the girls.

I closed my eyes and swallowed.

"Here you go." The waitress's voice was chipper as she handed me a menu. "Coffee?"

"Yes, please."

She put the mug down and poured it for me. I snatched two sugar packets and emptied them into the dark liquid before splashing in a little milk and stirring the heck out of it.

"Having fun with your whirlpool?"

My head snapped up to take in Kaplan's raised eyebrows before I whipped the spoon out of my overflowing cup and tapped it on the edge.

With shaky hands I lifted it to my lips, spilling a few drops onto my jeans.

"Look, calm down. You'll be useless to me if you can't control those emotions. Now, take a breath."

I sucked in a slow breath and closed my eyes. "Okay."

"You did fine with our last sting operation. You're going to be fine with this one, too, but I need you to stay focused. Can you do that for me?"

My eyes popped open and I met her gaze with a short nod.

"Good." Kaplan slapped a file down on the table. "Quella Maria Mendez."

I flicked it open.

"Born January 4th, 1998."

I gazed down at the photos. There were no really clear shots of her, just long-lens stuff, most a little blurry. She wore big glasses in over half of them and was surrounded by men in suits.

"I take it she's well protected."

"This is the first time Daddy is letting her roam free, which is why I'm suspicious. My guess is he's getting her out of the way while he starts up his new business."

I grimaced. "Human trafficking. How can you call it a business?"

"Because that's exactly what it is and that's how these men see it. These girls are just a commodity to him; something that will earn him big bucks. He doesn't care."

My eyes fell back to the page. "But he obviously cares about her."

"Yeah, well, she's his daughter. I guess she's the exception to the rule."

"But, how can someone who has children do this?"

"That's irrelevant," Kaplan snapped. "I don't care about the psychology. I just want you to help me get these girls back."

"Yeah." I nodded. "Of course."

The waitress approached and Kaplan snatched the file back. I flipped open the menu, feeling anything but hungry.

"Blueberry bagel, please."

"Is that all?" she asked with a friendly grin.

"Um...and a fruit bowl. Thanks."

"Egg white omelette." Kaplan handed the menus to the waitress and flicked her hand in an obvious *buzz off* gesture. The waitress took it with a kind smile, but I could see the glare behind her mask.

If she wasn't careful, Kaplan might end up with more than egg whites in that omelette. I squashed my grin, focusing back on the file slapped in front of me.

"The girl spent most of her life growing up in Albuquerque and Palm Springs. Those are where the two main family homes are. She has been home-schooled by several different tutors and she's basically been raised by two nannies who have been there since her birth. Her mother died when she was six."

"Wow, that's sad."

"She's had a charmed, sheltered life. I wouldn't feel too sorry for her. She was probably closer to her nannies than her mother anyway."

I'd had Kaplan's mask off since sitting down at the table, so it wasn't hard to miss the wave of jealousy riding over her features.

Jealousy? What was that about?

"I have a feeling Mendez owns one more home somewhere. We haven't been able to find any financial trace of it, but it's a gut-instinct thing. He has a business of operations somewhere and I need you to find it."

"If he's sending his sheltered daughter off to UCLA so he can start up some shady business, he's not going to be bringing her back to his hub of operations."

"Mendez hasn't been seen in either Albuquerque or Palm Springs for the last two months, and his daughter arrived in L.A. from an undisclosed destination. My guess is he's sending her off to iron out the kinks in this new operation of his, but as soon as he has it up and running, he'll want her back. Even if you can't get her to take you wherever the hell he is, at least you can do some snooping into the other places. There has to be something somewhere, some little clue that will open up the can of worms we need."

I could feel my eyes narrowing at the corners as I

watched Kaplan's face. Her desperate need to get this guy was showing again. She was hungry for it, ready to sacrifice anything, and everything, to get it...including me.

I sat back with a cautious frown. "You know, you didn't say anything about me sneaking into someone's house. You just said get to know this girl, that's all."

"Yeah." She nodded. "Enough to get inside her father's life. I need you to read her in order to get to him...and then read him. We need evidence, Caitlyn. We need the location of these girls."

"You don't know for sure he has them."

Kaplan slammed the table with her fist, making the coffee mugs dance. "It's him." She pointed at me. "Caitlyn, it is *him*."

I leaned back from her rancor, licking my lips and breathing in through my nose. "I don't want to go to some hidden location."

"You won't be alone. We'll keep a close eye on you throughout this entire thing. We need to find these girls. Whatever it takes." Kaplan's eyes were sharp and unrelenting. "You can't back out now; you've already said yes."

I couldn't help firing a cold glare right at her. Trying to hide the sick foreboding brewing in my stomach was a challenge, but I kept my expression hard and angry.

She smirked at me before taking a slow sip from her mug. Placing it back on the table, her expression snapped back into business mode. I threw her mask on, tired of watching the hard emotions within her. She was right, I had said yes, and those girls needed me to stay strong. I couldn't back out on them.

The breakfast arrived just as I sat back. I thanked the waitress and she smiled at me before simpering at Kaplan behind her mask. I squashed my grin and looked away from the egg whites. Oh, yeah, they definitely had something gross in them.

Kaplan doused them in salt then grabbed up her fork.

"Now, Quella has been at Rush all week trying for a place with Lambda Theta Alpha and has unfortunately missed out."

"Thanks to you?"

Kaplan's tight smile told me she was responsible.

"So I've pulled a few strings and she's going to be moving in with you."

I swallowed, hating that idea. It burned so much more knowing that I had the chance to be out of the dorms and living with my boyfriend.

"You need to watch everything she does, get her talking. Go through her stuff when she's not there, be a real sleuth about it, okay?"

I squirmed in my seat, pushing my bagel around the plate as Kaplan shoveled in a forkful of food.

"I don't like the idea of going through her stuff."

"Please don't be a princess about this. The sooner we get the goods, the sooner we can find these girls...before they're sold. If they're purchased by someone across the border, which is highly likely, they are gone for good. You understanding me?"

I gave a stiff nod and tried to swallow the lump in my throat.

Placing her fork down, Kaplan reached inside her bag and pulled out a black phone.

She placed it next to my plate. "You need to call me every night with an update. Even the smallest comments can be researched. We need to know exactly what's going on at all times. Rex and Eddy will be on a rotation, keeping an eye on you, so you don't have to worry about your safety."

"Why would I be worried about my safety? I'm just making friends with a freshman, right?"

"Right." Kaplan accented her T, making nerves skitter down my spine. Peeling her mask off confirmed the fact she was making this job out to be far less dangerous than it actually was.

She could sense me reading her and tried to open up her expression, but it didn't really work. All I got was a true snapshot of her desperation. This case seemed so much more than work and I wanted to know why.

"You seem pretty desperate to get this guy."

"He's selling underage girls for sex; of course I'm desperate to get him. I want this asshole locked up for life." Her venom was sharp and exposing.

"Are you related to one of the girls or something?"

Her eyes snapped to mine. "No! Why would you think that?"

I shrugged, trying for casual in an attempt to dampen the fiery warning on her face. "You just seem more emotionally invested in this case than you were in the Hoffman one."

"Slap my mask back on, sweetheart, and stop reading into everything. The stakes are higher this time, so obviously I'm more invested," she finished sarcastically.

Liar. The way her eyes had rounded when I said the words "related to" definitely pushed a button. Something pretty big was fueling her and it worried me. What kinds of lines would she be willing to cross in order to axe the demons haunting her?

"We need you, Caitlyn. You can't let us down."

The lump came back into my throat with a force so strong it was hard to swallow. If she'd said *me*, I could have brushed it off, but she used the word *us* and I knew she was talking about those helpless girls.

It didn't matter if Kaplan was doing this to settle some past vendetta. It wouldn't change the fact that those innocent girls needed rescuing.

All I could do was nod.

"And I'm serious about keeping this to yourself. Do not let Eric know what you're up to. It'll be a challenge, but you put on the best damn show you can, you got me?"

I kept nodding, the lump still thick in my windpipe.

Images of those young girls' faces buzzed in my brain for the rest of the meeting.

I was in, and there was nothing I could do to stop it. I felt like I was on an express train heading for a broken bridge.

Yes, that did sound kind of dramatic, but the responsibility I felt for those girls was enough to paralyze me. If I screwed up, we could lose them to a life of slavery...and I couldn't live with that.

I drove back to UCLA in a daze, feeling overwhelmed and under-prepared.

It wasn't until I pulled into my spot on campus that I realized my phone was off. I quickly turned it on and it dinged with a message from Eric.

Hey babe. Move went well. I'm hitting the water now if you want to come down and join me. Love you xx

I smiled and checked the time. He'd been out for just under an hour. If I hurried, I could make it down to the beach in time to meet him.

I scrambled out of the car and raced up to my room, the idea of seeing Eric helping to dull the buzz in my head. Yes, it was going to be hard to pretend around him, but I couldn't let that stop me from seeing him. I just needed to come up with a good story.

Swinging my door open, I kicked off my shoes and rummaged in my suitcase for a bikini. I needed to unpack again. I rolled my eyes, hating the idea.

Pulling off my shirt, I unzipped my shorts and wiggled into my bikini. It wasn't until I was tying the neck strap that I spun around and noticed the three Louis Vutton suitcases on Piper's old bed. My legs gave out and I slumped onto my mattress.

Those bags belonged to Quella Maria Mendez.

Holy crap, this shit was suddenly real and there was no backing out now.

twelve

eric

The waves were sweet. The sun was shining and my entire body felt relaxed as I bobbed in the water on my board. I could see a new set rolling in and watched them, eyeing up which wave I thought could give me the best ride. Spinning my board around, I lay flat, ready to paddle. The energy in the water flowed through my fingertips. It was like the ocean was talking to me, telling me what to expect.

Pulling in a breath, I paddled hard until the wave caught my board. Jumping fast, my feet landed on the board and I balanced quickly, twisting my body and bending my knees. I couldn't help a smile as the ocean moved beneath me, the board flying across the wave. I banked up, hitting the top of the wave and spinning back down. My eyes caught the beach when I came down and I spotted my girl, her hand raised against the sun as she scanned the water for me.

It was a relief to see her. I'd tried calling a couple of times that morning, but her phone was off. I was glad she got my message.

I slipped from my board and dove into the water. Yanking on the leash around my ankle, I pulled the board toward me and slid on top of it, paddling for shore. The waves carried me in and I jumped up, snatching the board beneath my arm and running up the beach.

Caity's sundress fluttered in the breeze, flashing her turquoise string bikini. She looked so damn hot in that thing I could barely stand it. Her long legs were sun-kissed, the rich tan giving her an edible quality. I grinned as I dug the board into the sand beside us then gathered her into my arms.

Her breath tickled my skin as she laughed into my shoulder.

I squeezed her against me and kissed her face, then worked my way to her lips. They were a hot contrast to my cold, salty ones, but she didn't seem to mind. Her fingers gripped a handful of my wet hair and she dove into the kiss with a fervor I wasn't expecting.

Finally, I pulled back for some air. I kept her firmly against me, though; otherwise, the entire beach would be able to see the effect she had on me. I blushed just thinking about it.

She felt me against her and gave me a wicked grin— the little minx.

I cleared my throat. "So, how was your morning?"

"Good." She shrugged, her nose wrinkling. "Just went for a drive to clear my head."

"Did it work?"

"Sort of." She nibbled at her lip. "How was Piper?"

"Fine." I tucked a lock of hair behind Caity's ear. "The move went smoothly and when I left the house, she was pinning up posters in that third room...just in case you change your mind. As far as I can tell, no one else is going to be invited to live with us."

"That doesn't make you feel like a third wheel, does it?"

I grinned, hoping to ease her worries. "It's okay, babe. We don't have to talk about this again."

She sighed, looking a little glum.

"Are you sure you've made the right decision? You seem really sad about it."

She closed her eyes and pressed her forehead against my shoulder.

"It's what I need to do for now," she mumbled.

Placing my fingers against her chin, I gently forced her to look at me. Her dark look fled and she replaced it with a smile. "It won't be forever and knowing there's a place waiting for me feels good."

I couldn't help a niggle. Was she telling me the truth? She seemed so torn.

Caity's blue eyes narrowed at the corners, went large for a second, and then suddenly brightened. She stood on her tiptoes, pressing her lips against mine before letting out a cheerful laugh.

"I need to stop worrying so much about letting you guys down. I think that's what's making me feel so unsettled."

"You do worry too much about that."

She drew in a breath. "I've made the right decision and I need to stick with it for a little while. If I change my mind next week or three months down the track, that's still cool, right?"

"Right."

She grinned. "So I just need to let go and not be so afraid of hurting everyone's feelings. This is right for me."

"And you're happy?"

"Yeah." She nodded. "Well, more peaceful, if that makes sense."

I nodded.

Her smile seemed strained but then she chuckled again, erasing my concerns.

"And Piper will forgive me."

"She'll probably make you sweat a little first." I winked.

"And you're not mad with me?"

My head tipped to the side. "Of course I'm not mad with you." I squeezed her waist. "It's more important to me that you're happy. I just hope you get a decent roommate."

I nearly said, "*Or maybe I don't, because then you'll want to move in sooner*," but I bit my tongue. She didn't need that kind of pressure.

Caity's chuckle faltered. It had a nervous quality that I wanted to understand. Although she said she felt peaceful about her decision, she wasn't really acting like it.

Caity cleared her throat and smiled. "There were suitcases on the bed when I went back to change."

"What was she like?"

"I haven't met her yet, but you know what..." Caity licked her lower lip. "I'm gonna make a real effort this year. She's probably a freshman and feels nervous. I want to take her under my wing and make her feel welcome, you know?"

Her eyes were locked on the horizon over my shoulder as she spoke, her head bobbing robotically. I brushed her cheek with my lips.

"That sounds like you, Caity. Always looking out for those in need."

"Yeah." The word came out in a breathy laugh and then she swallowed, her eyes still gazing past me. I thought I saw a wave of sadness washing over her again, but I didn't have a chance to look properly because she pulled me tight against her and wouldn't let go.

Part of me wanted to pull back and figure out what was going on, but another part of me—the louder part—told me to stay quiet.

So I kept my concerns to myself and held her, soaking in the feel of her perfect body clinging to mine.

thirteen

caitlyn

"See you tomorrow." I grinned again and planted a farewell kiss on Eric's lips.

I stood there waving as he pulled away, and waited until his jeep was out of sight before finally letting my shoulders droop. Usually, spending time with Eric relaxed and rejuvenated me, but the afternoon had been draining. I pulled my sundress straight and headed up the path to my dorm.

Wearing my game face around my boyfriend was the last thing I wanted to do. I'd never had to be anything but me around him and it was hard to keep my emotions in check. Every time I caught him trying to analyze my mood, I snapped into a brighter, fake version of myself. I tried to be subtle about it and I think I did an okay job, but talk about feeling like a schizo.

Eric would tire of me quickly if I didn't get myself together around him. He'd probe in that sweet, gentle way of his until I'd let everything spill...and then Kaplan would be super-pissed and I didn't know if I was brave enough to face that.

Besides, letting my protective boyfriend in could jeopardize this investigation and I couldn't do that to the girls.

They needed me to succeed and if Eric knew what I was up to, he'd do everything in his power to persuade me against it. And when it came to persuading me, Eric was a freaking Einstein.

I mean, yes I could probably argue my case and eventually win him around in my soft, gentle way, but Kaplan would have a hissy fit.

I placed my hand on the glass door entrance and sighed.

Was that so bad?

I closed my eyes.

Yes, that was so bad.

I didn't think I had it in me to fight Eric on one side

and Kaplan on the other.

"Just think about the girls," I murmured. "What do they need you to do?"

They needed me to shut my trap and get on with finding their captor. If Kaplan's hunch was right, which I got the impression it always was, then I had to stay the course.

Eric could live without the truth for a little while and then when it was over and the girls were safely back in their homes, I could tell him everything. Yes, he'd be annoyed with me, but after his rant, he'd calm down and let me explain...and then he'd forgive me.

Oh, man, I hoped he would.

He loved my compassion, my inability to turn my back on those in need, but he hated it when I put myself in danger. I'd just have to be extra careful not to do that.

I sighed. This was going to be harder than I thought.

Plodding up the stairs, I reminded myself of the girls and their plight. They would have to stay my central focus or I wouldn't make it through this.

I reached the top of the stairs and turned for my dorm room. The door was ajar and I peeked my head in with a smile.

Quella was standing over her suitcases. They were flung open, clothes spilling out of them and over her shoulder.

"Hi, you must be Quella." I slipped into the room, pasting on a sunny smile and instantly missing Piper.

Thankfully I'd had lots of practice with forced enthusiasm throughout the afternoon, so it was easy enough to hide my disappointment at being in this position.

I'd be a freaking smile expert when this was over, I could feel it.

Quella's head snapped around, her dark brown eyes gauging me. Her head tipped to the side like a sparrow, assessing her surroundings.

"Hi." She gave me a wave, her long, skinny fingers wiggling in the air.

"I'm Caitlyn, but you can call me Caity." I stuck out my hand and she hesitantly grasped it. It was like shaking hands with a limp fish. I slipped my hand into my back pocket and bobbed my head. "So, welcome to UCLA."

"*Gracias.*" She smiled and shook her head. "I mean thank you."

Her Spanish accent was relatively thick. It was obviously her first language.

She tucked a lock of straight, brown hair behind her ear and began playing with the long strands, running her fingers over the ends.

I pulled her mask away to see how nervous she really was and had to press my lips together to fight my surprise.

Well, wasn't that interesting?

The coy, little rich girl was anything but. I could see the spark in her eye. There was a wildness to her that was desperate to break free. She was just weighing me up, seeing if I was the girl who could make her college fantasies come true. She was ready to let loose, party, experience every indecent thing college had to offer her.

I could see her hunger for it.

This sheltered home-schooler was ready to unleash, and with no Daddy around to stop her, she was going to do exactly that.

"So, um, can I help you unpack?"

"Oh, no, that's okay. I'm trying to decide where I can fit all my clothes. It may take some time." She was not impressed with the closet space. Lucky for her I wasn't a shopaholic like Piper. There would have been major closet wars if those two roomed together.

I bit back my grin as I imagined the scene.

"I don't have that much stuff, so feel free to take more of the closet."

"Thank you."

Okay—so she was totally expecting me to say that. Probably because she was used to getting everything she wanted.

Putting back Quella's mask, I did a quick comparison.

She smiled sweetly and pulled out another shirt, draping it over her arm. "Are you sure it's okay? I do not want to be a bother."

"Absolutely. It's not a problem. I'm here to help you with whatever you need." I smiled.

Her mask slipped in time with my broad grin and I could see her disappointment. She probably thought I was going to turn out to be just like her sunny, over-helpful nannies. Someone else to mother her and lap at her feet like she'd had all her life.

I nibbled my lip. She was never going to open up to me if I was that to her. I had to give her what she wanted in order to break that sweet, innocent shell. I had to become that person she'd trust as a friend and confide in. I had to be her partner in crime.

Damn it!

I wanted to step away so bad. Let her find someone else to cause trouble with. College partying was so not my scene, but I had a job to do and if this girl would open up around me then the chances of a little rhetorical faux pas were that much higher.

Sucking in a breath, I closed my eyes while her back was turned and screamed at myself to man-up and just do it.

Think of the girls, Caity.

The breath whooshed out of me and as she turned to face me, I put on a smirk. "You know what, screw unpacking and closet space. We can do that any old time. It's Saturday night; we should be out having fun. I know this great bar just around the corner. You've got a fake ID, right?"

Her lips parted with a silent gasp before growing into an electric smile. "Not yet."

"Why don't we go and do something about that." I

winked.

She let out a little squeal as I reached for my phone and did a quick search. I'd overheard two guys chatting in my class the other day about a guy in Rieber Terrace who supplied IDs for the newbies. It cost eighty bucks and he'd do it on the spot if you paid more. I Googled his name and soon found his room and contact details.

I linked to his Facebook page and sent a message.

Got a newbie who needs a rush ID. Heard you're the man for the job. You around now?

Grabbing my wallet, I flicked out the ID card Stella had given me two years ago—Martha Woodgrove. I cringed, still unsure why I'd kept it for so long. Maybe it was for such a time as this. Snatching my skinny jeans off the end of my bed, I wiggled into them and threw off my sundress, picking out my pink, low-cut tank top. I kept my bikini underneath, not feeling comfortable enough to change my underwear in front of Quella yet.

I shoved the ID into my back pocket along with a few twenty-dollar bills, and turned to my new roommate who was wiggling into a tight black top that accentuated her breasts. I raised my eyebrows and nodded in approval.

She did a little shimmy and then covered her mouth, letting out a blushing giggle.

I grinned. "You're gonna need some cash; these IDs can be pricey."

"No problem. Money is never an issue for me." Her smile was demure, but I could see the pride behind it.

Hmmmm, spoiled brat hiding behind a good girl mask.

I was going to have to play this one carefully.

My phone dinged.

In room for the next hour. Come over right now and I'll set you up. $150 for a rush job.

"Let's go." I slipped the phone back in my pocket and reached for the door.

Quella snatched up her purse, her smile a mixture of jitters and sheer excitement. She'd never done anything like this before and she was loving it.

She followed close behind me, falling in step once we got outside.

"When I missed out on Rush, I was so worried I'd be lumped with some geeky roommate who wanted absolute silence so they could study all the time. It's such a relief to meet you, Caity."

"Yeah, you too." I was desperately trying to think of my high school bestie, Stella, and how she used to behave. She was a party-chick to the max and always played it cool and casual with me.

She was always going on about being hard to get.

Be mysterious and hard to get, Caity. It entices people.

Well, it damn well better work, because what I was doing went against every instinct in my body. My only comfort was that Quella seemed to be a party virgin. Her sheltered upbringing would do me a world of favors, because hopefully she wouldn't notice what a total novice I was.

My mind raced with all the things I needed to consider...

How to get her to open up, yet also keep her out of trouble.

How to keep this new act hidden from my boyfriend.

How to make this work while still keeping everyone around me blissfully unaware of what I was up to.

I rubbed my temple, quickly dropping my hand and shaking it out when Quella looked at me. She didn't need to know my head was pounding. I was party-girl Caity right then and I needed to act like it.

I threw on a smile as we rounded the corner and headed into Rieber Terrace, silently crossing my fingers that I'd be able to claw my way out of the huge hole I was digging myself into.

fourteen

caitlyn

The bar was noisy and chaotic. We got in without a sweat. The IDs both withstood the test and now, we sat at a little round table drinking beers. Quella offered to buy the first round. I ran my thumb up the cold bottle, carefully sipping at it and hating the flavor. It was an effort not to grimace with each swig. I'd tasted beer before, but never really loved it. If I ever wanted to get rip-roaring drunk, my best bet would be shots—quick and fast.

Quella gulped down another mouthful of Corona, trying to hide her grimace. She obviously wasn't used to it either. I'd kept her mask off all evening so I guessed all her expressions were exaggerated to me. She wanted me to think she was cool. The idea of coming across as anything other than sophisticated was humiliating to her. I narrowed my eyes a little, wondering how I could play on that.

I looked across the bar, scanning faces and trying to think how I could get Quella talking with information that would actually help the case. It was pretty damn hard with the pulsing music thrumming through my head, not exactly conducive to intimate conversation, but I highly doubted she'd want to go hang out at the beach.

My eyes traveled back to my drinking buddy, bobbing in her seat like an excited school kid as she sipped at her beer. I noticed some guys leaning against the bar and checking us out. Quella blushed, her lips quirking with what she thought was a flirty smile. That was the last thing I needed.

Leaning forward, I touched her arm.

"Don't be so obvious about it." I flicked my head at the guys. "Play it cool. Mysterious and hard to get is way sexier."

Her face blanched. Swiveling away from the guys, she rested her beer on the table. "So, how would you play it then?"

Man! This was so not me.

I didn't know.

Conjuring up every image I could remember about Stella, I sat back in my chair and swung one leg over the other. "Pretend you haven't even noticed them or you have, but they're really not worth your time."

"Will that make them want me more?"

"Oh yeah." I took a swig of my beer and licked the gloss off my lips, feeling like a total fraud. Like I honestly knew how to pick up guys! It was a freaking miracle I ever scored Eric! But he wasn't like these guys. He didn't lurk around bars trying to pick up chicks; he was all about the genuine article.

I swallowed, guilt singeing me.

"Once we're done here, we could maybe hit the dance floor." She wiggled her eyebrows. "That would really make them hungry, don't you think?"

I nodded and shrugged, trying to play it cool while screaming in my head, "*I don't want to make those douchebags hungry!*"

"Let's finish our drinks first." I tipped my bottle at her.

Quella nodded enthusiastically and started gulping hers back.

I raised my eyebrows and shook my head. "You don't drink much, do you?"

She pulled the bottle away from her lips, her expression asking me if once again she'd let her complete naivety show through.

I snickered. "Stop trying so hard. Play it cool. You don't want to get completely wasted while the night is still young. Stretch it out, have some fun." Okay, Stella would so never say that, but I had certain lines I wasn't willing to cross. I'd be useless to everyone drunk. Although, it would probably work in my favor to get Quella a little tipsy.

I raised my beer again and took a sip. I subtly spat my mouthful back into the bottle. Super gross, but it was starting to make me queasy and I had to keep my head in the game.

Thankfully, Quella didn't notice and took another sip, but some of it dribbled down her chin and she scrambled for a napkin. I handed one to her and put on a pitiful look.

She wiped her mouth and winced. "I guess I am so obvious. I scream small town, don't I?"

I wrinkled my nose. "Parents pretty strict, huh?"

She rolled her eyes. "My father. Yes."

Although her tone was scathing, I could see how much she adored the man. She obviously had no idea of his creep factor. I couldn't help wondering for a split second if Kaplan had it wrong. Was Mendez really behind this?

"It is a miracle he even let me come here."

My insides pinged. Was I about to get some goods on her dad? I took a second to respond, wanting to maintain my casual, slightly disinterested demeanor.

"Oh yeah? Where did he want you to go?"

"Correspondence school."

"No shit! That would have sucked."

"I've been home-schooled my whole life and dreaming of this day for years. I begged to go to a real high school ever since I was thirteen."

"Well, high school kind of sucks, so you got the better end of the deal. Believe me."

Considering she'd been so sheltered, I was surprised by her confidence. If I'd been in a sheltered, home-school situation all my life, going into a crowded bar and throwing back beers would have been like stress city! Quella was obviously not like me.

"So, what do you think changed your dad's mind?"

"I don't know." She shrugged. "We fought about it for nearly a year and then one day, about two months ago, he suddenly surprised me with college applications." She grinned, looking triumphant as she took another mouthful of beer. "He said I had to go to a school in either California or Arizona."

"Is that where you're from?"

"We have houses in several places, but we spend most of our time in the south-west."

"Nice. Your dad must be loaded."

Her grin was wicked and a little smug. I was starting to get a picture of her upbringing. This girl had never wanted for anything.

"What does he do?"

She shrugged, her face giving me nothing. Damn it!

"Some boring job where he travels and meets with other businessmen. He does not talk much about his work, but I would say my father is an entrepreneur."

Okay, so she obviously didn't really know.

"Always looking for ways to make money, huh?" I smiled.

"He is a smart man. Many fingers in many pies and it makes him mucho money, so I will not complain." She giggled.

I raised my beer, forcing myself to look impressed. "To wealth."

"To freedom." She lifted her bottle and clinked it against mine, letting out a loud whoop. "Come, Caity. We must dance!"

Her command was hard to argue with, especially when she grabbed my wrist and yanked me away from the table. We jiggled our way onto the squished floor and I tried to look as though I loved it.

Quella was in her element, her hips swaying rhythmically. She was a damn good dancer and I had two left feet. It didn't take long for the guys to swarm us. I inched back, not really wanting to get into their line of fire, but it didn't work. I bumped straight into a tall guy with dark green eyes, short wood-dust hair and a well-manicured beard. It was short, like a fine dusting of hair on his face.

He had an angular look about him, square jawline, prominent nose, but what really drew my attention was his intense expression. He was in a bar, surrounded by revelers, and he looked completely serious.

Why the hell was he out on the dance floor when he obviously didn't want to be?

Moving to the beat, he forced a few subtle moves, but I could see behind his mask and he was hating it as much as I was, which meant he was either here because his partner was forcing him out of the house to have a little fun or he had something else on his mind.

He smiled down at me, yelling above the music. "You seem pretty young to be in a place like this."

"Maybe I'm not as young as you think." I didn't know what made me get cocky, but I somehow wanted to prove myself.

"I don't know. You seem pretty out of your depth."

My eyes narrowed.

Wait a second. The guy knew me.

He wasn't forced there by a girlfriend—he was there for work.

I stopped dancing and resisted the urge to put my hands on my hips. "So which one are you then? Rex or Eddy?"

His eyes rounded slightly and I threw his mask back on, realizing he'd actually been playing it pretty damn cool.

I chuckled. He frowned.

Placing his hand on my hip, he forced my body to get dancing again before finally muttering, "You can call me Rhodes."

It was hard to hear him, but I watched his lips and

leaned toward his ear. "Rex Rhodes?"

He made a face.

"Eddy then." I nodded. "Nice to meet you."

His green eyes turned a shade darker before flicking over my shoulder. His unmasked expression blanched and he threaded his arm around my waist, pulling me closer to him.

I started to push back, but he squeezed me to him and mumbled, "She's looking at us."

I pressed my lips together and reluctantly swung my arms around his neck. "I thought you were supposed to be monitoring this situation from a distance."

"I would have kept my distance if I hadn't been watching your underage self get drunk in a bar."

"I'm not drunk." I rolled my eyes.

"Either way, you're supposed to be on the job."

"I am." I scowled. "Look, Kaplan wouldn't have asked me to do this if she didn't think I was capable."

"If she knew what you were up to right now, she'd be seriously second-guessing her decision."

My eyebrows rose. I found it interesting that he hadn't told her already. So it wasn't Kaplan who had ordered him in here after me. If anything, he was breaking the rules to give me a lecture.

Interesting.

"I can see you don't trust me."

He flinched, his eyes narrowing.

"This is my in with Quella, okay?" I glanced over my shoulder and watched her cozy up to one of the bar guys. I'd have to break that up soon. She was having way too much fun, although underneath her mask I could see that quiver of uncertainty. I turned back to Rhodes, needing to wrap this up. "She wants to party and let loose. She's not going to open up to some goody-two-shoes. She's already told me a little about her over-bearing father. I'm telling you, I know what I'm doing."

He didn't believe me. "You better not screw this up."

"Hey, I want to find those girls as much as you do."

A wave of agony coursed over his expression. The very idea of those girls suffering hurt him and I found myself softening toward the serious guy...until I kept reading him and noticed how little faith he had in me.

I sighed. "I know you think this isn't going to work and I'm just some shitty babysitting assignment."

His forehead wrinkled, his grip around my waist loosening.

"And now you're a little afraid because you thought you were hiding that."

He frowned and I took the chance to really prove myself.

"The truth is, you *are* hiding it...from everyone around here, expect me."

The green of his eyes swirled with uncertainty and he licked his lips.

"I know Kaplan's told you about my ability and you didn't believe her." I gazed up at him. "But now you're starting to, and that makes you feel vulnerable."

He let me go and I dropped my arms from around his neck. Very slowly his expression shifted, his disbelief ebbed away, replaced with a glimmer of awe.

I grinned. "Thank you."

The awe scuttled into hiding behind his scowl. "I still don't think you're the right person for the job."

"I know." I nodded, trying not to be irked. "But there's nothing much you can do about it, is there?"

His scowl deepened. I really had to end the conversation.

"Thank you for watching my back." I slapped his arm. "It's nice to know someone so capable is close by."

He appreciated the comment. My smile grew as I watched him fight a small grin.

With a little huff, he realized I could see it all and spun away from me before I could read anything else. I couldn't help a small giggle before spinning back to find Quella. Her arms were raised in the air, her head tipped back with a laugh. She had three guys around her now, their hungry expressions making my stomach turn.

I muscled my way in between them and tugged on her arm.

"Let's get out of here!" I yelled in her ear.

"But I'm only just getting started," she whined.

"This place is getting boring." I matched her tone. "There's another place we can check out down the road. Let's go!"

Quella stumbled after me with a giggle. We collected our stuff and I pulled her out of the bar before the guys could follow us. I really didn't want to go anywhere else, but Quella wasn't drunk enough to let me get away with lying, so we hit one more bar before heading back to our dorm.

It was a more sedate setting, but after another beer, Quella didn't seem to mind. I certainly appreciated the calmer atmosphere. Unfortunately, I didn't get too much more out of her. I tried to bring up her father again, but she waved her hand and said she didn't want to talk about him.

"Let's talk about that cute guy you were dancing with instead."

My chuckle wobbled with nerves; I couldn't help it.

"It was nothing." I waved my hand, trying to keep my movements floppy. I didn't want her to think I was still completely sober.

"It didn't look like nothing." She wiggled her eyebrows.

"Well, that's what it was." I shrugged. Nerves getting the better of me, I leaned across the table. "Hey, Quella, promise me something."

"What?" She frowned.

"When we go out like this, whatever we get up to, has to stay a secret, okay?"

"You live a double life or something?"

I grinned. "I have a boyfriend who isn't really into the

party scene."

"Oh!" She tapped the side of her nose and pointed at me. "I understand." Her head swayed slightly as she nodded. "Don't you worry, Caity. I am very good at keeping secrets."

Awesome...and also not.

I slumped back into my chair, confident she wouldn't spill the beans to Eric, yet also a little discouraged. I wanted her to be a gossip queen.

How the heck was I supposed to get the goods on her family if she was a first-class secret keeper?

Maybe Rhodes had been right. For all my cocky proof on the dance floor, he was spot-on about one thing—I was way out of my depth on this one.

fifteen

eric

I couldn't help worrying about Caity. She was a little off when she arrived at the beach the day before, but then she perked up. The afternoon had been worn away with laughter and light chatter, but I couldn't shake the odd sensation she was hiding something. I tried to call her later for a goodnight chat, but she hadn't answered her phone.

I was being stupid. She wouldn't hide anything from me and I hated that I couldn't shake the feeling.

The toaster popped and I pulled out my two pieces, dropping them on the plate quickly and blowing on my fingers. I reached for the peanut butter and popped the lid, wondering what Caity had gotten up to the night before. I went to catch up with Mom and the girls. I'd invited Caity to join me, but she'd declined saying she wanted to meet her new roommate. I wondered what she was like.

Checking my watch, I bit off a piece of toast and reached for my phone, sending her a quick text to see how it was going.

"Morning." Scott slumped into the kitchen, rubbing his eyes and running long fingers through his spiky ginger hair.

He pulled two mugs from the cupboard and placed them down beside the coffee machine.

"So, sleep well?" I grinned at him.

He threw me a dry look that was swiftly overtaken by a hot blush. His pale, freckly face was neon red while he cleared his throat.

I laughed and lightly punched him on the arm.

"How's your mom?" Scott's voice still had that morning croak. He pulled out a K-cup and popped it into his Kuerig. Steaming coffee poured from the spout and into his waiting mug. He pulled it from the machine and set it up for a second cup.

I finished off my first piece of toast and brushed my

fingers over my board shorts to clean them.

"It was a good night. We just played a board game with the girls and watched a movie. Cliff wasn't around so it was kind of like old times...just the four of us. We had fun."

"It's cool that you still check in. I'm sure the girls appreciate it."

"Yeah, they were a little sad that Caity didn't come with me."

"Didn't she?" Scott moved to the refrigerator and pulled out a carton of half and half, adding a little to each mug.

"Nah, she wanted to go meet her new roommate."

A disgusted humph came from the doorway and I turned to see Piper tying her bathrobe. She adjusted the collar then reached for her coffee, giving Scott a quick peck before glaring at me.

I rolled me eyes and turned back to my toast. "She did what was right for her. Would you drop it already?"

"I can't believe you just let it slide so easily...unless you don't really want her moving in."

Spinning back with a scowl, I made sure she saw it before I relaxed my expression. "Of course I'd love her here, but she's not ready. And to be honest, I'd prefer she didn't move in, rather than her living here just to make us happy. You know what she's like. It took a lot of guts for her to make that decision."

"Yeah," Piper mumbled, taking another sip before slumping against the counter. "I just wanted her to come with. I hate that she's living with someone else."

"She's not gonna like her more than she likes you." Scott rubbed Piper's shoulder.

"How do you know that? She's probably been out partying all night."

I cracked up laughing, nearly spilling the glass of orange juice I was pouring for myself.

"I'm sorry, are we talking about the same person?" I put the carton back in the refrigerator.

Piper gave in with a small smile, running a finger over her eyebrow.

"You know she'll have a better chance at staying your best friend if you just call her." Scott pulled out his phone. "Come on, invite her over for lunch or something. You can't stay mad at her forever."

"She was kind of worried yesterday." I backed up Scott.

Piper huffed out a sigh. "Okay, fine."

She grabbed Scott's phone and found the number, quickly texting my girl.

Without saying anything, we all moved to the table to finish our breakfasts. Piper ended up grabbing a banana while Scott poured himself some cereal. He was really sweet with his girlfriend, asking if he could get her anything. They were so natural and easy around each other. I could fast-forward a few decades and still see them doing this as their morning routine, murmuring to each other as they ate, sharing secret looks and laughs no one else could decipher. I gazed down at my plate and wondered if Caity and I would be like that.

A smile spread across my lips. Yeah, we could be.

My phone buzzed.

All good. Roommate is Quella. Seems nice. How was your night?

I was about to respond when a new message popped up.

Is Piper for real or is she being coerced by Scott?

I chuckled and wrote.

Real

A few seconds later, I got back a big smiley face and...

So relieved. Okay, will be over soon.

"Caity's coming." I tucked my phone into my back pocket and finished off my toast with a grin. I couldn't believe we'd been dating well over a year and I still got a small thrill at the idea of seeing her.

****

An hour later, Caity's Mini pulled up outside our

place; I noticed her out my bedroom window as I was towel-drying my hair. I threw the towel in the laundry hamper and walked to the front door, opening it before she could knock. I was about to scoop her into my arms when I noticed a girl behind her. She had a long face, long nose, long hair. Everything about her seemed long...and tired. Her dark eyebrows shifted as she took me in, a small smile pulling at the edges of her mouth.

"Hi there." I spoke over Caity's head after giving her a quick kiss.

"Hi." The girl swallowed, seeming nervous, and stuck out her hand. "I'm Quella, Caity's new roommate."

"It's nice to meet you. I'm Eric, Caity's boyfriend." I shook her hand and welcomed her in, trying to interpret the little smile on her lips. I let her pass us before looking at Caity.

"Sorry," she whispered. "She kind of had nowhere else to go today and asked if she could come. She doesn't know L.A. at all and I felt bad for her. I couldn't say no."

"That's cool. I don't mind. I just hope Piper doesn't get shitty about it."

Caity's eyebrows dipped. "Piper will just have to get over it," she mumbled, dropping her keys and wallet on the side table.

I smiled at Caity's unusual show of feistiness and gave her a proper greeting.

She giggled against me when she tried to pull away

from our long kiss and I wouldn't let her.

I'd missed her last night and damn it, I kind of wanted a breakfast like Piper and Scott had just had. I tucked my thoughts away and cleared my expression before letting Caity go. I didn't want her reading anything on me and filled my mind with calm, supportive thoughts.

She stepped past me before really looking anyway and walked into the living area just as Piper and Scott appeared. Piper stopped short when she saw Quella and her lips parted. A frown was forming on her face until Caity gave her the best set of puppy eyes I'd seen in a while. Piper's expression was dry as she tipped her head, but then her lips twitched and she broke into a smile, rolling her eyes.

"Hey, who's this?" Piper's voice was bright.

Quella spun around and studied the company before breaking into a smile of her own. "I'm Quella."

"Nice to meet you."

They shook hands and then Quella took a moment to take in Scott. Man, I wished I could read people like Caity did. Quella's expression was so bland, like maybe she wasn't all there, but I bet Caity saw something else. Scott's bright orange locks and freckly face often drew some kind of reaction. People were shamefully obvious sometimes.

"I'm Scott." He stepped forward. "You're new to L.A., right?"

She nodded.

"Welcome." He grinned, his freckled nose wrinkling.

Quella's lips twitched and the room pulsed with an awkward silence I had to fill. "So, can I get you guys a drink?"

"Sure, strong coffee would be great." Quella winked at Caity who did a little laugh in her throat before looking at me. I frowned at her, wondering what their secret joke was.

She cleared her throat. "Let me help you."

I followed her into the kitchen and quietly waited as she helped me get the coffees ready. I loved that she knew where everything was.

"Something you want to tell me?"

She spun to face me, her cheeks heating with color. "Yes. No. I don't know."

Her shoulders drooped and she leaned against the counter.

"Babe, what's going on?"

"We went out last night, because she really wanted to."

"What'd you do?"

Caity rubbed her temples and cringed. "We went bar-hopping."

"What?" Surprise made my voice loud.

Her eyes bulged and she slapped her hand over my mouth. "Keep your voice down. What's so wrong with bar-hopping anyway?"

I gently flicked her hand off me and whispered, "Nothing, except for the fact that you're both underage.

How'd you even buy a drink?"

She looked to the floor and mumbled, "How do you think?"

"Martha Woodgrove?"

She cringed.

I remembered pulling the fake ID from her wallet months ago and the hysterical laughter that ensued when I tried to imagine her as a Martha. "You've got to be kidding me. I thought you kept that ID as a joke, not to actually use it."

"I know, I know." She squeezed my arms, looking guilty.

"I don't get it." I peeked my head around the corner and heard polite small talk coming from the living room. "She doesn't even seem like the partying kind and I know you aren't. What were you thinking?"

"I don't know. I just wanted her to feel comfortable around me and I asked her if she wanted to go out and then one thing led to another."

It was impossible to hide my bafflement. If she'd pulled off my mask, all she would have seen was an amplified version of what I was already showing her. "No wonder she looks so tired. How are you feeling?"

She gave me a sheepish grin before looking to the floor. "You want to know the weirdest thing?"

"I'm not sure." I crossed my arms.

"I didn't get drunk, but I ended up pretending to get as drunk as her. The beer was so gross, I kept spitting it back into the bottle. It was pathetic."

"Why did you do that?" I chuckled. "Why didn't you tell her you're not really a drinker?"

"Because I want her to like me."

I threw her an incredulous look. "What are you, thirteen again? This isn't a popularity contest."

"Yeah, but you don't have to live with her."

"Neither do you." I shrugged, and then cleared my throat as her expression changed.

There was a long, uncomfortable pause before she finally huffed. "You're so not okay with my decision."

"Yes, I am. I said I am."

"Then act like it!" Her hands flicked through the air.

"I—" I held my breath for a moment, not wanting to start a fight. "I just don't understand why you're pretending to be something you're not."

Her jaw clicked to the side and she took way too long to answer me, like she was somehow trying to think of the right answer. Eventually, she sighed. "I don't know either. It was just a slip in judgment, but...we had a really fun time." She shrugged. "I'm not saying I want to go out partying every night or anything, but it was cool. She really let loose and she was funny. I know I made her feel welcome and relaxed and I've set us up for a good year."

"Caity." I placed my hands on either side of the counter, boxing her in. "You've made her believe you're something you're not. That's not a good set-up."

"I'll make it right." She leaned forward and kissed the sweet spot on my neck.

I closed my eyes, finding it hard to think straight with her lips caressing my skin like that.

"It was just one night of weekend fun. This won't become the norm, I swear." She looked up at me with those vibrant eyes and smiled. "The main thing I wanted was for her to feel comfortable around me. I don't want to kick things off like I did with Piper. Trust me, I may have acted a little wild last night, but I was totally in control and this is not going to be an everyday thing."

With gentle fingers, I brushed a long curl off Caity's face and smiled at her. It was so unbelievably typical of my girl to pull an idiotic move like last night just to make someone feel comfortable. At least she was smart enough not to get drunk. I only hoped that Caity's will to help Quella didn't end up changing who she was.

sixteen

caitlyn

My fingers felt sweaty as I gazed at Eric's text message. Exactly three weeks ago, I had stood in his kitchen and told him that my night of fun with Quella was not going to be the norm. I'd bullshitted my way through a story about how I wanted to make Quella feel at home. My first instinct had been to hide our night of revelry, but on the drive over I'd been inspired and decided that letting Eric in on as much truth as I could, would make it easier to hide the big truth.

It wasn't.

Drawing in a breath, I replied to his invitation of a quiet night at the beach. It sounded like heaven, way better than where I was currently standing.

Would love to, but am out with Quella. Why don't you come join us? We're at Club Ultron.

My fingers jittered as I waited for his reply.

He'd hate this. He'd read my text and wonder what the hell I was doing. I was a fool to invite him, but I missed him. Quella was taking up a lot of my time and it was starting to show. The only time I ever really saw Eric was on our study dates in the library and Taco Tuesday, which was sacred and would remain so. There was no way Kaplan or Quella were stomping on that one.

Eric still hadn't replied. I shoved the phone into my pocket with a scowl.

This sucked.

I wanted the beach, the moonlight, Eric covering me with his hot self, but instead I was out at a loud dance club, pretending to be a party diva so Little Miss Wild Child could shake her booty and get plastered.

We'd done it every weekend since she arrived and every weekend I worked my ass off to get her to spill something, *anything* about her precious father. So far, I knew he was a ba-gillionaire, a coffee snob and owned two mansions—one in New Mexico and one in Palm Springs. Yeah, well, thanks to Kaplan I already knew that.

Quella let out a whoop and waved at me from the dance floor, indicating I should join her. I raised my hand and nodded, pointing to the bar and pretending to be waiting on some drinks. She gave me a thumbs-up before throwing her head back and shimmying closer to a young Latino man who seemed to be fully into her.

I glanced away, imagining my phone call with Kaplan later that night.

Oh yeah, hey, Kaplan. No, nothing new. The only stuff this girl likes talking about is fashion, dancing and hot guys. In fact tonight, she spent most of it gyrating on the dance floor with some dark and handsome man who looked like he'd stepped straight out of a Spanish soap opera. So, can I quit now please, because I'm really not enjoying this and I'm sick of my boyfriend asking me out on these amazing dates and having to decline because I'm babysitting a spoiled, rich kid!

And she'd reply with...

You're not working hard enough, blondie. Stop messing around. Get her drunk, get her talking, make sure you're beside her at all times. Have those girly heart-to-hearts and get her to open up.

That was all well and good, but how did you get the world's most shallow person to open up?

Think about the girls.

The statement hit me like it did every day. It varied in pitch and volume, but it always had the same effect. Time was not on our side. I needed Quella to spill something—anything—that would get me a step closer to the truth.

I'd been reading her like crazy, flipping her mask on and off so I didn't slip up when I saw something new. I was aware she adored her father in spite of the fact she wanted to break free of his protective reign. She felt guilty sometimes, but when she was drunk, her inhibitions ran into hiding. She'd spout off about not being a little girl anymore and how he couldn't keep her locked up forever.

Last week, I'd had a little breakthrough when she'd confessed that her UCLA stint was only a one-year trial. If she didn't behave herself he'd haul her back home, which was why she used her sweet-as-pie voice whenever she spoke on the phone. "*Yes, Papá. I am being very well behaved.*"

If only he knew the truth.

With a sigh, I reached up on my tiptoes and looked across the dance floor. Quella's arms were now draped over the Latino man's shoulders. He was holding her hips and they swayed together as if connected with super glue. I frowned. I knew she was a virgin; she'd told me that late one night, as well. I'd tipped my head, thinking it was cool that she was opening up, but wishing she'd say more.

The phone in my pocket vibrated against my butt. I yanked it out.

Okay. I'll see you soon.

No kisses this time.

I frowned. That probably meant Eric was annoyed with me. Heck, I was annoyed with myself! How could I pass up a romantic night at the beach with my man?

Because of the girls!

I closed my eyes, wishing I could tell him.

A new song started up, blasting through the speakers. Quella glanced over her partner's shoulder and beckoned me to join them. I really didn't want to. I yelled that I was waiting for Eric. She couldn't hear me and gave up quickly as the guy spun her around. She giggled at the move, but a second later was facing away from me. I gazed at the back of her head, but quickly noticed that Mr. Soap Opera was watching me.

I smiled at him. His narrow lips rose with an easy grin, his dark eyes glinting with charm.

Narrowing my gaze, I ripped off his mask and saw it. His dry expression, the calculated look in his eye. He was checking me out and not in a flirty way. He wanted to make sure I was not going to harm the girl in his arms.

I waited until he turned away before letting my

expression fold into a frown.

Who the hell was that guy?

He spun Quella in his arms with a laugh. I put his mask back in place to check I was right before whipping it off again to see that everything about him was robotic and emotionless. His eyes darted around the room, his gaze skirting me numerous times.

He seemed more interested in me, and the crowd around him, than he was with Quella.

I thought of the black phone hiding beneath my bed back on campus. Kaplan was going to want to know about this guy. With a sigh I pushed off the bar and headed into the claustrophobic fray. Telling her about some guy who looked suspicious wouldn't be enough. Kaplan would want to know everything she could about the man pretending to flirt with Quella Mendez.

seventeen

eric

When I first walked into Club Ultron, all I could see were flashing strobe lights, all I could smell was drunken sweat, and all I could think was, "Why the hell would Caity pass up a skinny dip in the ocean for this?"

I scanned the room, bustling my way through people to find my blue-eyed beauty. She was on the dance floor, shuffling to the beat, looking stiff and awkward.

What was she doing?

It so wasn't my girl and it kind of worried me that she was trying so hard to fit in with Quella. I thought she'd gotten over that in high school. She used to be so caught up in pleasing everyone that she'd always gone with the crowd, but then her eyesight changed and the girl who was hiding underneath started to shine through. It'd been impossible to resist her after that.

Turning sideways, I plunged my way through the crowd until I reached the dance floor. Quella was swaying to the beat, her hands raised as she backed into some Spanish guy behind her. They moved together, looking as though they were lost in the music, although Quella's limbs moved like overstretched elastic.

Was she drunk?

I placed my hand on Caity's lower back. She spun in surprise and her expression washed with relief as she wrapped her arms around my neck. "I'm so glad you came."

Pulling her against me, I lifted her off the floor and gave her a quick kiss.

"You done dancing?" I yelled above the music.

"Definitely!" Her eyes rounded.

I chuckled, grabbing her hand and walking her off the floor. We found a couple of spare stools around a tiny table that looked out over the lowered dance floor.

The music was still blaring, making easy chatter impossible.

Caity scratched her arm, keeping an eye on her roommate.

"What's going on?" I leaned toward her so I didn't have to yell so loud.

She shrugged. "Just keeping an eye on Quella."

"Why? Why are you doing this, Caity?"

Her head swiveled in my direction and I caught a brief glimpse of something.

She gave me a closed-mouth smile and touched my arm, leaning up to my ear. "I told you. I want to look out for her."

"By falling into this lifestyle? It's not you. I don't get it."

"She needs me to be her friend right now."

"Aren't you taking things a little too far?"

"Look, it's not that bad. We've been having fun." She pulled back from me and looked at the dance floor again, laughing at Quella's lucid movements.

I frowned.

She saw my expression and sighed, nibbling her lower lip and looking at the round tabletop.

"I—" She swallowed. "It's hard to explain."

Her expression was pinched.

I hated that this was happening again. We had a communication breakdown at the beginning of last year, over the whole Connor taking drugs thing, and it nearly broke us up. I'd been a stubborn ass about it and could have lost her out of sheer pride and fear. I didn't want that to happen again.

I reached for her hand. "I'm always here to listen, you know. You can tell me anything."

Her blue gaze filled with agony for a minute, her lips parting. She hesitated for a beat, her tongue skimming her lower lip. "I want to, but..."

She glanced at the floor again, wincing and closing her eyes.

I waited, trying to be patient when all I felt like doing was dragging her out of the noise-pit and demanding the truth.

"It's a girl thing." She turned back to me, blinking a couple of times before looking me straight in the eye. "Quella told me something in confidence and I swore I wouldn't say a word, even though I really, really want to tell you. But she's vulnerable and she needs me to look out for her."

"Is everything okay? She's not in any kind of danger, is she?"

"No." Caity shook her head. "Nothing like that, just...some stuff about her family and her past and.... She's just really trying to make each day count at the moment, and I want to help her do that."

"As long as you're not compromising who you are to make that happen."

"I'm not, I just...this is something I have to do." Her eyes begged me to accept this. "You didn't see her face, Eric." She looked to the ground, her expression sad. "They need me."

"They?"

"*She.* I meant she." Caity shook her head with a bashful smile. "I'm just trying to do the right thing."

I could only guess what demons Quella was fighting. There were multiple scenarios, but there was one thing I knew for sure: my girlfriend was a sweetheart. She cared so much about people. She was a girl you could trust, and she wouldn't spill Quella's secret if she'd ask her not to.

And knowing Caity, she'd go to the ends of the earth to give Quella what she needed to be happy.

That was the part that concerned me.

I needed to keep a close eye on her and make sure the lines of communication stayed open this time around.

Caity gazed up at me, looking like a kid waiting for approval; her eyes were bright, still imploring me to accept what she was doing.

I gave her a tender smile.

"You're a good soul," I whispered.

She wouldn't have been able to hear me, but her smile told me she'd read my lips. Her white teeth glowed as the black lights went on. She moved toward me, her slim body pressing against mine as our lips met. I held her close, loving every inch of her.

The urge to drag her out of the bar and down to the beach was intense. As we pulled away from the kiss, I checked out the dance floor again, wondering if I could pitch the idea to Caity. We'd be gone for no more than an hour; just a snapshot of fresh air, the feel of the sand beneath us, a quick make-out session with the ocean waves as our soundtrack. Quella probably wouldn't even notice we were gone.

I was just opening my mouth to suggest it when I spotted Caitys' roommate. Her head was leaned back against her dance partner, her eyes closed, her skin pale.

I jerked out of Caity's arms. "Hey, is she okay?"

Caity followed my pointing finger and gasped. "She looks like a ghost!"

We scrambled through the crowd to reach her.

"Quella!" Caity tapped her shoulder.

The girl lurched up as if coming out of a sleep. She spotted Caity in front of her and tried to smile, but then her body convulsed once and she threw up...all over my girlfriend.

I cringed in disgust, pulling Caity away from the spray. She stood still on the dance floor, her arms spread out as if holding an invisible beach ball. Vomit dripped off her arms and ran down her shirt. Her lips wobbled as if fighting barf of her own.

"Okay, time to go." I quickly took control.

Grabbing Quella's arm, I gently pulled her off the guy she was leaning against. He scowled at me as if to say, *Who the hell are you?* I ignored him, more concerned about getting Quella home to bed and Caity cleaned up.

Quella tripped as we neared the stairs, falling against me and letting out a bourbon-infused burp. I grimaced as the smell wafted up my nostrils. She stumbled again and I swept her into my arms, the need to get out overpowering my will to not touch her. Most of her puke landed on Caity, but a little still clung to her clothes.

It was so completely foul.

I turned to see Caity slopping out behind us. The Spanish guy was still giving me an evil glare.

Whatever.

To say I was pissed with Caity's roommate was an understatement. If that guy thought I was trying to steal her away from him, he was insane. I had no idea who he was, but what kind of moron let a girl get that drunk?

The idea that he may have had plans for her sent a shudder down my spine. Quella was walking a dangerous line hanging out in bars and getting drunk off her ass. Caity was trying to compensate and make her feel better about whatever the hell was bugging her, but this was not the way to do it.

I'd have to talk to her about it. Surely Caity would see reason.

Glancing over my shoulder, I waited for my smelly girlfriend to catch up with me.

Quella groaned and leaned her head against my shoulder.

"If you're gonna puke again, let me know."

She mumbled something in Spanish before going floppy. I hitched her into my arms, her sleeping weight becoming that much heavier with each step.

"You okay?" I asked over my shoulder.

"Fine," Caity muttered.

"The keys are in my back right pocket."

She dug into my jeans and pulled the keys free, racing ahead to unlock the doors of my jeep. I laid Quella down in the backseat.

"Do you have a towel I can sit on or should I just walk back?"

I yanked a towel free from the trunk and threw it at Caity. She caught it with an apologetic smile. I waved my hand to indicate it wasn't her fault. She had enough to deal with; she didn't need me harping on at her.

I could tell the only thing Caity wanted to do was get Quella into bed, then go and sterilize herself in a boiling hot shower.

So much for the beach.

eighteen

caitlyn

Eric carried Quella up to our room. I flung the door open and made room for Eric to shuffle past. He laid her on her bed while I whipped off my shirt and decided just to throw it in the trash. As if I'd be able to get the stench out with my washing skills.

I stood there in my bra, gazing down at my roommate. She was still pale, but her color had improved a little since she puked all over me. I sniffed and glanced down at my hair.

"Gross," I muttered, flicking it over my shoulder and wanting to cry.

I'd never felt so filthy in my life.

"It's on your jeans, too." Eric pointed to my thigh.

I tipped my head. "If you're trying to get me into bed, you should know that I've never felt more unsexy."

He chuckled. "As much as I would like to take your fine form to bed and make sweet love to you, I think you have more important things to deal with right now."

His gaze adored me as he stepped forward and nipped my nose, running his finger between my breasts and down to my belly button.

"I'll take you up on it tomorrow, though. You, me, a private cove." He wiggled his eyebrows and I had to laugh. He was so cute when he did that.

I ran my hand over his shoulder and into his hair, wrapping my fingers into his long, straight locks. "Thank you for being there tonight."

"I'm always here for you." His gentle look had a serious edge. "I know she needs to deal with some demons and I know you can't tell me what they are, but I don't know if this is the best way."

Caity stepped back with a sigh, placing her hands on her hips. "I know, me either. I'll try to talk to her tomorrow, once she's sobered up."

"Good idea." He winked at me. Man, it was so damn tempting to invite him into my shower, but I still had to get Quella undressed and washed. He couldn't really stick around for that.

"I'll see you tomorrow, okay?" Eric pointed at me as he backed toward the door.

"Sounds good." I nodded.

He flicked the door open.

"Hey, Eric."

"Yeah?"

I drank in his sexy body and the beauty of his face, wishing I could just tell him everything. My lips wanted to say it, drag him back in and confess all. Even though he'd bought into my Quella lie, it still felt so incredibly wrong.

My lips fought for the right words, eventually breaking into a soft smile. "I love you."

His grin was instant. "I love you, too, babe."

And with that, he quietly slipped out the door.

I slumped onto my bed and gazed across the room at Quella. I hadn't meant to let her get quite that drunk. I hadn't realized how much she'd been throwing back...and now she was basically in a coma. I wasn't going to get anything out of her and it felt like such a waste.

With a sigh, I stood up, pulling off her boots and placing them on the floor at the end of her bed.

"*Hubiera deseado que me vieras visto esta noche.*"

I paused at her mumbling.

"*Mi amor, podríamos haber bailado por siempre.*" She giggled. "Danced the night away."

I stood, gently squeezing her shoulder. "Hey, Quella. It's Caity. I'm just getting you ready for bed."

"*Yo lo amo.*"

"What are you saying?"

Her eyes fluttered open and she stared straight at me. "I love him."

"Who? The guy you were dancing with tonight?"

"No." Quella's giggle was high and squeaky as I pulled her forward to help her take off her vomit-splattered shirt. She raised her arms so I could wiggle her out of it, then flopped back onto the bed. She was still giggling. I pulled her mask away and caught her yearning. She was gazing at the ceiling as if the man of her dreams was floating above her. Her mask-less face gave whomever he was a dreamy smile, growing wider with glee. "I will see him soon at the secret mansion."

I stilled.

Was she giving me something?

I swallowed, fighting to keep my tone casual. "What mansion?"

"*El castillo escondido.*"

"What does that mean?"

She ignored my question, throwing her hand in the air. "It is in the hills. We will hike and make love in the sunlight."

"Which hills? Where is this mansion?" I sat on the edge of her bed, flicking the hair off her face.

"Shhh." Her long finger smushed my lips to the side. "No one can know." Her eyes grew large and she whispered with a dreamy smile. "All that matters is that he will be there. He is always there."

"Who?"

"My true love." She giggled again and then broke into a warbling rendition of a Spanish song I didn't recognize. It was slow and painful, making me wince when she tried to hit the high notes.

"Quella. Quella!" I tried to quiet her. "Tell me more about this mansion. What's it like?"

She ignored my questions, her voice growing stronger as she came to the end of the song. Her floppy arms fell onto her stomach and her body shook with laughter as she rolled onto her side. Ten seconds later, she was snoring.

My shoulders drooped with a heavy sigh as I rolled her onto her back and wrestled her out of her skinny jeans. Throwing them in the laundry hamper, I then pulled Quella's sheet back and with a little effort managed to get her floppy body under the covers. She curled into her pillow like a little kid and fell into oblivion.

I stepped back with a sigh, rubbing my lower back and cringing.

I smelled disgusting and as desperate as I was to have a shower, I had a phone call to make first. Grabbing a shirt that was still hanging over my desk chair, I threw it on, scrambled under the bed for my phone and snuck outside.

"Kaplan," she answered in her usually curt tone.

MELISSA PEARL

I pressed my back into the dark alcove just outside my dorm. "Yeah, I think I got something."

"Finally!"

My eyes narrowed, hating her attitude. She was such bitch sometimes.

Or all the time!

"What've you got?"

"Okay, so two things...we were out dancing at Club Ultron tonight and I noticed this guy hanging out with her. He looked a little suspect to me. He was definitely eyeing the crowd and way more interested in them than Quella, yet he hung out with her all night."

"What was his name? Did you get any details?"

"I think he said it was Carlos, but it was kind of hard to hear. I don't know if we'll ever see him again, so it could be no big deal."

"You said he was scouting out the club?"

"Yeah, I guess. He just seemed on high-alert, if that makes sense."

Kaplan cursed.

"What?"

"It's probably one of Mendez's bodyguards, sent down here to keep an eye on Quella."

"He'd do that?"

"It's Mendez; of course he would."

"Do you think he'll pull Quella out if he knows what she's been up to?"

"Maybe. We need to cool it on the party vibe, Caitlyn."

154

"But that's how I got her talking tonight."

"What'd she say?" Kaplan snapped.

"Most of it was in Spanish, but she said something about a secret mansion in the hills. She said *el castillo escondido* or something; I don't know if I'm saying it right."

Kaplan muttered my terrible Spanish back to me and said, "That means hidden castle. Did she say anything else about it?"

"Her true love is there."

"Who the hell is that?"

"I don't know." I nibbled my lip. "She didn't say anything else. She's pretty hammered, and after throwing up all over me, she fell asleep."

Kaplan snorted. "She threw up on you?"

"Yes," I clipped.

Kaplan snorted again and I was tempted to throw the phone into the bushes and quit on the spot.

"Listen, Caitlyn, you're doing a good job."

I nearly dropped the phone. Was that a compliment?

"Keep working on the true love angle. Girls love to chat and we might be able to get something out of her that way. And watch your back with this Carlos guy. I'll see what I can find out, but if my bodyguard guess is right, he'll probably be hanging around a lot more."

"I don't think Quella knows that's what he is."

"I guarantee she has no idea. After what you told me about her dad finally letting her go free, she'd be pretty pissed if she knew he didn't trust her and was sending out a bodyguard."

"Maybe rumors have reached him that she's partying."

"Hmmm, we could use this, though. If Mendez thinks you're the girl who's going to lead her astray, he's going to want to meet you. He'll definitely be looking into your history."

I swallowed, my stomach bunching into a tight knot. "I don't—"

"Don't worry, we're making sure your files are clean and there's no mention of your involvement in either the Donovan or the Hoffman cases."

"I was going to say, I don't really want to meet him, especially if he thinks I'm leading his daughter astray. Won't he be super-pissed with me?"

"Let's not focus on that just yet. Stay close to Quella, get her to keep talking and we'll see where that leads us."

It took me a second to find my voice.

"Caitlyn?"

"Yeah, o-okay."

"Keep up the good work."

Kaplan hung up, but it took me a minute to move. Mendez might want to meet me? And do what with me?

I mean, I knew this was what we wanted, but it sounded terrifying.

I blinked at the unbidden tears and sucked in a breath. My pride at doing well for Kaplan disintegrated as the reality of where it might lead hit home. I felt paralyzed as I stood in the alcove imagining my fate.

What the hell was I doing?

If Mendez was stealing girls and selling them, what could happen to me?

I closed my eyes. "No, surely not. Not his daughter's friend. Besides, you're too old."

The statement made me sick. Images of the girls' faces fled through my mind. I leaned my head back against the building and wanted to weep for them.

"Don't let fear stop you, Caity," I whispered. "Just remember these girls are going through far worse and you have the chance to save them."

Standing tall, I sucked in a breath and headed back inside to shower and get some sleep. I needed to stay focused and fresh. I had a job to do.

nineteen

caitlyn

So much for my job.

Since Quella's drunken confession and the arrival of Carlos into our friendship, it was basically impossible to get anything out of her.

Oh, yeah, Carlos was still around. She'd given him her number that night, before she'd puked all over me, and he'd called it. In fact, he'd called it every day that week, and in spite of the fact that she claimed to be in love with some mystery guy back at her secret mansion, she didn't seem to mind getting cosy with Carlos.

Hopefully her true love wasn't the jealous type.

Quella seemed drawn to Carlos's charm, but when I looked behind her mask, it was obvious she wasn't overly interested in him; she was just enjoying the flirt-a-thon.

She woke up with the world's worst hangover on Sunday morning, which had dampened the whole party scene for her just a little, so there'd been no mid-week bar-hopping or drinks after class. And with Carlos wheedling his way onto the scene, we'd ended up doing a lot more quiet, subdued things like going out to dinner, watching movies and shopping, shopping, shopping. Unfortunately, this did not bring out Quella's imprudent chatty side...I really needed liquor for that, and thanks to Carlos she wasn't getting much anymore.

I guessed it was a good thing. It really wasn't cool to get an underage girl drunk just to get her talking. Part of me wanted to screw my conscience and start spiking her drinks, just so I could get the damn job over with. I was sick of hanging out with Quella and Carlos—the refined, snobby Spaniard who didn't know how to smile...or relax...ever!

Oh, yeah, and they spoke in Spanish all the time—so not helpful! It totally made me feel like a third wheel, too.

I missed my friends. I was sick of lying to them and

constantly saying I couldn't join them for stuff. I missed hanging out at Eric's place, watching him surf, chatting with Piper over coffee. I hadn't seen her in forever.

I wasn't even conscious of it happening, but over the last month, basically since she moved in with Scott, we'd drifted apart.

It sucked!

And the worst part was, I was about to head into yet another weekend where I *could* actually see her, but I'd be forced to hang out with Quella instead.

Checking my watch, I hitched my bag onto my shoulder and glanced at the sky. A light shower was starting. No big deal, but the sky was pretty grey and the light shower looked to be strengthening. I had no rain jacket or umbrella. Thankfully it wasn't too heavy, so I decided to enjoy the wet sweetness and amble back to my dorm. It didn't really matter if I got there soaking wet.

Quella was still in class, Eric was surfing—a little rain would never stop that from happening. Piper and Scott were no doubt tied up with other things. I kind of had the afternoon off to do as I pleased.

The idea of popping home and catching up with Holly flittered through my head, but I quickly dismissed it. We'd no doubt end up talking about babies, and I wasn't ready to see what they'd done with my bedroom.

Feeling a little lost and sorry for myself, I blinked the raindrops off my lashes and wiped a wet curl off my face.

My phone started singing. I ducked beneath a tree and pulled it out of my bag, answering it just in time. "Hey, Scott, how's it going?"

"Not great. This day is falling to total shit and nothing's going as planned. I really need your help."

"O-kay." My eyes narrowed as I listened to the slight panic and major frustration in his voice. "What do you need me to do?"

He sighed. "I need you to meet Piper after her class and stall her...for about an hour."

"Can I ask why?"

"I—" He cleared his throat and let out a breathy chuckle. "I have something special planned."

My eyebrows wrinkled as I tried to think what it might be. It wasn't Piper's birthday and I didn't think it was their dating anniversary.

Wait.

It couldn't be...

My eyes grew large as a thought hit me. "No way. Are you going to propose?"

"Please, help me," he whispered, his voice pitching with either excitement or terror; I couldn't quite tell. Man, I wished I could read him at that moment. "It was supposed to be a gorgeous day and I was going to take her to the beach and this really fancy restaurant that overlooks the ocean, but the place just called and said there was a fire last night so all bookings are cancelled for the next month. Damn it, Caity, it was going to be perfect."

"Why don't you just wait?"

"Because I picked up the ring this morning and I can't stand the idea of it not being on her finger as soon as possible."

A smile bloomed on my face. "You're so cute."

"So, you'll help me?"

"Of course." I giggled. "This is so exciting."

"Don't make it worse." He puffed. "Just be calm."

My laughter grew. "Are you talking to me or you?"

He let out a shaky chuckle.

"Where do you want me to deliver her?"

"Bring her to our place. I'm setting everything up there."

"Okay. Where is she now?"

"The Humanities Building."

"Cool. I'm not too far from there."

"Her class is due to finish at four."

I glanced at my watch. "I can make that. Good luck."

"Yeah, thanks, and don't say anything."

"Of course I won't. I'll fudge my way through and give nothing away, I promise."

I hung up, wincing at the fact that I was getting pretty damn good at fudging my way through things.

The rain was falling steadily. I jumped into it, running across campus to the Humanities Building. I hovered around the main entrance, hoping I wouldn't miss my friend.

After about ten minutes of leaning against the wall, a wave of students emerged. I stretched on my tiptoes to see above the crowd and waved.

"Piper!"

Her head popped up and she jerked in surprise when she saw me. "What are you doing here?"

I shrugged. "I had the afternoon free and was wondering if you wanted to hang out."

Piper eyed me up with a hard gaze that could strip paint off walls. "You're not busy with Quella?"

I gripped my bag strap. "Nope." I shook my head and grinned. "Besides, I'd rather hang out with you." Her lips twitched with a little smile and I threaded my arm through hers. "Come on, let's go get a coffee or something."

We paused at the entrance so Piper could look at the weather. With a sigh, she pulled a small umbrella from her bag and opened it up. I ducked underneath it and we awkwardly shuffled along the pathways. We decided to head to Ostin Music Center and grab something at the cafe there. It was close to the Humanities Building and although it wasn't anywhere near my car, it would give the rain a chance to die down.

Once we'd bought our coffees and were sitting by the window, looking out at the gloomy day, Piper finally started talking. "So, tell me about your life. I feel like I haven't seen you in forever."

"I know." I sighed. "School's busy and I'm definitely not making it to your place as much as I wanted to."

Piper's eyebrow arched and she took a sip of her

coffee. "How's the roommate?"

My nose wrinkled before I could stop it.

Piper scoffed before I had a chance to answer. "You should have just moved in with us."

I rolled my eyes, not wanting to get into it...again! I scraped the foam onto my teaspoon and sucked it off, licking my lips and stalling on the conversation.

"It's not too late, you know?" Her green eyes searched my face.

"I know," I sing-songed.

She grinned at me and I ripped her mask off. She wasn't really mad; she just missed me.

My insides crumpled. That was so sweet.

Man, I couldn't wait for the job to be over!

I picked up my coffee cup and gazed out the window, trying to not let it get me down and just enjoy this time with my friend. I thought of the upcoming proposal and couldn't help a grin. Man, I couldn't wait to see her face. I wondered if I was allowed to stay and watch. Maybe if I hid in the kitchen or something. I wondered what Scott had planned. I had no idea how he was going to make the house romantic enough to propose in.

I couldn't wait to meet up with Eric later and tell him.

This was so—

"What are you smiling about?"

"Nothing." I took a sip of my coffee and licked the foam off my top lip.

Piper's eyes narrowed so I pulled a face, trying to

throw her off.

She laughed at me and shook her head. "You're such a spoon."

I shrugged. "That's what you like about me."

"That's what I miss about you," she mumbled.

I swallowed back my guilt and felt the tears burn. It was so tempting to launch into it. She'd understand. She'd been mistreated by Cameron and the professor last year, and she knew the sick terror, that feeling of being unable to control her future. She wouldn't try and stop me; hell, she'd probably help me, especially if I showed her pictures of the girls.

Piper came across as a hard-ass sometimes, but she had a heart of pure gold.

I licked my bottom lip, shuffling in my seat and loving the idea of unburdening myself...but then my phone buzzed. It was a text from Scott.

Ready to go.

I drew in a quiet breath and pressed my lips together. "Hey, do you want to go back to your place? I really feel like watching a girly movie and hanging out like we used to."

Piper's lips twitched. "You don't have any other plans tonight?"

I picked up my phone and quickly typed back.

We're on our way.

I shoved it into my back pocket with a grin. "Not anymore."

She smiled at me, quickly draining her coffee and standing up from the table. "Where's your car?"

"Back at the dorm." I grimaced.

"Bluch." Piper grabbed her umbrella and poked out her tongue. "Let's get this over with then."

We ran though the rain, giggling and puffing as we splashed through puddles. It took us about fifteen minutes to get to my car. We slammed ourselves inside, two drowned but happy rats. My hair was beginning to frizz big-time while Piper flicked her perfect locks off her face and still looked like a beauty queen. I started up the car and backed out of my parking space, my nerves jittering with excitement.

I couldn't believe she was about to get engaged. It was so damn exciting I could barely contain myself.

As we drove the ten minutes towards the house, I felt free for the first time in weeks. It was like Quella and Kaplan didn't even exist in my world. I was just Caity, hanging out with my friends and having some fun.

That was what I wanted for my life and it was something I feared I'd never get.

If I succeeded in this job, which I was determined to, Kaplan would no doubt use me again.

Was this my life? One lie after another?

How would I ever settle down and be normal?

I shoved the unsettling thoughts from my mind as I

pulled the car into the driveway.

"Oh, great, the guys are here." Piper pointed to the cars. My eyebrows rose. So that was how Scott managed to pull off whatever he had planned. Eric had forsaken his surfing to help him out.

My insides squeezed. Man, I loved my boyfriend.

We raced through the rain and up the stairs.

Piper swung the front door open and called out, "Honey, I'm home!"

She threw a wink at me over her shoulder and giggled her way into the living area, stopping short with a gasp.

I crept up behind her to take a quick look.

The entire room was strung with fairy lights. The guys had draped black fabric and frost cloth over every wall in the living area, including the ceiling, and fairy lights glittered like fireflies. The floor was covered with rose petals and soft strains of "Monkey and the Tree" by Lindsey Ray wafted into the air. What a perfect song for the moment.

Better yet, Scott was standing in the middle of the room...in a tux.

I pressed my lips together, tears lining my lashes as I took in the magical atmosphere and the sweet look on Scott's face. I ripped off his mask and he was shining like the sun, the love pulsing from his gaze powerful and electrifying.

Piper sucked in a shaky breath and covered her mouth. "I can't believe it."

Scott grinned, stepping toward her and lightly taking her hands.

"Pip, my one and only." He kissed her nose. "You already know how much I love you and I know we've talked about waiting until we graduated, but why?" He hitched up his pants and lowered himself to one knee, pulling out a box from his jacket pocket. "I know we're young and I know it's probably insane, but I've been saving for this since that day you told me you loved me." He chuckled. "You let it slip at senior prom, do you remember?"

She nodded with a soft laugh.

"And I just knew...I wanted to be with you for the rest of my life." He popped the lid of the box open. I couldn't see the ring, but Piper's head tipped to the side and she touched a hand to her chest. "Piper Vaughan, will you marry me?"

She sucked in a breath, covering her mouth and nodding frantically. "Yes." She dropped to her knees, wrapping her arms around Scott's neck and squashing the ring between them. "A thousand times yes!"

He cupped the back of her head, laughing and kissing her before leaning back to slip the ring onto her finger. She looked at it and squealed before reaching for his face and running her dainty fingers over his freckly cheeks. He smiled at her, looking like a giddy schoolboy as she drank him in.

Tears were falling freely down my face. I wiped them away with a smile and caught a movement in the hallway doorframe.

Eric was leaning in the space and gazing at me.

I gave him an excited *can-you-believe-it* smile. He chuckled softly, his expression going mushy.

"I love you," he mouthed.

"I love you, too," I mouthed back, unable to tear my eyes away from his ardent gaze.

I wondered if that would be us one day. If I peeled off his mask, I'd be able to tell. I saw the edge fall, but chickened out, pushing it back into place. His grin grew as if he knew what I was doing. I blushed and bit the edge of my lip.

His gaze turned serious and I was certain, without having to peel his mask off, that he wanted this for us, too...one day.

A thrill raced through me, my insides dancing with a dizzy rush.

The idea of spending the rest of my life with Eric was the sweetest thing in the world, and it wasn't until I saw Scott slip the ring on Piper's finger that I realized how much I wanted that, too.

twenty

eric

I wished I could read Caity sometimes.

I knew her pretty well, but that look on her face as we stared at each other...I wanted to know exactly what it meant. I thought I did. My guess was no doubt right, but it would've been great to have it confirmed, because when your girl is giving you her *I love you* eyes and you've just watched your best friend propose, it's damn tempting to drop to one knee right then and there.

I glanced back into the living room before I screwed up everything and stole Scott's thunder. I wouldn't do it to him. He and Piper were still kissing, the small diamond on her fourth finger looking so shiny and new. I'd helped him pick it out—damn hardest job in the entire world. We both knew how fussy Piper was. When it came to fashion and jewelry, that girl knew what she liked. Scott was sweating blood by the time we'd finally picked it. I told him since they'd already talked about it, he should just bring her to the jewelry store and let her decide, but he wanted the surprise to be faultless, so we'd fumbled our way through the purchase and he'd picked up the perfectly sized ring that morning.

To be honest, the way Piper was gazing at him, she could be wearing a pebble from the bottom of a fish tank. I chuckled; only those closest to her would ever know what a pure nugget of gold her heart was.

Pushing off the doorframe with my shoulder, I crept into the kitchen and slipped my arms around Caity, quietly lifting her off the floor.

She giggled softly into my ear. "Love this day."

"It's the best, right?"

I placed her on the floor and grinned down at her. "You're all wet."

She shrugged. "When have I ever carried an umbrella?"

I chuckled. "One of the things I love about you."

She squeezed my biceps and grinned. "The room looks amazing; you did a great job."

"When I got home to get changed and head to the beach, he was sitting on the couch looking lost and heartbroken. It was really sad." Eric laughed. "I had to help the poor guy out."

"You did good."

A squeal from the living room pulled us apart as Piper jumped up and came to show Caity her ring.

She gently held Piper's hand oohing at the solitaire. I thought it was just okay. When I proposed to Caity, I wasn't going to do anything by the book. I wanted to get her a sapphire to match her eyes, something unique and different that would suit who she was. It'd be none of this traditional stuff for us. I was thinking a beach wedding and bare feet. That was the way to do it.

Caity glanced over Piper's head and caught me dreaming, so I swallowed back my smile and winked at her before heading for the table to uncork the champagne bottle. We filled the four flutes and I raised mine in the air.

"To a happy life." I grinned.

"To a beautiful wedding." Piper smiled.

"To the one and only person in the world who knows absolutely everything about me." Scott winked at Piper. "And always will."

We all chuckled and then looked to Caity when she didn't pipe up with her toast. Her eyes were glistening as she stared at Scott. After a beat, she swallowed, her smile looking slightly melancholy. She cleared her throat. "To the best couple I know."

Scott let out a little cheer.

The glasses clinked together and we all took a sip, Caity's smile returning to full splendor and chasing my doubts away. She always cried at weddings and romantic stuff. It was sweet.

But as the evening wore on, my doubts came back. Something was definitely up with my girl. The more Piper talked about wedding plans, the quieter Caity became.

Piper squeezed her arm and Caity forced another soft smile. "I'm so excited I can barely stand it. I can't wait to plan this with you."

Caity patted her friend's hand. "It's going to be awesome; I can't wait. Thank you so much for including me."

"Of course! During the Thanksgiving break, we'll get together for the day to talk wedding dresses and bridesmaids outfits and venues and—"

"Hey, don't I get a say?" Scott nudge Piper's arm.

"Of course you do. I meant get together as a foursome." She winked and we all laughed at her. She blushed red then leaned over to kiss Scott on the lips, murmuring some sort of apology.

I gazed across their heads and looked at Caity. She glanced at her watch, wiggling it on her wrist before looking up at me.

"Do you want to stay?" I mouthed.

She pursed her lips and looked at her watch again.

"Please?" I put on a pouty face and batted my eyelashes, no doubt looking like an idiot.

Caity silently giggled.

Biting her lip, she looked at the front door then back at me, and after a long pause she nodded. "Okay." Her eyes lit with a desperate hunger.

I flicked my head toward the hallway, slowly getting up from the table.

Caity joined me. "Have a good night, you guys."

Piper and Scott jerked apart.

"We'll talk more in the morning." Piper waved goodbye and I tugged Caity down the hallway before she got caught up in more wedding conversation. I was happy for those two, but my girl was staying and I didn't want to waste it.

The second she made it through my door, I closed it behind her, pressing her into the wood with my body and kissing her hard. She met my heat with a passion of her own, her fingers scraping through my hair as she hooked her knee up against my hip. I grabbed her leg, running my fingers down her jeans and cupping her butt.

There wasn't room for words. We just let our tongues and bodies do the talking, ripping each other's clothes off and making love in a passionate frenzy. When we were done, I lay on top of her, panting heavily in her ear. Her lips were feather-light on my shoulder, kissing their way up to my sweet spot.

I sucked her earlobe gently and she squeezed me with her legs, digging her heels into my lower back.

"I love you," she whispered then sniffed.

I frowned, leaning back on my elbows and noticing the tears on her lashes. "Hey, what's the matter?"

"Nothing." She shook her head and sucked in a ragged breath.

With my thumb, I gently wiped the tears away.

"I guess the proposal is just making me emotional or something."

I rolled off her, lying on my back and pulling her against me. "It's not just that, though, is it? What's bothering you?"

"I—" She sucked in a breath and then huffed it out, burying her face into the crook of my neck.

"What are you not telling me?"

Her hand ran up my chest, her fingers splaying over my shoulder before gripping my neck. She was crying again; I could feel the tears on my skin.

"Caity," I whispered. "What's—"

Her phone started singing. She jerked in my arms and scrambled for her jeans.

"Leave it." I tried to pull her back to me, but she shook off my hand.

"I can't." She fished the phone out of her pocket, a frown flickering across her features before she pressed the screen. "Hello?" A muscle pinged in her neck. "No, I know....Yes....Well, I was planning to—" She clenched her jaw and I sat up, running my hand lightly up her back.

She turned to me and forced a smile.

"Yes, I can understand that." She rubbed the back of her neck then glanced at her watch. "With my friends.... No, of course not." She rolled her eyes. "Now? But—" She pressed her lips together. "Yeah, yeah, I understand. I'll be there soon."

Pulling the phone from her ear, she touched the screen and then threw it down beside her.

"Who was that?"

"Um..." Caity swallowed. "Quella."

My eyes narrowed. She saw my expression and she huffed out a dry laugh, running her hands into her hair. "She needs me to head back. She's become quite...annoying."

"What do you mean?"

"You know, she wants to know where I am all the time and if I don't check in she calls me. It's like she's anxious or suspicious if I don't call her every night."

"Every night, what do you mean? Aren't you guys sharing a room?"

Caity blushed and shook her head. "I'm not explaining myself very well. What I'm trying to say is that she likes to know where I am and what I'm up to all the time and if I'm not with her when she thinks I should be, she freaks out." Caity spat out the last word. "It's getting kind of exhausting."

My frown was sharp. "Why didn't you tell me this?"

She shrugged. "I told you, it's private, girly stuff. I

can't break my promise. She's really insecure and maybe I misread just how much. All I know is that she needs me, Eric, and just because it's getting irritating doesn't mean I can turn my back on her."

I scoffed. "Caity, she sounds like your personal stalker. Calling you up in the middle of the night and asking where you are? That's just plain weird."

"I know it is." She rubbed the back of her neck again. "She...she has a lot of issues."

I rubbed my chin, hating this on her behalf and okay, yeah, worried for her.

"You know how much I love that you care about people." I held my breath for a second, wanting to get the wording right. My fingers drew circles on her back. "But you don't have to save the world, and if being nice is making you feel unsafe or unhappy, you've got to stop."

"How can you say that?" She turned to me. "So my happiness is more important than anybody else's?"

"It is to me."

"I can't walk away. This isn't about me. It's about taking care of those in need."

"And Quella's in need?"

"Yes!" Caity turned away from me, pulling her knees against her naked chest. "Emotionally, she's very unstable and I—I don't feel like I can walk away and pretend this isn't happening."

I couldn't help my frown. "You're not a psychologist. Shouldn't you be referring her to someone who's a professional in this field?"

"No, it has to be me! I see things others can't. I've been chosen for this and I can't back out."

My forehead wrinkled with a frown. "Caity, you're not actually making sense. What is happening that you can't back out of? Who chose you?"

She sighed and buried her face into her knees. "I mean like cosmically," she mumbled.

My head jerked back in surprise. Since when had she been into any kind of higher power? It felt so weird to be sitting next to this girl, who I thought I knew so well, and realize that maybe I didn't know her at all.

My frown was so deep it was actually starting to hurt, but what bothered me more was Caity's palpable tension.

Her arms were wrapped so tightly around her legs, I could see her spine protruding out of her back. Hating this, but not wanting to make it worse, I lowered my voice to a gentle whisper. "I know this gift is a huge responsibility and I get that you want to be there for Quella. I think it's admirable and really nice." I licked my bottom lip. "But if your job is to think about her and what she needs to get better, then I want my job to be thinking about you and what you need to be happy."

Slowly her head turned, her large blue eyes looking at me sideways.

"What do you need, babe?"

She looked past me, tears lining her lashes. "To forget the world exists. To forget all the badness and pretend like I'm normal and I don't see anything. To escape this weight of responsibility and be with you, somewhere where no one can find us or ask anything of us."

Her sad voice pinched my heart.

The first tear dribbled down her nose, trickling to the edge of her mouth. I leaned forward and kissed it away.

"I'd take you away in a heartbeat if you needed me to. Fly your butt all the way to Bora Bora if you wanted."

Her glum smile turned into a soft giggle.

"You can count on me, okay? I'll do whatever it takes to ease this burden for you, babe."

"I know." Her head popped up. "And that's why I love you so much." Her hand was soft on my face as she leaned over to kiss me. "I wish I could tell you everything."

"A promise is a promise." I shrugged. "Just...be careful."

"I will." She rubbed her thumb over my cheek and kissed me again. "I better go. She needs to talk."

"Okay." I slid my arm down Caity's side, hating that she had to leave.

She stood and walked to the edge of the bed, stepping off and collecting her clothes. I lay back against the pillows and watched her get dressed, the mood still bleak and somber.

She slipped on her shirt and looked at me, an apology on her lips.

I raised my hand to stop her. "It's okay. I love you."

Her smile was sweet. "World's best boyfriend, I swear."

"I'll take it." I winked, enjoying her giggle.

As soon as she slipped out the door my smile fled. The room was dark and cold without her; my worry over her need to help others was crushing. I pinched the bridge of my nose and muttered a curse, wondering what I could do to make it better, because if there was one thing I could not stand...it was seeing my girl cry.

twenty-one

caitlyn

Quella was sound asleep when I slipped in the door. I gazed down at her, wondering what she'd think if she knew the lies I was making up about her. Kaplan calling me at Eric's was so unexpected. How dare she disturb what could have been a perfect night?

I should have listened to Eric and just ignored her damn call, but no, I had to answer it and get my ear chewed out. She ordered me back to my dorm...and stupid me, because I sucked at standing up to her, agreed. I left my super-hot, naked boyfriend in order to wake up in the same room as Quella, on the off-chance that she might say something meaningful to me.

It was ridiculous. I was tempted to call Kaplan back right then and tell her to shove it up her ass. I was going back to spend the night with my boyfriend, so that when I woke up in the morning I could be surrounded with more exciting wedding talk. Instead, I'd be waking up in Quella Town, listening to the world's most self-absorbed eighteen-year-old talk about how she spent the previous day getting a mani-pedi and eating a quail egg salad for lunch.

I threw myself back on the bed, not even bothering to undress. I'd already done that tonight and if I'd had my way, I would have stayed naked next to the man I loved; the most patient guy ever to buy into my sack of lies. When I told him the truth, it was going to hurt him. He'd had so many people lie to him in the past, so he was super-sensitive on the whole *be honest with me* thing. I got that. I respected it. That was why I promised him I always tell the truth.

But I broke that promise.

I'd dug myself into a hole of deception that could bury me alive. Once he got over his anger, he'd understand about the girls, but that still wouldn't change the fact that I'd broken his trust. I should have let him in from the start, but he would have wanted me off the case. It wasn't that he didn't care about those girls. He'd want them found just as badly as I did, but he would've fought for a way to ensure my safety throughout the case.

My well-being was paramount to him and although he loved the fact I put others first, it also drove him crazy. My compassion was one of the things he fell in love with, but it seemed to keep putting me in harm's way, and Eric didn't cope with that.

I covered my face with my hands, more tears threatening to break free.

What if he couldn't get over my lies? What if he didn't forgive me?

What if Kaplan found out I'd told him?

She was working way outside the boundaries of the law on this one, driven by something I hadn't been able to figure out yet. I could only imagine how livid she'd be, and I had a sinking feeling that if I told Eric, he wouldn't be able to just sit by with his lips sealed while Kaplan sent me into the house of a human trafficker. He'd insist on going with me, and that could blow the whole operation.

Scrubbing my hands over my face, I gazed up at the ceiling and let the scenarios run through me, each one more brutal than the last: Eric storming away from me in outrage that I'd made him buy into one lie after another, Kaplan screaming at me for breaking the rules.

By the time my imagination was done, I was in tears again, my soul splintering like a smashed pane of glass.

I had to tell him.

I could risk Kaplan's wrath, but I couldn't risk hurting Eric and potentially losing him.

Yeah. I nodded. Kaplan could shove it. My boyfriend was more important than her reputation. Besides, I'd make Eric see reason. Surely, he'd let me rescue these girls, and so what if he came with me? He could play undercover. He'd done it once before. Sure, it didn't go to plan, but he'd stopped Cameron from mauling me and Kaplan had still nabbed her bad guys.

My chin jutted forward, determination rippling through me. It was settled. I was telling him and everything would work out fine. And then when it was over and those girls were safely back home, Eric and I could get engaged and be as happy as Scott and Piper!

****

Sleep was a joke and remained a joke for the rest of the week.

I barely got any, my nerves wound so tight I thought they might snap. I'd made my big decision to tell Eric the truth; now I just had to find the right time and place.

The noisy diner we were sitting in was definitely not it.

Quella played with the salt shaker, pouring little piles of salt onto the table and drawing patterns in it while we waited for our dinner orders to arrive. I glanced across at Eric and forced a smile, trying to pretend the awkward double date with Carlos wasn't actually happening.

Carlos had called that morning inviting Quella out for a midweek date, and for some reason she couldn't say no. She didn't really want to go and had begged me to join her. I wasn't willing to give up my evening with Eric, so I begged him to join me.

And there we were.

I tapped my finger on the table, my brain too foggy to even think of small talk. It was pretty damn painful. Eventually Quella sat back.

"The food is taking forever. Carlos, go and find out what's wrong. I'm going to the bathroom."

She nudged Carlos out of the way and he reluctantly walked up to the main counter.

As soon as Quella was out of earshot, Eric turned to me.

"Okay, so I've had an idea," he spoke quickly. "I know you feel a huge responsibility to basically everyone, but it's time you broke a few rules."

My eyes narrowed.

"Hear me out. Quella has Carlos to look out for her now and you look exhausted. How about a trip to San Diego?"

I sat forward.

"It'd only be for the weekend. We'll leave after class on Friday and then be back on Sunday afternoon. Gramps is so easy to stay with and would love the company."

My nose wrinkled before I could stop it. "He wouldn't mind?"

"I called yesterday and asked him. Whether you say yes or no, I'm going down there. He sounded kind of lonely."

I blinked slowly, trying to ignore the searing pain at the idea of Eric being out of town for the weekend while I was stuck with Quella.

Kaplan wanted me to spend every waking minute with her, but what was one weekend? If Eric and I could sneak off to San Diego, it'd give me a chance to tell him somewhere private. Kaplan could live without me for two days.

But what about the girls? What if something important happened while I was gone?

What about my sanity? What about my relationship with Eric?

I nibbled my lip, rushing to think it through so I could respond.

"Okay, yes." I said the words before I changed my mind.

"Yes?"

"Yeah." I nodded with a grin. "Yeah, it'll be great."

I still felt nervous. Kaplan was going to kill me for doing this, but she'd just have to understand. I needed a weekend off. I didn't think that was too much to ask.

I called Kaplan that night, tapping my finger against the phone as I waited for her to answer.

"Kaplan," she snapped.

"Yeah, just checking in."

"Got anything for me?"

"Nothing new from today. Carlos seems to be keeping her on track, which is great for her, but bad for me. She doesn't talk as much when he's around all the time and she really needs to get a little plastered to loosen that tongue of hers."

"Okay, well make that happen. Take her out this weekend. Get her piss-drunk and talking."

"Actually, this weekend, I was wondering—"

"I'm not interested in your ideas. I just want you to do your job."

"I was kind of hoping—"

"Get me something new by Sunday afternoon. I don't care what you have to do."

"I'm thinking—"

"Don't think, just do it."

She hung up before she could interrupt me again.

I glared at my phone, wanting to scream at it, throw it to the ground, then grind my heel into that damn thing. Nobody could piss me off like that woman could.

Crossing my arms with a huff, I looked at the night sky, hating that I'd have to sacrifice my weekend away just to please that woman.

But I wouldn't please her. I'd do exactly what she'd ask me to and it still wouldn't be enough.

"Screw you," I muttered at the phone.

Quella could get drunk *next* weekend. Tomorrow night, I was going away with my boyfriend!

twenty-two

eric

Caity hadn't stopped smiling since we got into the car. It was like something had been set free inside her and the further we drove from campus, the more relaxed she became. Breathing in through her nose, she let out a happy sigh and leaned her head back against the headrest. Her arm was out the open car window, her fingers fluttering through the breeze as we drove down to San Diego. The sun was setting, bathing her in amber light. She looked like an angel.

To say it was a relief to have my girlfriend back was an understatement. I hadn't realized how badly she needed the break. I was hoping by the end of the weekend I could convince Caity that she really didn't have to shoulder the burden of Quella anymore. It was getting too much and she needed to back off, for her own sake.

We were about twenty minutes out from Gramps's house. It always felt like home when I walked in the door, and I was looking forward to that feeling again. That man had saved my life. I didn't know what I'd do without him and every time I came to visit, I always left feeling re-energized.

I reached over and squeezed Caity's knee. Her smile was golden as she turned to look at me.

"Nearly there."

"I know." She dropped her feet off the dashboard and sat up. "You going surfing tonight?" She ran her fingers up my arm. "Or are you going to keep me company instead?"

She wiggled her eyebrows, making me chuckle. It'd be impossible to resist her. I'd just have to go surfing in the morning.

Caity's phone dinged. She reached for her bag, still grinning until she pulled it out and read the screen. Her expression changed instantly, her lips twitching before pressing into a thin line.

"Everything okay?" I stole a glance at her.

Her fingers hovered over the screen before she let out a sigh and sent a quick text. "Yeah, everything's fine."

It didn't sound fine.

I watched her out of the corner of my eye. I couldn't see who she was replying to, or what she had written, but I could tell it was a very short text. When she was done, she pressed the top button on her phone and held it down, actually turning the phone off.

Throwing it into her bag, she crossed her arms and slumped back against the seat.

"Quella?" I asked.

"Not this weekend. I just can't do it." She kept her eyes out the window, not looking at me.

"Then turning off your phone was probably the best idea."

She glanced back at me, her lips tipping into a grin. "It was, wasn't it?" With a small giggle, she shuffled closer, sliding her arm behind my neck and kissing my cheek. "Thank you for this," she whispered in my ear before resting her head against my shoulder.

I kept my eyes on the road, glad she couldn't see my frown. I should have been happy that I was taking her away and making her feel better, but the grip she had on my shoulder told me it wasn't over.

Clenching the wheel, I decided that all I could do was give her the best weekend I could, remind her what it was like to not be burdened by someone else's problems and then when we drove back on Sunday, I could hopefully convince her to let this Quella thing go and move in with me.

****

Gramps appeared in the doorway as I turned off the engine and flicked off the lights. His broad grin was highlighted by the porch light, his blue eyes wrinkling at the corners as he spread his arms wide and pulled Caity into a hug.

He lifted her off the ground with ease before dropping her back down and wrapping me in a hug, pounding my back twice like he always did. For a guy in his seventies, he was still pretty damn strong and capable. I couldn't imagine anything stopping him. He was just as tall as I was, with a broad chest and hardy muscles from years in the military. He'd spent the last fifteen of his career training new Marines at the Marine Corps Recruit Depot in San Diego, before he retired to come save my ass. He could be a hard man, but I didn't know anyone who didn't respect him.

"Welcome home." He squeezed my shoulders before taking Caity's hand. "Come on in, I've got dinner all ready."

Caity looked at me with an adorable grin before following him.

In spite of his tough exterior, when it came to the ladies, Gramps was all sweetness and charm. I shook my head with a grin, wondering how it was possible that he'd never re-married after Grandma died. I'd never met her, she'd passed away before I was born, but pictures still hung all over the house. He must have loved her more than anything.

I watched Caity skip up the stairs ahead of me, her long curls bouncing on her back, and I understood that feeling. I wasn't sure I could ever move on from a girl like Caity, and I hoped I never had to.

We bustled into the small living area and I dumped our bags on the wooden floor. Like it always did, the large photo my father had taken slapped me in the face. I turned my back on it and strained to hear the sound I lived for. A smile lit my lips as the faint rolling and crashing of waves wafted in the front door.

Gramps had owned the small house near Blacks Beach for over fifty years. Houses had been torn down around him, replaced with big mansions, but he'd stood strong, maintained his little place and kept a hold of the sweetest spot in San Diego.

I, for one, was very grateful.

Just across the road and down the little slope was one of the best surf beaches in the area.

Jogging back out to the car, I grabbed the boards off the roof and tucked them under my arm, checking the car was locked. Climbing up the three short steps, I leaned them against the wall of the closed porch area before heading inside. Caity was already seated at the table and grabbing a bread roll out of the basket.

"Sounds good to me." She smiled, ripping off a piece of bread and popping it into her mouth.

"What sounds good?" I sat down beside her.

"Poker with Gramps after dinner." She winked at me then mouthed, "No cheating; I promise."

I chuckled, pecking her lips and reaching for the salad bowl Gramps held out to me.

The meal passed with easy chatter. Gramps could make a killer spaghetti and meatballs. We sipped our Cokes as we laughed at another of his military training stories and that look on Caity's face was back...the relaxed, no-cares-in-the-world one that I wanted her to live with permanently.

Gramps stood from his seat, clearing the plates. Caity jumped up to help him.

"Let me. You cooked." She kissed his cheek and took the plates from him.

Once she was in the kitchen, he leaned over the table and whispered, "That's a catch right there. Don't you ever let her go, boy."

"Not planning on it." I grinned.

He slapped me on the shoulder with a chuckle. "Why don't you go grab the chips and we'll get started."

I did as I was told and thirty minutes later was sitting at the table with two cards in my hand, clinking my chips together. We were playing Texas Hold 'Em...a little more complicated than the five-card draw, but Caity wanted to get her head around it.

"Okay, so you've dealt the flop and then the turn, so

there's another round of betting now?" Caity asked Gramps.

"Yes, you can either fold, raise, check or call to match Eric's bet." He nodded.

Caity nibbled her lip, eyeing the cards in her hand.

"Remember now, you still have the river to go, so there's one more chance of bettering your hand and one more round of betting before you have to show us anything. If your cards are really bad, get out now before you lose more money."

"But you told me aggressive players do better."

"No, I told you to be a better, not a caller, but I also said wait on the good cards and throw the bad ones away."

I grinned as I watched my two favorite people talking. Gramps had a Southern lilt to his voice, having been raised on a farm in Kentucky. In spite of the fact he'd spent most of his life living in California, he'd never lost it and I loved that about him. Caity, in contrast, was a California beach bunny through and through and I most definitely loved that about her.

She nodded, a large curl dropping over her shoulder as she leaned forward and gazed at the four upturned cards in the middle of the table.

Gramp pointed at her. "Keep that poker face, girl. You don't want to give anything away now."

Her lips tipped up at the corners, her blue gaze brushing mine before dropping back to the tabletop.

"Okay," she nodded, looking at me. "I'll call and

raise you two dollars." She threw four chips onto the table.

My eyebrows rose and she gave me an innocent blink, her lips still fighting a smile. I narrowed my eyes at her and she started giggling, squeezing her eyes shut.

I tapped her foot under the table and shook my head. She'd said no cheating, the little deviant.

"Fold." I placed my cards on the table, annoyed that I couldn't get my bluff past her. I should have known; she probably hadn't even meant to read me, but my mask would have slipped away and she'd probably spotted something before pulling it back into place.

Gramps frowned between us before calling Caity's bet.

He then burned the top card by placing it on the table, face down, before dealing the river card. I gazed at the five upturned cards, glad I'd folded. After three rounds, I was already down on chips, which was why I'd decided to go for the bluff, but I hadn't taken into account the Caity Factor.

I glanced at her pile, wanting to be mad at her for cheating, but not quite making it. She was just too damn cute and adorable and I secretly loved that she kicked ass at this game...especially when she beat jerks like her brother, Toby.

In the end, Gramps won the round with two pair, queen high. Caity had two pair, tens high. With a good-natured groan, she threw her cards down as Gramps scraped the pot toward him.

"Oh, come now, this is the first hand you've lost, little lady."

She chuckled. "I'm happy for you, honestly I am." She winked and then smiled at me.

"I tell you, you've got the gift." Gramps shook his head with a grin.

Caity's face blanched while my back pinged straight in the chair.

She cleared her throat. "What do you mean, Clayton?"

He shrugged, his eyes still on the chips he was staking. "Poker comes natural to some. Now, you take Eric's daddy; he was one mean poker player." He shook his head, his eyes going distant as if watching a memory. "That boy had the most uncanny luck...or maybe it was just skill, I don't know, but I hardly ever beat the kid."

I pressed my elbows into the table.

"Yeah, a lot of good it did him," I mumbled, sharp memories attacking me. One in particular dug in deep, feeling like a saber through the gullet.

Gramps's lips formed a tight line the way they always did when his son was insulted. It was the only thing we didn't see eye-to-eye on, which was why we never really talked about Declan Shore.

To me, he was the biggest asshole on the planet with a father who wanted to forgive him and a son who wanted to hate him for all eternity.

"You be careful, son. He wasn't all bad," Gramps

warned.

But I wasn't ready to listen. I couldn't help a soft gibe at my father. "He was hardly good."

Gramps' nostrils flared, his voice stretching tight with checked anger. "Boy, do not ruin tonight. I know you've got your issues, but you don't bad-mouth my son around me."

I made two fists with my hands, fighting the urge to throw back my chair and storm from the room. Gramps had hung a punching bag in the garage for occasions like this. It'd been well used in the past, but I wasn't going to lower myself to it tonight. Not with Caity staring at me with those beautiful eyes of hers.

Pressing my lips together, I slumped back in my seat.

I should have kept my dumb mouth shut. Never engage in battle with a decorated Marine; you'd always lose.

But I couldn't help it. He'd just compared my pure, sweet Caity to a guy who had left his eight-year-old son standing out in the rain after school one day for nearly two hours. I knew I could have walked home, but my loyal soul hadn't wanted to give up on the man I'd adored. It'd been dark by the time he finally arrived with a puffy eye and a cut lip.

I'd gotten into his car, my anger being overridden by my fear.

"What happened, Dad?"

He gazed out the windshield with a sigh before

starting up the engine. "Know when to hold 'em, buddy."

That's all he'd said and I hadn't figured out what he'd meant until three years later when I heard that Kenny Rogers song, "The Gambler." Mom had been singing along to it in her car and I'd listened intently until it had finished, flicking off the radio and demanding she tell me what that country guy was singing about.

It'd broken my heart, figuring out that my dad had left me in the rain in order to gamble his money away on a card game. Thanks to him, I'd scored myself a really bad cold, which turned into bronchitis. I'd been on bed rest for over a week, which for an active eight-year-old felt like an eternity.

My adoration for him had started to stumble and trip by that stage, but my stupid self had clung tight for a few more years. It wasn't until he left me hanging outside Dodger Stadium for an entire day that I really gave up on him. He never showed, never called, and I hadn't heard from him or seen him since. His promise to turn up with the tickets and spend the day together had been the final one he'd broken, and I couldn't forgive him anymore. He'd used up all his chances and I no longer cared where he was...or even if he were alive.

Caity rubbed my shin with her foot, giving me a tender smile before quietly shuffling the pack. She kept glancing at Gramps, and I could tell by her expression that she was seeing something I wasn't. I was smart enough to realize that Dad's disappearance probably hurt Gramps as much as it hurt me, but I couldn't bring myself to ask. Talking about my father always put me in such a foul mood and I didn't want to spoil the weekend.

"Deal up," I said softly, lifting my chin at Caity.

She did as I asked, but it was safe to say the mood in the room had been crucified by my snarky comments. Without meaning to, I had ruined the evening.

twenty-three

caitlyn

The best thing to get Eric out of a slump was for him to go surfing. So as soon as we woke up the next morning, I suggested we hit the beach. He knew what I was trying to do and gave me an appreciative kiss for the effort.

It had meant our Saturday started on a much sweeter note, which it most definitely needed to.

I rode my wave into shore, bending my knees and flicking the board up one last time before jumping off into the ocean. The salty water was crisp and cool, waking me up thoroughly. The day was going to be a big one. I had decided as I lay beside my gloomy boyfriend that the next day, I would definitely tell him about Kaplan and what I was doing for her.

He deserved the truth and seeing the agony on his face as he sat across the poker table from me just confirmed it. We didn't talk about Declan Shore...ever. I'd heard little snippets here and there, and I knew about the Dodger Stadium incident. It'd been told to me in short, sharp sentences and when I'd try to venture into an in-depth conversation about the reasons why his dad might have done it, I was cut off. Eric didn't want to go there and I had to respect that.

I stood up, slicking back my hair, and noticed that Clayton Shore was sitting on the beach watching us. His elbows were resting on his knees, his toes buried in the cool, morning sand.

Collecting my board, I glanced over my shoulder.

"Hey, Eric! Going in now!" I raised my hand and waved at him.

He gave me a thumbs-up and turned back to the ocean. I could tell he was in a zone, working through his feelings. Tucking the board under my arm, I walked up the beach, swamped by nerves. How the hell would he react to my revelation this afternoon? I could see a night surf in his immediate future. I cringed. I really didn't like him surfing in the dark, but he'd probably need it after I revealed my lies.

"Looking good out there." Clayton smiled as I dropped the board onto the sand and unfastened the leash around my ankle.

"Thanks." I grabbed the towel he was holding out to me and rubbed my face dry before flicking it out and unzipping my wetsuit. I wriggled out of it and sat down beside Eric's grandpa, mirroring his stance.

"You sleep okay?" The sand felt good against my damp skin as I wiggled my toes, feeling the grains grind between them.

Clayton shrugged. "As well as I could." He huffed out a sigh and ran a hand over his bald head. "I shouldn't have been so snappy. The kid's got a right to be mad with his father; the guy let him down big-time. I just thought...*hoped*...by now that he would have forgiven him. He's been harboring that anger and hurt for too long."

"I guess it's hard to forgive when there's been no resolution. For all Eric knows, his father could be dead. To just disappear like that is so bizarre." I stole a sidelong glance at Clayton, wondering if I'd snatch a glimmer of what I caught the night before. The mask began to slip, so I ripped it off and went for it. "I'm surprised you've never tried to find him."

Bingo.

There it was.

A flash of guilt, knowledge, something. He had a

secret, something he'd never shared with his grandson, a nugget of truth locked away inside him.

"You did, didn't you? What happened?"

Clayton sighed, a long, heavy one this time. His face washed with pain.

"It was partly my doing." His brows bunched together, tears springing into his eyes. I threw his mask back on and noticed his tough facade was dry and void of emotion. I let the mask slip away as he kept talking. "After the last time he let Eric down, that day at Dodger Stadium. Shayna called me in a rage, telling me my son was a loser and what he'd done to Eric. I was livid, humiliated that my own offspring could treat his kid so badly. I called him that night and told him to leave the boy alone. If all he was going to do was break his heart, it was better if he wasn't even around. I told him he was a loser and to never call me again. I was so mad." His unmasked tears started to fall as regret and anger grew with force. "I never expected him to actually listen to me, but he did. Went AWOL on us all."

His lips wobbled and he sniffed.

It was heartbreaking to watch and I felt my own tears forming, so I quickly pulled Clayton's mask back up. It would be easier to hear the stone-faced recount, I was sure of it.

I gazed at Clayton's calm expression, finding his mild sadness easier to bear. "So you stepped in, took on the role of dad for Eric?"

"Not at first." He shook his head. "I still had my

responsibilities with the Marines and at the time, Eric's mom was with a pretty good guy, but then things changed..."

"Oh, you mean Shayna scored a new man?" I couldn't help the dry tone; that woman had been around.

Clayton didn't react to my sarcasm. Instead he went still, his lips deepening into a frown, his eyes locked on the horizon. Fear skittered through me.

"Clayton, what happened?"

"He made me swear never to tell," the old man whispered.

"Who?" I turned my body to face him properly, peeling back the mask again and seeing the anguish, the fear. "Declan? Your son called you?"

Clayton's jaw clenched. "About a year after I told him to leave us alone, he left a message on my phone telling me he'd gone too far. The boy sounded scared, real genuine fear. Maybe that's why I believed him." Clayton's voice was down to a low whisper now, like he was retelling a dramatic ghost story. The scary thing about it was, it felt real...because it actually was.

"What did he do?"

"He didn't say. He just told me he had to disappear for good to keep everyone safe. He told me to take care of his boy and that if a guy called Marchant ever came looking for one of us, I had to get Eric out of there as fast as I could." Clayton sniffed. "He also said he was sorry for letting us both down and begged me to keep an eye on Eric, make sure he didn't turn out to be like him." Clayton scrubbed a hand over his face and blinked a couple of times. "I tried to get in touch with Dec after that, but he was gone. Maybe I should have called the police, but something in my gut told me to trust my son and leave it alone. I don't know who Marchant is, but the way Dec said his name..." Clayton pursed his lips. "The man's a threat, and thank God he's never surfaced." Clayton pointed out at the ocean. "My son asked me to do one thing: look after that kid in the water. Eric was fifteen by that stage and I had to admit, I was scared. I had no idea what Declan had gotten himself into." He huffed and closed his eyes. "But I promised myself to watch over my only grandson, and that's why I stepped in when Eric got real bad."

"His rage stage," I mumbled.

"That's the one. Had a temper just like his daddy. I'd seen it all play out before. When my beautiful May died, Declan was eighteen and he didn't cope too well. Hell, neither of us did. I was in so much pain, I threw myself into work and Declan just..." Clayton shook his head. "Got lost."

I gently squeezed his shoulder, actually feeling his torture as if it were my own. "It's not your fault," I whispered.

"Yeah, it was," he croaked. "That's why I couldn't fail Eric."

"You know, he always says you saved his life. Taking him out of school and into the wilderness like you did. It was just what he needed."

"Probably should have done the same with Dec, but it was too late by then."

"Why have you never told Eric this?"

"I'd planned on it, but when I finally got a hold of that hurting little kid, I couldn't do it. His rage toward his father was unshakeable. I figured if I told him the truth, he'd just hate Declan more for being a loser and putting us all in danger."

I turned back to the ocean in time to see Eric jump up on his board and ride the wave, blissfully unaware of our conversation. "I wonder what your son did."

"I have no idea. Probably got himself into debt to this Marchant guy. That boy couldn't resist the money or the cards. The amount of times I had to bail him out…" Clayton punched out a hard laugh that quickly dissipated. "That call, though, that one was different." His lips pursed and he shook his head. "You know, for all Eric's hatred towards the man, I think Declan really loves his son, and I think he'd do anything to save Eric's life."

"You should tell Eric that."

"It's been too long now; the boy'd no doubt turn all his anger back at me for hiding the truth for so long. You know how fragile his trust is. I don't want to be the one to shatter it."

I swallowed; dread bubbling in my stomach. The afternoon was going to suck. Closing my eyes, I drew in a breath.

One conversation at a time, Caity.

I turned back to Eric's grandpa. "He needs closure over this whole thing. Maybe if he knew his father disappeared out of love, he'd be able to move on."

Clayton grunted, his right shoulder hitching up as if he agreed with me, but didn't really want to.

His expression changed to a sunny smile and I glanced back at the sand to see Eric running up the beach toward us.

"Mouth shut, honey. I'll tell him in my own good time." Clayton rose from the sand before I could argue, wiping the sand off his shorts before waving at Eric and heading back to the house.

"He still mad with me?" Eric laid his board down next to mine and snatched up his towel.

"No." I shook my head. "He's just going in to get breakfast started."

Eric gave me a skeptical frown.

I raised my hands and forced a light laugh. "Can you seriously imagine that guy holding a grudge against you? His cherished grandson? Come on."

Eric snickered, tucking the damp locks behind his ear before kneeling down in front of me.

"Feeling better?" I ran my foot up the side of his leg.

"You know I do."

I chuckled, brushing my teeth over my lower lip as he came toward me for a kiss. I relished the taste of his salty skin, tempted to pull him on top of me. The beach was practically empty bar a few surfers in the water.

They wouldn't mind, would they?

I pushed Eric away before I succumbed to temptation. I'd die if Clayton came back down telling us breakfast was ready, only to find us tangled up together on the sand. Touching Eric's face, I soaked in his adoring expression then peeled off his mask. Last night's conversation was still weighing on him. Peeling away a few more layers, I could see the hurt and disappointment. They weren't buried as deeply today and I wondered if I should be unsettling them even more. But I had to. I loved Eric and he deserved the truth.

"Hey, so after breakfast, I was wondering if you wanted to go hiking, just the two of us." I tried to keep my expression light, hoping he'd assume I had a little love-making session planned. The idea was actually to use that part to soften him up and then tell him. It was devious, but at least if he was going to storm away from me, he'd be storming away from a naked version of me and it might be a little harder for him to leave.

"That sounds like the perfect way to spend my day." His smile was exquisite as he stood and reached for my hand. I let him pull me up and we collected our stuff.

My nerves were in a frenzy as we walked up the beach. Yes, telling him was the right decision and that part felt great, but I was also really scared. I just hoped I could make him see my reasoning.

We paused at the road and checked both ways before crossing, my steps faltering as I spotted a familiar-looking car on the other side of the road.

Shit!

Was that Kaplan?

I squinted and noticed the shape was all wrong.

No, that shadow behind the wheel had to be Agent Rhodes.

How the hell did he find me?

I'd replied to Kaplan's *Where the hell are you?* text on the way down last night, saying I was out of town. I'd kept it brief.

Out of town. Will call when I get back.

Then I'd turned my phone off, vowing to leave it in my bag until I returned on Sunday.

She wasn't even supposed to be contacting my private cell anyway, and yet she'd gone and used it twice in the last week. I was still livid with her for calling me when I was in Eric's bed. What the hell!

"Babe, are you okay?"

"Huh?" I looked away from the car and forced a smile at Eric.

"What's the matter?"

"Nothing." I blinked innocently and headed across the road.

As we moved toward the narrow path leading up to Clayton's place, I stole a quick glance over my shoulder. Rhodes was getting out of the car and firing a look my way. Eric turned down the path and I glanced at the agent one more time. His shades were off and he was giving me a steely message that said we had to talk...and we had to talk now.

twenty-four

caitlyn

"Um," I wiggled my fingers out of Eric's hand. "Did I leave my shades on the beach?"

"I didn't think you took them down."

"Are you sure?" I flicked my thumb over my shoulder. "I'm just gonna go and check."

"No problem." Eric shrugged and turned toward the beach.

I flicked the board from under my arm and held it out to him. "Can you carry this back for me? I'll be right behind you."

"Oh, okay, sure." He took the board and turned back down the path.

I raced to the roadside, thanking my lucky stars that he hadn't made a fuss about coming with me. Peeking over my shoulder, I saw Eric turn right and disappear into his grandpa's backyard. I sucked in a breath and checked the road before running across it.

Hurrying down the sandy slope, I decided to check the sand and at least look as if I were searching for my shades.

Rhodes would subtly approach me, the way he always did.

"What the hell are you doing in San Diego?" His dry voice made my shoulders ping tight.

I kept my eyes on the sand. "Having a weekend away."

"You're not entitled to a break."

"Yeah, well, last I heard, I wasn't getting paid for this gig, so I think I can take some time off."

"I'm sure the girls would love to hear you say that."

I spun around to face him, not caring who saw us. "Don't pull that on me. I've been working my ass off trying to get the goods on where they might be. I'm hanging out with people I don't like and lying to the people I really care about in order to make this happen, so don't guilt-trip me, okay?"

Rhodes shrugged. "I'm just doing my job."

I let out a scoff and turned away from him.

"Kaplan thinks you came down here to tell Eric what you're up to."

My jaw clenched and I looked out to the ocean, determined to keep my gaze locked on the horizon.

"Thought so," he muttered. "You done it yet?"

I shook my head.

"Don't."

"It's my right."

"It's not your right," he snapped. "You agreed to take this on, and part of the agreement was to work undercover, which means you lie to keep those around you safe."

My eyes flicked toward him; I couldn't help it. Something in his tone made my heart seize.

Who was he trying to keep safe? Who did he regret lying to?

I opened my mouth to ask, but he cut me off.

"Kaplan is livid over this. She wants you back in L.A. ASAP, but knows you can't fumble your way through an early departure, so lucky you. You have the rest of the weekend off." He huffed and scratched the back of his neck. I wished he didn't always wear those shades around me; I'd love to get a proper read on him like I did the first time we met. Maybe then I could figure out what was really bothering him right now.

"The second Eric drops you off at your dorm tomorrow night, I'll be taking you to meet with Kaplan."

"Why? Can't I just call her?"

"She wants to bite your head off in person." He shrugged, his right eyebrow popping up in time with the move.

I snickered. "Look, I get that what I did was wrong, but I tried to tell her. She wouldn't let me."

"Well, she's a focused lady. She goes after what she wants, no matter what."

"Understatement of the year," I mumbled.

Rhodes' lips twitched, but he caught the smile before it had time to bloom. "Look, just do me a favor and toe the line. You don't want to get on the wrong side of this woman."

My eyes narrowed and I gazed at his profile. "She scares you, doesn't she?"

The tough-looking man swallowed, running his tongue over his lower teeth. "She's a viper on this particular case. I've never seen her like this before. She..." he sighed, obviously hesitant to tell me.

"What?"

"When she was a kid, her sister was taken— kidnapped. No one ever found her. She just disappeared without a trace. She could have been murdered...or something worse." A tendon in Rhodes's neck pinged tight. "When it comes to stolen girls, Kaplan's a pit bull. She's always on the lookout for cases like this and she jumped all over this one. It's like saving these girls will somehow make up for the fact she couldn't get her sister back. If she doesn't find them..."

He shook his head, clicking his tongue and looking down at the sand. "It'll be like reliving it all over again."

My heart actually squeezed in sympathy...for Kaplan. Something I thought it would never do.

"How old was she when her sister disappeared?"

Rhodes shrugged. "Just a kid. Old enough to know what the hell was going on, young enough to be scarred for life."

My face crumpled and I crossed my arms, pinching my bicep.

He looked over at me, his expression steely. "Don't screw this up, Davis, or we're all gonna pay..." I noticed his unmasked mouth dip. He pressed his lips together, trying to hide his reluctance before breathing out through his nose and muttering, "Including your boyfriend."

My breath hitched, my stomach squeezing tight as I watched the concern flitter over his expression.

I grabbed his arm. "What do you mean?"

Whipping off his shades, he gave me a clear view into his hard, green eyes. The mask fell away from the rest of his face, revealing something I never expected to see.

Guilt. Conflict. Dissent.

"What is Kaplan up to?"

He swallowed. "You'll find out when you get back to L.A. tomorrow night." He flicked my hand off him, sliding his shades back on. "But word to the wise, if you love your boyfriend, keep your damn mouth shut."

twenty-five

caitlyn

I did what I was told and sealed my confession up tight, locking it into the back recesses of my brain. Anxiety was the perfect padlock and kept me forcing sunny laughter and plastic smiles for the rest of the weekend. Eric and I did go hiking, and we made love by a secluded little lake and dozed in the sunshine. Eric softly snored while I lay in his arms, eyes wide open. My brain jittered with nerves and the exhaustion of playing pretend, but I held my ground and didn't fall apart until Eric's car disappeared into the darkness and Agent Rhodes pulled up outside my dorm.

I hopped in, throwing my bag in the back before slamming the door behind me.

"Nice weekend?" he asked quietly as we pulled away from the curb.

"Shut up." Tears lined my lashes as I looked out the window, reliving my final converation—argument—with Eric.

"Caity, you have to admit that the further we've gotten into this weekend, the more tense you've become. I know it's because you'll be seeing Quella again soon and you don't want to. Just move out and let her go."

"I can't. You don't understand."

"I do understand. I know that you find it really hard to turn your back on someone in need, but she's draining you completely."

"It's not that bad." I smiled and squeezed his knee. *"This weekend has totally rejuvenated me and I'm ready."*

He looked unconvinced.

"She needs me, Eric. I can't turn away."

He humphed and kept driving in silence.

I'd thought of a million things to say to break the

tension, but I hadn't uttered any of them. The only one to really work would have been the truth, and thanks to Rhodes freaking me out on the beach, I couldn't give Eric what he needed.

I closed my eyes and let the first tear fall.

Rhodes was wise enough to stay silent for the twenty-minute trip. We parked underground and I followed him into an elevator and up a few floors. I had no idea where we were; it looked like a hotel. We stopped outside room 204 and Rhodes knocked twice.

The door opened and there stood Kaplan, her expression cold enough to freeze the Pacific. I cast my eyes to the floor and slid past her, walking into the room and taking a seat at the small table by the window. The heavy drapes were drawn shut and I didn't have the courage to peek out and see where we were.

Instead, I tapped my nails on the polished wood and awaited my doom.

Kaplan let me sweat it out, taking her sweet time to extract yet another file from her black briefcase and take a seat opposite me.

"Proud of yourself?"

I ignored the question, keeping my eyes on the table.

"I sure hope you had a good time, Caitlyn, because until this case is over, it was your last."

"What does that even mean?"

Kaplan slapped the file down on her table. "It means that if you hadn't been attached to Mr. Dreamboat, you never would have felt the need to run away with him for a weekend of pleasure."

"It wasn't like that; I just needed some time off."

"You think you deserve that luxury? While twelve girls are suffering somewhere?"

My head popped up. "I thought it was only ten."

"Two more went missing on Friday."

I swallowed.

"The fact of the matter is, Caitlyn, Eric is distracting you from this case, which I knew he would."

"I haven't told him anything," I grumbled.

"And you won't, because you're going to break up with him."

"What!" I exploded out of my chair. "Forget it! You can't make me do that."

"An entire weekend was wasted while you flittered off for some fun! You need to get yourself an invite to Quella's place, preferably for Thanksgiving, which is less than two weeks away. How the hell are you going to sell that to him? There's no way he's not going to put up a fight and try to convince you to stick around. I've thought it through and this will work."

"No." I shook my head.

"You break up with him and run crying to Quella. You'll be distraught and desperate to get away. This will be your chance to drop a few hints that going to Quella's will give you time to heal. She likes you; she'll buy into that easily."

"No!"

Kaplan ignored my shout. "You go there for Thanksgiving, find the evidence we need and you're done."

"NO!"

"Look, Princess!" Kaplan stood from her seat and leaned toward me. "You can get back together with him once this is done. If you do your job properly, it should be over by the end of November."

"I can't do it." My voice caught.

"Yes, you can, and you will."

I shook my head.

"Geez, you can be stubborn when you want to be." She threw her hands in the air and looked at Rhodes, who was silently standing post on the other side of the room. His shades were still on, dammit, and I had no idea what their silent exchange meant, but I ripped off Kaplan's mask and a quick unease skittered inside me before she turned my way. "I didn't want to have to do this, but you forced my hand when you took off this weekend."

"Didn't want to do what?" I looked back to Rhodes. He flinched, pulling in a quick breath and looking away.

Kaplan cleared her throat. "Sit down."

My knees gave out and I fell into the chair, the ominous dread in the room making me want to pass out. What had she done? What the hell had she done?

"You forced me to find leverage."

"Leverage?" My forehead wrinkled as Kaplan tapped the folder on the table.

MELISSA PEARL

"I need you to play nice, and if I have to blackmail you into doing that, then so be it." She flicked the folder open and spun it around to face me. I couldn't reach for it. As much as I was desperate to look, I couldn't take my eyes off Kaplan's face. "I've had a very interesting weekend. When you went *non-communicado* on Friday evening, I knew I had to up the ante, so I got a little hacker friend of mine to help me out." She crossed her arms, her pristine jacket pulling tight across her shoulders. "While you were riding the waves with your boyfriend, I was discovering some very interesting things about his family."

She slid the folder toward me, forcing me to pick it up. I gazed down at the picture and gasped. The man staring back at me looked so like Eric it was freaky: the same intense gaze, the chiseled features softened by the floppy brown locks of hair.

"His name's Antonio Costa."

I glanced at her with a frown. I'd been expecting the words Declan Shore to pop out of her mouth.

"He also goes by the name Thomas Dunn and Patrick Kuntz, but his real identity is..." Her left eyebrow arched and she stared at me expectantly, like a schoolteacher waiting for the right answer.

I tore my gaze away from her, staring back at the picture and feeling my stomach turn over.

"His name's Declan Shore, son of Clayton, father of Eric." She tapped the folder, making it jump in my hands. I jerked in surprise and glanced at her smirking face. "But you already knew that, didn't you?"

I slapped the file closed and threw it onto the table. It slid to the other side, falling against the curtain and getting caught behind the table leg.

"Tut-tut." Kaplan wagged her finger at me, carefully collecting the file back up and putting it on the table. "You should really go through this. It's an entertaining read."

The mockery in her voice made me want to slap her. I ripped at her mask, wanting to eliminate that smirk, but it remained in place, growing more sinister until I finally reached that desperate little girl again...the one who'd lost her sister and never recovered.

"What was her name?" I whispered.

"Who?"

"Your sister."

Kaplan's gaze shot to Rhodes, who squirmed and looked to the floor, before she fired it back to me. Her stare was black and hard. I could feel my flesh burning. "Don't even try." Her tone was brittle. "I know you can see behind these layers. I've been to enough shrinks to recognize the truth: I am a woman driven by the tragedy of my past." Her granite exterior was hard to break through. I sat in the chair, forcing air to my light-headed brain. "I will never actually catch the person who stole my sister and we will never find her. I cannot repair the damage that was done to my family, but you know what I *can* do?"

I swallowed.

"I can catch every other fucker who tries to hurt, steal or kill little girls, and I will do whatever it takes to make that happen." I wanted to bolt from the room and run to Eric's. I wanted to crawl into his bed and pretend this moment was a nightmare.

But I couldn't move.

Kaplan's iron voice worked like manacles on my wrists. I was stuck in my chair and couldn't say a word as she flicked open the file and cleared her throat.

"Now, this little con man here." She tapped the photo of Declan. "He scored himself some major cash in a pretty short space of time and set up an account under his ex-wife's name. Kind of like a trust fund for his kid. Damn hard to trace, I can tell you that. It took my guy hours of hacking to find the money trail that linked Shayna Watson and Antonio Costa." Kaplan pointed at me, looking damn proud of herself as she spoke of Eric's mom. "We started with Eric, looking for anything we could pin on him, but he's pretty clean. I know he had nothing to do with that friend of his dying on the beach, so we had to go wider, start looking at his father...his mother. That's when alarm bells started ringing. Don't you think it's strange that a woman who can barely maintain a job as a nail technician is sitting pretty in Pacific Palisades? Haven't you ever wondered how Eric pays for his college education?"

"The trust fund is from her deceased parents," I tried to explain.

She responded with a scoffing laugh. "Well gosh, he

really has a lot of liars in his life, doesn't he? Shayna Watson's parents are alive and well."

I shot her a dark glare, about to tell her she was wrong, but I couldn't, because she wasn't lying.

She countered my death rays with a sticky sweet smile and kept talking. "What we know for sure now is that Eric's father is very good at covering his tracks. But where there's a will, there's a way, am I right?"

My glare grew a little darker.

"So we dug a little deeper and finally found out what this guy had really been up to. Luckily for us he screwed up big-time. Managed to con the wife of one of the meanest men in Vegas—Lucian Marchant."

The blood froze in my veins.

Marchant?

Was that the guy Gramps told me about on the beach?

"So, anyway, Marchant got his hands on Declan and beat him to a pulp, left him in the desert. Not a great way to go."

She pulled a face and my insides curdled. All this time, Clayton Shore had thought his son was in hiding, but he'd actually been caught and killed.

"Marchant got away with it, of course. With his kind of power, he gets away with a lot. Missing bodies, missing bones...no trace of evidence whatsoever. It helped that no missing person's report was ever filed for Declan Shore." Kaplan's eyes narrowed as she studied me. I kept my gaze steady. Like hell I was giving away my conversation with Clayton.

"I'm surprised you don't want to go after him," I muttered.

"One bad guy at time, Caitlyn. Don't worry, he's on our radar."

I grimaced, squirming in my chair. "Why are you showing me this?"

Kaplan leaned back in her chair, tapping her thumbs together. "I want to paint a picture for you."

I swallowed; dread restricting my airways.

"Marchant hates to lose, so can you imagine his humiliation at knowing that his wife had an affair with a conman and lost him close to half a million dollars of his money."

"What happened to her?" I whispered.

"She committed suicide. At least, that's what the police reports say." Kaplan shrugged. "500k is probably peanuts to a man like that, but it's the losing, the disgrace against his good name, that kills him."

My heartbeat was now thrumming in my brain, making it hard to hear.

"So just think what would happen if I mailed him this file and he found out that Antonio Costa was actually Declan Shore, and that he had a son living less than 300 miles away. For a guy like Lucian Marchant, finding and torturing the offspring of a man who shamed him would be well worth the time and effort."

The air in my lungs evaporated. I gripped the wooden arms of my chair and threw a desperate glance at Rhodes. He looked to the floor and shook his head.

I turned back to Kaplan and shouted, "You can't do that!"

"I think the U.S. Postal Service would disagree with you."

"You...you bitch!" I lunged out of my seat and went for Kaplan. I wanted to scratch her eyes out.

Rhodes caught me before I could, grabbing my arms and holding me back. I shook him off me and spun to face him, clutching his jacket. "Please, you can't let her do this."

"I won't have to if you do what you're told!" Kaplan snapped. "If you love your boyfriend then break his heart...at least you'll be keeping him alive."

Rhodes calmly loosened my grip and smoothed down his jacket, nudging me away from him.

I pointed at Kaplan, my lips wobbling as I fought for control. "You know, you're a really shitty FBI agent."

"Then why have I never lost a case?" Kaplan snatched an A4 envelope off the desk and slid the file inside. "It may look like I play dirty, but I do what it takes to win. This little operation is going to save multiple families from complete destruction, and you're going to help me do it. Eric's life is safe...as long as you do what you're supposed to."

I slumped onto the perfectly made bed, wanting to dissolve into a puddle of tears, but I couldn't. My eyes burned and my head screamed, but all I was capable of was a slow blink.

"From now on, I want you to wear a permanent wire. We're getting to crunch time, and I need to know exactly what you're up to. Go with Rhodes; he'll take you next door and make sure you're all suited up. The tech guys will show you how everything works." She gave me a tight smile. "Hey, look on the bright side: at least you won't have to call me every night now."

My body was too numb to form any kind of defense. Rhodes gently put his hand under my arm and helped me stand, leading me from the room and into what would be the beginning of an even bigger nightmare.

twenty-six

eric

Pulling out the loaf of bread, I sat it next to the peanut butter and gazed out through the kitchen window. It was dark out and I still hadn't heard back from Caity. After the awesome weekend we'd had together, I'd thought...

I sighed.

Okay, so the weekend hadn't been spectacular. Yes,

it'd had its beautiful moments, but it'd also been filled with imperfections, like the little spat over my dad during poker and then our final conversation on the drive home.

Caity knew what I was saying. Quella was a drain and she couldn't deny that, but she refused to back down. She was so incredibly stubborn sometimes!

I frowned, untwisting the tie on the bread and pulling out two thick slices of wholemeal. Not the world's most nutritious dinner, but I couldn't be bothered to cook.

It was Tuesday night. Technically, I should be at a little Mexican restaurant ordering two of my favorite tacos, but what was the point of going if Caity wasn't even going to be there? And why the hell had she not returned my text OR answered my call? Her phone was on because it rang what felt like a hundred times before going to her voice mail.

Unscrewing the peanut butter jar, I threw the lid on the counter and watched it skid to the edge then drop to the floor.

I hadn't bothered leaving a message. She'd see the caller ID, she'd read my text.

What is going on with you? Why are you not replying to me? It's Taco Tuesday and you weren't there when I came to pick you up! Since when have you ever ditched a date? Talk to me! This is driving me insane!!

Slapping a knife full of peanut butter onto my bread, I slathered it around then slammed the other piece on top, leaving finger indentations behind.

"Dude, what did that sandwich ever do to you?" Mr. Smiley ambled into the kitchen and opened the refrigerator.

"Shut up, man," I mumbled at Scott, collecting the lid and screwing it back on.

"You okay?" Scott pulled out the milk and poured himself a glass, his permanent smile dulled just a little.

"Yeah." I scrubbed a hand over my face, then shook my head. "It's Caity."

"Is she okay?"

"I don't know." I shrugged, snatching a plate out of the cupboard and throwing my sandwich onto it. "She won't call me back, she won't text me, and when I swung past her dorm this evening, she wasn't there. I was going to sit in the car and wait for her, but then felt like a total stalker so decided to come home."

"Yeah, I thought it was weird you were here. Taco Tuesday, right?"

I nodded, slumping into my chair and biting off a hunk of bread. It tasted like ash, but I chewed it anyway.

Scott poured me a glass of milk and set it down by my plate.

"Got anything stronger?" My eyebrow arched.

He chuckled. "Come on, man. It's not that bad, is it?"

I leaned forward in my chair, pushing my plate aside.

"It's weird. This is so un-Caity. I mean, yes, she forgets to charge her phone and she turns it off every now and then, but she never ignores me. I don't know what's going on."

Scott licked the residue milk from his top lip. "Do you think it has anything to do with her new roommate?"

I threw my head back with a groan. "Probably. She's bending over backwards for this girl, and I don't think Quella even notices or appreciates it. I hate that she's putting her before us."

"You know what Caity's like, though. She'll do anything for anyone."

"I know." I sighed. "But she's always been really good at putting us first. I didn't think she'd ever do anything to compromise our relationship."

Scott chuckled. "She doesn't call you for two days and the relationship is compromised? Dude, that's some pressure."

"I'm not that pathetic." I rubbed my eyebrow and ran a hand through my hair. "I'm just used to talking to her most days... and she's been different lately. Like she's trying to be happy around me or...I don't know."

"Do you think she's hiding something from you?"

My heart jerked in an unsteady rhythm. "She always promised me she wouldn't."

"Well, then you gotta give her the benefit of the doubt. Something else must be going on."

"I can't lose her, Scott."

He placed his empty glass on the table. "Sometimes you can't control those kinds of things."

I gave him a sharp look. "Don't you think I know that?"

"I'm not trying to piss you off or anything, I'm just saying..." He raised his hands as two white flags.

"Well, don't." My chair scraped on the floor as I stood tall and took my plate to the trash can, throwing out my uneaten sandwich.

"Eric."

"What?"

"Maybe it's a combo effect; you know, pressure from all sides."

I paused. "What do you mean?"

"Well, she's trying to help Quella, which she knows you don't like, but even so, she's putting on the right face for her and then when she's around you, trying to keep you happy, and then Piper's wedding mania has started and that has a pressure all of its own." He shook his head with a grin. "Aside from that, exams are looming and then you've got Thanksgiving just around the corner and I don't care how awesome anyone's family is, that celebration comes with its own special kind of stress."

Spinning around, I leaned against the counter and folded my arms. "So, what do you think I should do?"

"Well, maybe instead of trying to give her advice, like pulling away from Quella, why don't you ask her what she needs to get through this?"

I frowned at him.

He raised his hands. "It's only an idea, man. I'm just trying to help you out."

"No, it's good. I like it. Rather than saying 'you should be doing this', I can be like 'what do you need from me'?"

"Yeah." Scott nodded. "I can't guarantee it's going to work or anything, but I do know that I'm the kind of person who responds better to that sort of thing. When I feel like I'm being bossed around, I kind of dig my heels in and do the quiet stubborn thing."

My lips twitched with a smile. "Stubborn," I muttered, thinking of Caity.

"Good luck, man." He walked out of the kitchen with an impish grin.

Grabbing my phone, I gazed at the screen and sent my girl another text.

Hey, babe. I don't know what's going on tonight, but whatever it is, I'm here if you need me. Your Hercules forever xx

twenty-seven

caitlyn

I read Eric's text and blinked, tears making my vision blurry. This sucked. This *sucked*!

Kaplan wanted us broken up by the end of the week, so I could score myself a last-minute invite to Quella's. So far, my grand plan had been to completely ignore him, do the lame ass *don't call and we'll just naturally end it* thing. It was so cowardly, but I didn't know if I could do it.

How did I get words out of my mouth that I one hundred percent did not mean?

How?

How was I supposed to look at Eric's beautiful face and tell him I didn't want to be with him anymore?

"Just think what would happen if I mailed him this file and he found out that Antonio Costa was actually Declan Shore, and that he had a son living less than 300 miles away. For a guy like Lucian Marchant, finding and torturing the offspring of a man who humiliated him would be well worth the time and effort."

That was how.

The idea of Eric being found, stolen, tortured? I doubled over, fighting for air.

I had to do this and just pray that once it was over, he'd hear me out and take me back.

Sniffing at my phone, I quickly texted back.

Sorry. Got delayed. It's been a shitty night. Can't talk about it yet. Can you meet me tomorrow after class?

Less than a minute later, I got my reply.

Of course. Whatever you need.

I sent back the details of when and where. It took me way too long to think of a spot. I didn't want anywhere to be tainted by this horrible thing—not our willow tree, not our Mexican restaurant, definitely not the beach. In the end, I settled for outside Powell Library. It was close to his final class for the day and we could walk and talk. It'd be easier to run away from him in tears, which I could guarantee would happen.

Hating Kaplan with a new kind of passion, I sent my text and threw my phone onto the bed.

"Okay, I've just texted Eric. I'm doing it tomorrow night," I mumbled into the permanent wire attached to my bra.

"Good job," Rhodes said quietly. "Remember you're doing this to save his life. Just keep that in your head."

I let out a heavy sigh as Quella walked in. Straightening up, I pasted on a smile.

She paused, her head tipping to the side as she looked right through it.

"I feel like dancing."

I glanced at my watch. "It's nearly nine o'clock. I'm too tired."

"No, you are sad." She grabbed my wrist and pulled me toward the door. "I do not know why, but I do know that dancing will make it better."

I wanted to say no and curl into a ball on my bed.

"Don't forget your persona, Caitlyn," Rhodes whispered into my ear. I hated that he was there all the time...and so often right. I had to get this damn thing over with, and dancing with Quella would help.

Forcing another smile, I shrugged. "Okay, you win. Take me dancing."

She let out a squeal and yanked me out the door.

****

I got drunk.

I'd never done that before. Ever.

I usually hated the taste of alcohol, but I threw that stuff down my throat like my life depended on it.

My Martha Woodgrove ID was put to good use, that was for sure.

Shots.

Tequila.

Deadly.

Stumbling out of the club, I checked to make sure Quella was following me. She bumped her way around the large man by the door and giggled when he spilled his beer. He gave her an evil glare. My vision blurred as his mask disintegrated, my eyes bulging wide.

He wasn't really mad with her; he was too busy checking her out.

I sniffed and tottered toward her, yanking her arm and pulling her out of the bar.

"Let's go," I croaked.

She giggled again, tumbling into me until we both ended up on the grass, our feet flying into the air before we curled on our sides with more laughter. I had to blink really hard to see Quella clearly. The alcohol was doing something freaky to my sight; I couldn't figure it out, but masks weren't falling away tonight...they were evaporating. It was like watching a fire suck them into nothing. The alcohol burned through the layers rapidly. I had no control.

"Awwww." I brushed Quella's face. "You miss your mom. I'm sorry."

My words felt thick and heavy, oozing out of my mouth like viscous glue. I smacked my lips together and winced, my head starting to ache as I looked at Quella's wide, soulful gaze.

"How do you know about my mother? I never talk about her." She frowned, propping herself onto one elbow.

"I don't..." I licked the edge of my mouth. "Your mom.... People leave, but they don't mean to hurt you. Sometimes they do it to protect you."

"She did not want to protect me," Quella snapped. "She left because she did not love me enough to stay."

Quella's heated anger was harsh and uncompromising. I turned away from it and closed my eyes, my head spinning circles. The sky was seriously falling. I dug the heel of my hand into my eye socket and was struck with an overwhelming urge to cry.

"That's not always true," I wailed, my stomach jerking with sobs. "He's never gonna forgive me," I hiccuped. "I hate her for making me do this. I hate her."

"Who do you hate? What are you talking about?"

I never had a chance to answer. A strong hand clamped around my arm and hauled me to my feet.

"That's enough," he whispered.

My head flopped against his shoulder and I breathed in his scent. It had become familiar somehow, even though I'd only been close enough to smell him a couple of times.

"Let her go!" Quella stood on wobbly legs and tried to pull me back. "Who are you?"

"Security, miss. It's time you girls head home."

"Rhodes," I mumbled against him.

"Shhhh," he silenced me quickly, pulling my arm and marching me away from the bar. Quella trotted up behind us.

"Where do you girls live?"

I giggled. "Don't you already know that?"

"Of course he doesn't," Quella snapped, the idea of security sobering her up. She crossed her arms and huffed, still a little unsteady on her feet but able to walk unaided.

I glanced at her face as we waited to cross the street. Her nostrils were flaring, the muscles in her face pinched tight.

"Don't be scared. He's not going to arrest us." I patted Rhodes's chest.

"Would you shut up?" he whispered between clenched teeth. "Just stop talking."

I sniffed and tried to glare at him, but my head felt too heavy to lift off his shoulder.

By the time we crossed the road, the FBI agent had let go of my arm and actually had his arm around my waist. Quella walked ahead of us, leading the way with her tense, edgy shuffle.

My body groaned and ached as we stumbled along. It felt full of liquid, like whatever I'd been drinking was sloshing around inside me.

I glanced up at Rhodes as he hauled me along.

He looked worried, agitated.

"I know you hate this job," I mumbled. "You never signed up to be a babysitter."

"It's fine. Keep walking."

I teetered beside him and his arm clenched me tighter. "I know you think I'm an idiot, under-qualified, but you know I didn't sign up for this either. I—"

"I swear to God, if you don't shut up, I'm going to knock you out."

I giggled. "You don't mean that."

He glared at me and I swallowed, licking my lower lip slowly.

"Although you are tempted," I slurred then erupted with giggles again that swiftly turned into sobs.

"Hey," he said softly, squeezing me against him. "It's gonna be okay. He'll forgive you."

"I'm about to break his heart. You don't know Eric. He's been hurt. He puts up this shield to protect himself, but he let it down around me. He trusts me, and I'm going to destroy that."

Rhodes jerked to a stop, spinning me to face him. His fingers dug into my arms, holding me upright. "I've been watching you for the last seven weeks and I know for a fact that your boyfriend loves you...and if he doesn't forgive you after this, he's a fool. Guys don't give up on girls like you."

My insides jolted as I took in Rhodes's unmasked expression. His penetrating gaze drove right into my core, the gentle look in his eyes contradicting his usual, angry fire.

I sucked in a quick mouthful of air, unable to hide the fact I was seeing everything.

He quickly swallowed, his face blanching as he spun me back around and marched me forward. The revelation did wonders in sobering me up. I was still inebriated, but seeing Rhodes's tender side was like having a cold bucket of water thrown over me.

We didn't say anything more as he walked me back to my dorm.

I tripped on the pathway to the front door and would have face-planted on the concrete if Rhodes hadn't caught me. Swooping me into his arms, he muttered something to Quella and she led him up to our room. Halfway up the stairs, Quella swayed, covered her mouth and then made a lurching run for the bathroom.

With a sigh, Rhodes shifted me in his arms and walked to our door, plonking me on my feet.

"You have a key?"

"Um..." I frowned, patting my pocket, then giving him a little smile before fumbling the key free.

He rolled his eyes and let me lean against him while he unlocked the door.

We tripped into the room together and he caught me, half-throwing me onto my bed.

My sigh was wistful and luxurious as my head sank into the soft pillow.

When I opened my eyes Rhodes was standing over me, pulling his suit jacket straight.

"Thanks for bringing me home, security."

He cleared his throat. "Don't get drunk again. It doesn't suit you."

My eyes welled with tears.

"Hey." He gave me a gentle smile. "It'll be okay. You can do this. Just rip off the Band-Aid and end it. It'll be easier that way."

I sniffed and gave him a shaky nod.

"I'm here if you need me," he muttered before turning for the door and disappearing.

I pressed my fingers into my temples and bit my lip against the tears that threatened to overtake me again.

Kicking off my shoes, I heard them plop onto the floor then tucked my knees up against my chest. Something was digging into my butt. I pulled it out of my pocket and slid my thumb over the phone screen. Eric's text stared back at me.

My eyes filled with tears again and I decided the Band-Aid had to come off right away. Pressing the little phone symbol on my screen, I held it to my ear and waited five rings.

"Caity? Are you okay?" Eric sounded groggy. I had no idea what time it was.

"I need a break," I slurred.

"Excuse me?"

"From us." My voice sounded wooden. I squeezed my eyes shut.

"I don't understand what you're saying to me right now." There was a pause. "Caity, it's two o'clock in the morning. Where the hell are you?"

"In bed." My voice pitched.

"Are you—Are you drunk?"

"Eric, I can only tell you this once, okay? We're over...for now. I need some time to think and be away from you."

"What? What are you talking about?"

"I'm tired, so I'm gonna go to sleep now."

"No. I'm coming over. We have to talk about this."

"No, Eric. There's nothing else to say. You have to respect my wishes and give me some space."

"But—" He huffed. "Caity, where is this coming from?"

I licked my lips, suddenly regretting the fact I was attempting the call while drunk. "I'm just...I'm...I need..." I cleared my throat. "I'm starting to feel a little claustrophobic."

"You're lying," he whispered.

Tears stung my eyes, my face bunching into a painful frown. "Look, I know this is hard for you to hear and it's hard for me to say. I love you." I sucked in a breath, sobs making my belly quake. "I really love you."

"Calm down," Rhodes voice was back in my other

ear. "Just stop for a minute and catch your breath."

I sucked in a mouthful of air.

"And for the record, you're an idiot to do this drunk." His low voice and dry tone almost made me giggle.

Rhodes was funny.

My head lolled to the side and I grinned.

"Caity, are you still there?" Eric's voice was rough and unsteady in contrast to the FBI agent listening in on this call.

"End this and hang up. Now," Rhodes commanded.

"I gotta go, Eric." I sniffed.

"No, wait. You can't leave me like this."

"I gotta sleep," I whispered. "We can talk about it in the morning."

"Wait, Cait—"

"Goodbye, Eric." I hung up before he could say more. Clutching the phone to my chest, I curled into a small ball and let the sobs break free. They punched out of my mouth, broken and pitiful, my body heaving until exhaustion took over.

I heard Quella come in, mumbling some sort of thank you to security, but my puffy eyes were closed by then and I couldn't drag them back open.

Mercifully, sleep took me and I drowned in an oblivion of strange dreams, until I was jerked awake with a nightmare in the morning.

Squinting at the clock on my phone, I winced, my head feeling like it was made of bricks and being held together with sludge. It was nearly seven and I had a class in an hour, but that wasn't what made me jerk off the bed. What made my body move like lightening was the text message from Eric flashing on my phone screen.

I don't understand why you tried to break up with me last night, but we have to talk about this. I'm waiting outside your dorm and I'm not leaving.

I did what?

"Oh, shit."

I started to hyperventilate as patchy memories from the previous night flashed through my brain. When the hell did I call Eric? Pressing my hand into my chest, I flopped onto the bed and tried to yank on my shoes, my movements erratic and shaky.

"Calm down. You can do this," Rhodes whispered in my ear.

My response was a few quick puffs of air.

"Did Quella make it onto her bed last night? I thought it would look a little off to actually walk her right into the room. I escorted her from the bathroom to your door but then left, hoping she'd actually make it to the bed and not end up passed out on the floor."

I glanced at the bed. She was lying face down, fully clothed, her feet dangling over the side.

"Yes," I whispered, knowing he was trying to distract me in order to calm me down.

"Good. Now I want you to take in a deep breath, nice and slow."

I did as I was told.

"And then I want you to tell yourself that there are twelve girls who need you to pull this off and that once this is over, you'll be free."

I pulled in another slow breath, pressing my lips together.

"And then tell yourself that if you don't find the courage to do this now, that guy waiting for you downstairs is a dead man."

My throat restricted.

"Go and save his life, Caity, so that you can be together again once this is over."

I closed my eyes and dipped my head. "Thank you, Rhodes."

"I'm here if you need me."

twenty-eight

eric

I didn't sleep; I didn't even try after Caity hung up on me. Instead, I paced my room like a caged animal until I couldn't take it anymore. The three a.m. sand sprints down the beach were a great way to burn off steam. I ran until my lungs were heaving. My rubber band legs gave out on me eventually and I fell to the sand, burying my cheek into the grains.

I could tell Caity was drunk, which was a shock all its own, but to have her dump me as well, that was a backhand blow I never saw coming.

I didn't know what the hell was going on with her, but I had to find out and so at five in the morning, after I'd showered and changed, I headed for Caity's dorm and that was where I sat for nearly two and a half hours. I had a coffee in one hand and my phone in the other. The minutes ticked by in slow agony as the night sky began to light at the edges.

It was nearly seven-thirty when I saw her approaching. Her skin was pasty white, her expression somber. Large shades covered her eyes. I drank in the sight of her as she checked the street and then crossed, getting into my car without a word.

"Hey." I cleared the lump out of my throat. "You feeling okay?"

She rubbed her forehead. "I feel like a truck has smashed through my skull and is currently burning its back tires inside my brain."

I snickered. "The price you pay for getting off-your-ass drunk."

She bit her lip.

"What's going on with you? You've never gotten drunk before. You don't even like the taste."

"I know," she mumbled. "Quella started buying shots and then everything became a blur."

"Quella." I seethed the word.

She jerked to look at me. I wished she'd take off

those damn shades so I could actually see her.

"Did you mean what you said last night or was Quella putting you up to it?"

Her lips moved, but no sound came out. Her head flinched to look out the window.

I held in my huff and gently laid my hand on her leg. "Caity, I don't think you want to break up with me."

She swallowed and flicked my hand off her thigh. "You don't know what I want."

"I thought I did."

"Well, maybe you thought wrong. Maybe I've just been putting on a show to keep you happy and Quella is helping me to see that I can be whatever I want to be."

My expression marred with confusion. "I've never heard you talk like this before. I don't understand what's going on."

"Well, maybe I don't either." She threw her hand in the air. "But I do know that I need some space and time to figure out exactly what I *do* want out of my life. I'm too young to be settling down. There's a world of opportunity waiting for me, and I don't care that Piper and Scott are getting hitched. In fact, to be honest, I think it's kind of insane. They're like what? Twelve!"

"O-kay." I rubbed my chin, trying to figure out who the hell took over my girlfriend. "I thought you were happy for them."

"Of course I had to be happy for them. Can you imagine the hissy fit Piper would have had if I told her what I really thought?"

The short, snappy sounds punching out of her mouth were foreign to my ears. I didn't know who I was looking at, but it definitely wasn't the Caity I fell in love with.

"I'm not—" I cleared my throat. "I'm not sure what's going on here. I don't know if it's because you're hung over or what, but I don't think we can have a proper conversation with you in such a foul mood."

Her shoulders tensed and then she crossed her arms tight across her chest. "Thanks, Dr. Phil, but all I really need for you to understand right now is that I need a break from us. I want space and room to breathe. I don't want your constant pressure and demands."

"What pressure?"

"To move in with you! To stop hanging out with Quella! Who can be really fun, you know, if you just give her a chance. Something I know you hate doing with people."

I glared at her.

A huge part of me wanted to explode, tear into her with a verbal venom that would no doubt make her cry. If I was one hundred percent honest, I really disliked the Caity sitting across from me. Mean Caity was unattractive.

She glanced over at me, her face paling even further as she no doubt read me. Her lips wobbled, matching the creasing in her forehead. I was sure there were tears behind those glasses of her.

I went to gently pull them off, but she veered away

from me, scrunching herself into the corner.

It broke my heart. She'd never shied away from my touch before and it hurt like a hot poker on bare skin.

"I don't know what you're trying to achieve right now, but...I still love you," I croaked. "I want to make sure you're okay."

She gripped her biceps, her fingers pinching in tight. "I'm fine," she whispered. "I know this seems random and out of the blue, and I'm sorry I've kept—" She swallowed, licking the edge of her mouth. "I've kept it hidden for so long."

"I thought you were happy." I ran a hand through my hair.

"You know me, always putting on a show. You know how I hate to hurt people's feelings."

"But not me. You've always been yourself around me."

She pressed her lips together and sniffed. "Which is why I'm saying this stuff to you now. I can't pretend anymore."

My breaking heart was shattering, shards of ice tearing through my blood stream. Her words were poison ivy, making my insides itch and writhe. I didn't want to hear them; I couldn't quite make myself believe them.

"This doesn't feel like you. You're not like this. You don't want to be like Quella."

"People change, Eric." She reached for the door handle and it took all my willpower not to lock her in the car. If I could only steal her away, then maybe I could talk some sense into her.

I gripped the steering wheel, swiveling my body away from her. I could feel her gaze on me, but I refused to look across.

"I don't mean to hurt you. All I'm asking for is a little space to think. Please, give me that."

I had no words. Like hell I could say yes.

Instead, I kept my eyes straight ahead and listened with a sinking soul to the door open and slam shut behind her.

I'd never felt so lost. Even waiting outside Dodger Stadium for my dad hadn't hurt this much. With robotic movements, I started the jeep and pulled away from the curb, nearly clipping the motorbike behind me. He swore and raised his fist. I ignored him, driving slowly out of the university, toward the beach. I had no idea where to go or what to do. I just had to stay on autopilot for as long as I could, because if I stopped to think about what was really happening to me, I didn't think I could recover.

twenty-nine

caitlyn

By the time I returned to my room, my chest was heaving. I could barely breathe as I barreled through the door and landed on my bed. I clutched the pillow to my chest, tears streaming down my cheeks.

"It's okay. Everything's going to be okay," Rhodes said quietly.

"Oh, shut up!" I ripped the earpiece out and shoved

it under my pillow.

The door behind me clicked open and my insides skittered, thinking it might be Eric not letting me go.

Whipping a look over my shoulder, my heart slumped.

It was Quella.

Fresh tears descended and I turned away, propping my chin on my fisted hands.

"What is wrong?" She perched on the side of my bed, looking a hell of a lot better than me. The throwing up probably did her good the night before. At least the alcohol was out of her system.

I buried my face into the pillow, not wanting to talk about it.

But what was the point of breaking my heart if I wasn't going to do the job I was meant to?

Loathing tore through me—a black resentment I had to fight to speak past.

I squeezed my eyes shut and thought about those girls. Images of them beaten and afraid forced my head off the pillow and I looked up at Quella.

"Eric and I broke up," my voice quivered. "And Thanksgiving's next week and I don't think I can face my family and tell them what happened."

"What did happen?"

"I don't know!" I sat up, swiping at my tears. "I thought things were great and then bam, out of the blue, it's over. I'm so humiliated," I ended with a broken whisper.

"*Pobrecita, hombres son pendejos.* "

My brow wrinkled in confusion.

"Men are assholes," she translated with a shrug, rubbing circles over my back. It was a gentle comfort so I let her keep doing it.

"I don't know what I'm going to do now." I rubbed my forehead and sniffed. "How am I going to face everyone? I don't want to have to explain something I don't even understand. I think I'll just lie to my parents and say I'm going away, but actually hole up here for the holiday."

"No, you cannot do that. You have to get out of here."

"And where am I supposed to go?"

Quella nibbled the edge of her lip, her sharp nose twitching. I pulled her mask away and fought to keep my expression bland. I was about to get exactly what I wanted.

"Come with me. Celebrate Thanksgiving with my papá."

"Really?" I touched her arm.

"Of course. We would love to have you." She smiled.

"That's so sweet, but I don't know. I won't be very good company."

"I cannot let you stay here. You have to say yes." She squeezed my shoulder.

I fought a watery smile, going for uncertain a little longer, just to really sell it.

"Come on, *chica*, you know it is a good idea."

"Okay," I finally sighed and then sniffed. "Yeah, okay, I'd love to. Thank you." I wrapped her in a hug and squeezed tight. "Thank you."

She giggled at my unrelenting embrace. "We will leave next Wednesday. The car is arriving at four."

I forced a smile, letting her go and squeezing her arm one last time before she got off the bed and snatched up her bag.

"It will be fun." She smiled and winked. "Trust me."

As soon as she walked out the door, I scrambled for the earpiece under my pillow and shoved it back in.

"You hear that? I'm in." I smiled, expecting to hear Rhodes reply.

Instead, I got the sharp staccato of Kaplan. "I told you it would work. Now you better hold it together for the rest of the week. You stay strong and you get this job done. Are we clear?"

"Yes, ma'am."

"Good. Now get your ass to class before people start asking questions."

I checked my watch and swore, lunging off the bed and snatching up my stuff. My head spun, a wave of nausea surging through me.

"I think I might have to call in sick," I groaned.

"So pathetic," Kaplan muttered.

I flopped back onto my bed, holding my head with one hand and flipping her the bird with the other.

One week.

It felt like an eternity. Why the hell hadn't I waited for the weekend? Why had my stupid, dumb, drunk ass decided to call Eric and break up with him? How was I supposed to avoid him until I left?

Sure, I felt sick today, but holing up in my room for the week would not fly.

My mind swirled as I pictured what he was probably going through. I wished I could call and tell him the truth, but another part begged that he'd leave me alone.

Tears burned as I curled into a ball on my bed, praying I could survive the week without bumping into the guy whose heart I'd just annihilated.

thirty

eric

I ran my thumb over my phone screen before plonking it onto the table with a heavy sigh.

"Still not answering, huh?" Scott's soft question felt loud in my ears.

I shook my head, struggling for words.

Hell, I'd been struggling all week. It'd been seven days of hell since Caity slammed out of my car. I'd spent the first day numb, the second day sleeping, the third day desperately trying to call her, but she'd ignored every message.

Piper, with her usual flair, got in on the action and finally got in touch with her. I stood there in agony listening to her bawl out Caity on her psychotic behavior. After that, Caity turned her phone off and none of us had been able to reach her since.

I'd even called around to her parents' place to see how she was doing. They were as perplexed as me.

"She won't tell us anything. She called two days ago to let us know she's going away with a friend for Thanksgiving."

"Who?"

"Some girl named Quella."

Since that moment, the sick nausea in my stomach had not abated. I was plagued by it. My head was in a constant state of fuzziness, making lectures impossible to hear. As I walked the campus my eyes constantly roamed the pathways for Caity, but I never saw her. It was like she'd disappeared off the face of the earth.

"Dude, I know this hurts, man, but she obviously doesn't want to talk to you right now."

"But why?" I whispered. "I never saw it coming. I never expected this from her. I feel totally blind-sided."

"You've got to admit that she's been acting a little different since Quella moved in. You knew something was up."

I closed my eyes as Scott took a seat at the kitchen table.

"I didn't think she could be influenced so easily."

"Remind me of her words again?"

"Don't make me relive it." I leaned back in my chair and crossed my arms.

Scott shot me a glum smile. "I just recall you saying that she needed a break for now...that doesn't mean forever. I don't think calling her every day is helping. Maybe you need to respect her wishes."

I grimaced, spinning my phone on the table. "I can't give up on her. I can't just let her go."

"It's not your choice, man."

I met Scott's sympathetic look with a dark wrath. Shooting out of my chair, I kicked it away from me. It toppled to the floor with a loud crash. "I can't buy it! I can't believe that she would go from loved up to breaking off in one weekend."

"What happened down in San Diego?"

"I don't know! I thought things were pretty good! I mean, yeah, I probably lectured her a little too hard on the way back, telling her to stop feeling so responsible for Quella, but I didn't think she'd take it to this extreme. Is her roommate a witch or something? Has mind-controlling powers?"

Scott snickered, but swiftly swallowed it down when I looked at him. "Or maybe Caity just needs some time to figure out what she needs."

"If I could talk to her...if she'd only listen to me, I know I could change her mind."

"People need to walk their own journeys, in their own time. Forcing a feeling doesn't work, dude."

I shook my head, unwilling to listen. "School gets out today and then she's taking off with Quella. I can't let that happen."

"Eric—"

"I've got to find her." I spun out of the kitchen, snatching my keys off the side table. "If I can talk to her, I know I can make this right."

"She wants space!"

"I've given her a week!" I threw my arms wide. "She's not leaving without talking to me."

I wanted to punch the pained expression right off Scott's face. "What!"

He shrugged. "I guess I'm kind of worried that you'll only push her away even more."

Letting out a soft curse, I squeezed the keys in my hand until it hurt.

"I'll hate myself forever if I don't at least try. If I see her today and she still doesn't want me, I'll walk away." The words fell out of my mouth, broken and splintered.

Scott didn't say another word as I walked out the door.

I drove in tense silence, not even bothering with the radio. All I could think about was Caity and what I'd say to her. I only had one class that morning and I'd driven back home straight after it. I had no idea what I wanted to do for Thanksgiving anymore. Caity and I were supposed to have lunch with her family and then watch football with my mom and Cliff. Those plans were shot to hell...unless I could say the right thing.

It took me a while to remember which classes Caity had. I started at her dorm, but no one was there. Her room was locked up tight, freaking me out for a second.

Had she left already?

But then I remembered that she had a Comparative Literature class at two.

I checked my watch and raced down the stairs. If I hurried, I'd be able to catch her as she was coming out.

There was a nip in the air as I burst out of the building. Winter was well on its way and it felt like it could be a cold one. I ignored the chill and strode toward the right building, trying to figure out a good place to wait.

I was scanning the area when my body froze.

There she was, walking toward me with her head lowered and her binder hugged tight against her chest.

She glanced up and tucked a lock of hair behind her ear, coming to an abrupt stop when she saw me. Her blue eyes grew large, a look of delight fluttering across her face before she caught herself. She made a move toward me, but then jerked still.

Her smile evaporated, a look of annoyance taking over her expression. Her eyes quickly glassed with tears. She blinked rapidly, biting on her lip and shaking her head.

"Caity, I just want to talk." I took a step closer.

She backed away.

Her lips pinched into a tight line, like she was wrestling a demon on one shoulder and an angel on another.

"Please."

She shook her head again, punching out a sharp, "No."

"Caity, come on."

"No." It was more of a sobbing whine this time, her face cresting with agony. Closing her eyes, she spun on her heel, her movements sharp and tight.

"Caity, wait!"

"NO!" She shook her head again. "I told you to leave me alone! I don't want you." The words punched out of her like machine gun fire...and they killed me.

I couldn't move for a minute. I just stood there, watching her run away from me, awkwardly holding her folder and pumping her arms, creating a distance between us as fast as she possibly could.

She didn't want me.

My throat burned, my eyes stung and it was suddenly impossible to breathe.

I had to get out of there.

My limbs felt like they were made of brittle wood as I turned back for my car.

She wouldn't even let me talk to her.

She didn't want me.

Those four words hammered themselves into my

brain, like some sick mantra I had heard a million times before.

People didn't want me.

Sucking in a ragged breath, I picked up my pace and sprinted to my car, wanting to punch, kick, kill.

I had to get out.

I had to get to Gramps before my reckless anger made me do something stupid.

thirty-one

caitlyn

"Okay, Caity, you need to calm down." Kaplan's voice was sharp in my ear.

"Shut up! Shut up!" I sobbed. "I ran, okay. I ran from him." I seethed out the words, hating her with every fiber of my being. Nestling myself into a small alcove, I doubled over, sucking in lungfuls of air and trying not to relive the broken despair on Eric's face.

I'd told him I didn't want him. I knew that'd be the only way to get him to leave me alone...and I hated myself for it.

The second I saw him, I'd wanted to run into his arms, but Kaplan had been yelling in my ear, telling me to back off.

"I am watching you and if you take one more step, I'm heading to the post office and mailing that file to Marchant. Walk away! NOW!"

My lips quivered and I struggled to rein in my emotions. I'd been a ball of nerves all week. If I wasn't stressing about breaking my boyfriend's heart, letting down my family and pissing off Piper, I was freaking out about getting in a car with Quella and traveling to a den of lions.

I couldn't do this.

I wasn't capable!

"It's three-fifteen. You need to start heading back to the dorm to get ready. Quella's car leaves at four."

"Just give me a minute."

"You don't have a minute! Move your ass."

"Kaplan," I snapped. "For the record, I hate your fucking guts!"

There was a long beat of silence. I breathed into it, anxiously awaiting her retaliation. With a frown, I pressed the plastic piece into my ear, making sure it was still working.

"Luckily for you," she finally quipped, "I don't give a shit what you think...as long as you do what you're told."

I closed my eyes and leaned my head back against the cold stone bricks. I didn't want to move; I wanted to stay frozen to this spot until it was over, but my logical brain kept shouting at me.

It won't be over unless you move!

With a heavy sigh, I pushed off the wall just as Rhodes's voice came into my ear.

"You know, I'd normally say language like that from a mouth as cute as yours is really quite ugly, but..." He chuckled. "That was pure poetry, Caity. I'm so glad I was standing in the van to hear it."

I snickered, comforted by the sound of his voice.

"Where are you guys?"

"On the road, outside your class. We'll be moving with you as you head back to the dorm."

"Where's Kaplan?"

"Ahhh, she's taking a...break."

"Oh, man," I mumbled, trying not to look like a crazy lady talking to herself. "She's gonna pay me back for that, isn't she?"

"Nah, I actually think she appreciates it when you show a little fire. But you did piss her off."

"As long as she's not going to the post office."

"I'll make sure of it."

I closed my eyes, his soft words acting like a balm. "Thank you."

"You know I've got your back."

I nodded, hoping he meant it. The weight of my

upcoming weekend crashed over me again, restricting my chest. I opened my eyes, forcing my body back to my dorm when, for the second time that day, I jerked to a stop.

Scott was walking toward me. He was looking the other way and part of me was tempted to duck my head and keep moving, but I couldn't.

The idea of a chance flickered inside me. Nerves scuttled through my body like hungry crabs. I clutched the binder to my chest and stepped into his path.

"Hey." The word punched out of my mouth, sounding sharp and unfriendly. I cringed.

Scott glanced over at the sound of my voice, his stride faltering.

"Hi." His smile was soft and sweet as always. Scratching his short hair, he came to a stop beside me, his warm gaze quietly analyzing me before saying anything.

I looked to the ground.

"You okay?"

I bit my lip and nodded.

He was still studying me; I could feel it. My lips twitched as I fought the question, but then I couldn't help myself. "Did you see Eric, just now?"

"No." He shook his head. "I was heading to my last class before break." He pointed at me. "Did you see him?"

I pressed my lips together and went for a lie, shaking my head. "I—I just wanted to know if he was okay."

"In all honesty, Caity, he's not great."

I flinched. I already knew that. I'd seen his face as I made it a million times worse. All his childhood wounds would have been unearthed with my one soul-destroying statement. If only I could take it back, make it better, give him a reason to forgive me.

My face crumpled, worry skirting through me as I entertained my idea. Kaplan would kill me and then head straight to the post office.

But only if she found out.

I had to tell Eric. I couldn't go away with my *I don't want you* statement hanging between us. I had to let him in on my lies. I'd be gone in an hour anyway; Kaplan would get what she wanted and Eric would stay safe.

And standing in front of me was my one and only chance to do it.

I flipped open my binder, tearing out a sheet of lined paper.

"What are you doing?" Rhodes voice shot into my ear.

I cleared my throat, forcing my stance to relax. "I hope he's going to be okay."

"He's pretty cut up, Caity."

"I know." I stared at the concrete beneath my feet, my mind working overtime as I tried to think how to pass on my message without Kaplan finding out and unleashing some foreign mafia on my boyfriend.

"Look, it's none of my business." Scott waved his hand. "I guess we're just kind of surprised."

I nodded. "Yeah, it does feel out of the blue, which is totally my fault. The curse of being a people-pleaser, I guess." I punched out a hollow laugh.

"I thought Eric and you were really great together. I thought he made you happy."

My nose wrinkled as I fought off a fresh wave of tears.

"Time. I just want a little time." I cleared my throat. "Hey, listen, um, I'm heading out of town for a couple of days...for Thanksgiving."

"Yeah, Eric told me. Quella, right?"

I frowned, wondering how Eric knew that.

"Yeah, she invited me, so..." I shrugged.

Scott nodded, obviously not impressed that I was choosing Quella over my original plans.

"You probably think it's weird, but this feels like the right decision for now."

Scott nodded. "I guess you gotta do what you gotta do."

"Yeah, uh-huh. That—that's what I was thinking."

"Would you wrap this up? You're leaving in thirty minutes and Kaplan will be back any second," Rhodes softly barked in my ear.

It was a real effort not to react to his warning. My lips pushed into a tight smile before I gazed down at the note of paper I'd ripped from my binder.

There was no way I could get this note to Eric without Rhodes seeing. I gazed across at Scott as a handful of new lies filtered into my head.

I dug into my bag for a pen and yanked one free.

"Hey, can you pass on a message to Piper for me. We were supposed to get together on Friday to talk wedding plans."

"Were you?" Scott frowned.

"Yeah, you guys are spending Thanksgiving with your cousin this year and since you're staying in town, we wanted to take advantage of that." I gave him a wide-eyed stare, nodding my head emphatically and probably being way too obvious.

His eyes narrowed and I looked away from his suspicion with a shaky laugh, clicking on my pen and scribbling out my note.

"After her last phone call, I didn't think she'd want to, but I checked my phone this morning and she hasn't cancelled on me yet, so I'm guessing she still thinks it's on."

I glanced up at his reluctant expression. "Why don't you just call her...or text her with the truth. I'm sure she'd be a listening ear if you needed her to be."

Shaking my head with a quick snigger, I wrote the name on the front of the note and put the pen back into my bag. "She'll probably spend the whole time telling me off for breaking Eric's heart and I don't think I can sit through that again." I zipped up my bag and looked at him.

He gave in with a small nod and chuckled.

"I don't want to get into a texting frenzy with her, either. I just need to get away and if anyone can talk me out of it, it's her." I held out the note to him.

His hands remained in his pockets as he stared reluctantly at the folded piece of paper.

"Please. Give her the note. At least by the time she gets it, I'll already be gone."

With a sigh, he took it from my hand. "Chicken."

I gave him a sheepish grin and tucked a lock of hair behind my ear, unable to take my eyes off him as he read the name on the front.

ERIC

His eyes snapped to mine and I held his gaze, silently pleading for him not to ask.

A wave of understanding washed over his expression, followed by instant concern.

"Thanks for your help, and I hope she doesn't shoot the messenger." I chuckled, grateful when he forced a grin of his own.

"I'm sure I can talk her around." He slid the note into his back pocket. "I'll give it to her as soon as I get home."

"Thanks." I nodded, my eyes burning with unshed tears.

"Have a good time away." Scott's sincere gaze nearly crushed me. "You take care of yourself."

"I will. Thanks for understanding." My smile was watery and I couldn't help myself. With a sniff, I wrapped my arms around his neck and squeezed tight. He hugged me back, patting my shoulder a couple of times before letting me go.

"See ya later, Scott." I raised my hand with a short farewell wave and spun away from him before he could say anything else.

I didn't want to turn around to see if he was still watching me. Instead, I rested my chin on my binder and scurried away.

"Okay, now that all your gush is behind us," Kaplan spat. I cringed, hating that she was back in my ear again. "Can we please focus on the job at hand? You're leaving in twenty minutes, so start running, blondie."

I did what I was told, picking up my pace and hurrying back to my dorm. A small smile tugged at my lips as I raced up the stairs to my room. I closed the door behind me, checking the room was empty before leaning my head against the wood and letting my smile grow.

I'd gotten a note to Eric.

Thanks to Scott, the truth was now heading straight for my boyfriend. The security in knowing that outweighed the fear of my impending trip.

The fact that I'd managed to do it right under Kaplan's nose was freaking epic. Insanely, I felt like doing a little happy dance. The relief was intense. Eric would read my note and finally have a chance to understand my bizarre behavior. It would explain everything...and then he would forgive me.

My job now was to make this Thanksgiving trip count. My brain switched into work mode, snapping off my emotions as I hauled my bag off the bed and checked that I hadn't forgotten anything.

The trip better work, because when I returned, I was winning my boyfriend back. I didn't care what it took. As soon as these girls were safe, I was washing my hands of Kaplan and making sure she could never touch me, or Eric, again.

All I had to hope was that he'd get my note before writing me off for good.

thirty-two

eric

I packed up the car and hit the road late afternoon. My plan was to make it to Gramps' by sunset. My day had been total shit.

Watching Caity run away from me hurt like hell, her words open bullet wounds in my chest.

I felt like such an idiot.

I drove home in a mindless stupor, which eventually

bubbled into my standard rage. By the time I got back to my house, I was fuming. If Caity had been there to read me, she would have given me that sympathetic smile and told me it wasn't my fault. People didn't reject me because of who I was. They all walked away for different reasons.

But no matter how anyone put it, the truth remained the same.

People left me, and there was nothing I could do about it.

I'd walked to my room, fighting despair and an overwhelming sense of hopelessness. It hadn't help that draped over the chair in the corner was Caity's sweater. The shards of ice running through my veins had become chunks of wood that sliced and tore, leaving behind painful splinters.

I'd squeezed my hands into fists and punched the wall. It fucking hurt.

I glanced at my swollen, red knuckles and grimaced.

I needed to get to Gramps. He'd be the only thing to calm me down, help me think straight. I had no idea where Piper and Scott were when I pulled out of the driveway, but I was determined to leave before they got back.

I didn't bother with a note. Scott would probably guess where I'd taken off to anyway.

I gripped the steering wheel and kept my eyes fixed on the road, trying not to think about the last nightmare week.

The phone on the dashboard buzzed. I collected it and saw the caller ID.

Scott Ferguson.

"Not in the mood to talk, man." I threw the phone back down and let it ring.

After three more, it went quiet and then a minute later I got a voice mail notification.

I shook my head. I was driving. I couldn't check it and I didn't think I had the will to check it later, either. Whatever he needed could wait.

About ten minutes later, the phone started up again.

Snatching it up, I saw Scott was trying once more.

"Forget it," I muttered, pressing down on the top button and switching my phone off.

With an angry huff, I flung it onto my backseat, not even caring if it broke.

If Caity wanted space, I'd damn well give it to her. It was probably a good thing we were apart for the long weekend. It'd give me time to think about what I really wanted out of life, too.

That morning, I'd been convinced it was Caity.

"Now, I'm not sure!" I spat out the words and thumped the wheel...not believing one word of my lie.

thirty-three

caitlyn

A limo picked us up from UCLA at four p.m. sharp. I handed my bags to the hesitant driver and slipped in behind Quella. As soon as he'd closed the trunk and gotten behind the wheel, he swiveled in his seat and asked Quella a question in Spanish.

"*Quien es ella? Tu padre no le gusta tener invitados de sorpresa.*"

Her nose lifted into the air and her mask slipped away. Nervous guilt maybe? Had she not told her father I was coming?

Oh, shit. This was so not cool.

"Bueno, el va tener que lidiar con esto. Ella es mi amiga y yo la puedo traer conmigo si yo quiero."

What had she just said?

The driver chewed the inside of his cheek before making a clicking sound with his tongue. I tried not to squirm beneath his scrutinizing gaze. A smile quivered over my lips and he humphed, turning in his seat and driving slowly out of campus.

I couldn't be one hundred percent sure what they were arguing about, and it didn't help that when I gave Quella a questioning look, she just waved her hand in the air telling me not to worry about it.

My guess that I was not supposed to be in the limo with her was yet again confirmed when the exact same thing happened at LAX. The limo pulled up next to a private jet. I slid my shades off as I got out of the car, my lips parting. I'd never been on a private jet before.

Quella once again argued with the crew, her lips drawing into a stubborn line, her eyebrow arching defiantly.

She threaded her arm through mine. "Fine then. Take me back to the dorm. I am not spending Thanksgiving without my friend, Caity."

With a resigned sigh, the security guard huffed. *"Usted pequeño niño obstinado. Luche contra tus propias batallas entonces."*

He flicked his hand at me, indicating that I should spread 'em. I did so, shooting Quella a nervous look, grateful I wasn't actually bugged. She rolled her eyes and gave me an apologetic smile as he waved a bug sensor over me. When it came away clear, the guard reluctantly ushered us onto the plane.

"Are you sure it's all right that I'm coming? I feel like this is kind of a surprise for everyone."

"It is." Quella winked and then giggled at my shocked expression. "Do not worry about it. My father is very strict on security. He never lets me bring friends home, so I figure if I am going to get what I want then I have to surprise him."

"But what if he doesn't let me stay?"

"He will. You are my first friend outside of my family and you make me happy. He cannot deny me." She grinned, pretending to wrap an invisible thread around her little finger. "Besides, it would be rude for him not to welcome one of my guests. Above all things, he is a gentleman."

I grinned at her, desperately trying to hide my disquiet. She actually believed that. She had no idea what her father was really up to. Poor thing. When he got arrested for his crimes, it would really hurt her.

I closed my eyes and drew in a breath, forcing myself to think of the kidnapped girls.

"How are you feeling today?" Quella's question was quiet and filled with concern.

I opened my eyes and looked across at her, giving her a glum smile, which was in no way forced. She was referring to Eric, and just the very thought of him was like a wound to my soul. The look on his face as I ran away...

My eyes glassed with tears. "Heartbroken is probably the best way to describe it."

I sniffed and turned away from her, not wanting to give away my small smile. He'd have read the note by now. I clutched the bag on my lap, wishing my phone was in it, but Kaplan made me leave it behind. I hoped he didn't try to call me. I silently begged him to hold out for the long weekend. I'd be back soon to make everything right. If only I could speak to him telepathically. That would solve all my problems.

"You will be okay." Quella nodded and gave the security guard a pointed look as he boarded the plane.

He humphed and shuffled past us before plonking his large frame into the seat across from me. I shrunk away from his intense glare.

I leaned toward what felt like the only safe thing on the plane and whispered, "So, where are we going?"

Quella shrugged. "I am not sure. I find out when the plane lands. My father likes surprises."

Nibbling the edge of my lip, I sat back in my seat and tried to relax. Knowing Diego Mendez's paranoia for security, Kaplan had made me de-bug before getting into the limo. She'd of course waited until I was nearly out of the dorm before barking the order into my ear. I'd had to veer off to the bathroom where Rhodes was waiting for me. I'd had to take my shirt off in front of him, which wasn't humiliating or anything! I forced myself not to read his face while his fingers lightly brushed my skin, removing all technology from my body.

"And your phone." He held out his hand.

"Why?"

His face crested with empathy. "This is a business trip. You have to put your life on hold for the next few days; no distractions."

With a dark glare, I slapped it into his hand. He turned it off and shoved it in his back pocket.

"I promise I won't peek at any of your stuff." He winked.

I huffed a short breath out of my nose and crossed my arms.

"You've got the black phone Kaplan gave you, right?"

I nodded.

"There's an app installed on there so we can track you the whole way. Make sure you have it on you at all times so we know exactly where you are." I swallowed at the grave look on his face, my insides exploding with nerves. "We'll be nearby the whole time. I've got your back, I promise."

I gripped the soft leather of my bag as the plane

took off, hearing Rhodes's soft voice in my head and reading the truth behind his mask. He was worried for me, scared that something would happen to me...but he was also determined to keep me safe. That part felt good and I was more than relieved that he was on this assignment, too.

****

It was dark when we landed. I followed Quella down the plane stairs and was met by another surprised driver. He eyed me up and down, and then barked something at the security guard who barked right back at him.

Quella rolled her eyes and grabbed my arm, pulling me into the limo. The ninety-minute drive passed quickly with Quella rabbiting on about all the things she was going to tell her father and all the things I had to promise not to say.

"He will not approve of the drinking...and probably not the dancing. And do not mention Carlos to anyone."

I didn't have the heart to tell her that her father probably knew exactly what she'd been up to thanks to Carlos.

The long limo slowed. I peered out the window, but the combination of tinted glass and a moonless night made it impossible to see anything. My butterfly nerves turned traitorous, and cold sweat broke out on the back of my neck. I rubbed at it, squeezing my neck and holding my breath as the limo pulled to a stop at the end of a very long driveway.

I went to open the door.

"Not yet." Quella touched my arm with a smile. "I know where we are now and the parking is underground." She winked and chuckled.

I paused and heard a soft whir in front of us. A few moments later the car descended. The lower we got, the lighter it became and we were soon pulling into a large courtyard. The limo pulled around the bubbling fountain and came to rest outside a Spanish-style villa.

My door popped open and I hopped out, taking in the ornate tiles below my feet and the plush, rich garden around us. The fountain created a soothing soundtrack for the idyllic space. I couldn't believe it was all underground. No wonder Kaplan couldn't find it.

I gazed up at the high ceiling and captured a few stars. There was a massive hole at the top of this mountain. It was like being inside a volcano, minus all the lava of course. I'd never seen anything like it.

Quella let out a little squeal and raced away from the car, jumping into the arms of a man who was about the same height as she was. He had thick, black hair and bitter cocoa eyes set deep in his hard, narrow face. His tanned skin crinkled when he smiled, flashing a set of straight, sharp teeth.

Deigo Mendez.

My stomach clenched.

"*Bienvenida, mi princesa preciosa. Te he hechado mas.*"

Quella's father held her at arm's length, drinking her in. I could instantly see how much he adored his daughter. His warm, unmasked smile showed me how protective he felt of his little girl. Sending her away to college had been hard for him, and he hated the mischief she'd gotten up to. I pulled another layer free and saw the faint whistle of guilt resting beneath the surface. He'd rather die than have her find out what he was really up to.

He pulled her back into a tight embrace and then his gaze hit me. It was like being shot by a bullet. Unmasked, his intense stare cut straight through me. He was taking me in, assessing what kind of threat I might be, checking me out, finding me slightly attractive, but also a total nuisance. He didn't like me; that much was clear. I was the girl who was leading his precious princess astray.

I tried to stand tall against his scrutiny, smiling bravely and hoping he couldn't smell fear.

"I see you brought a friend."

Quella giggled. "Sorry to surprise you, Papá, but Caity is my roommate and she has looked after me."

"Has she?"

I didn't miss his dry tone. He was holding me responsible for all the party antics. Carlos had obviously given him very thorough reports.

Quella threaded her arm behind her father's back.

"Please." She rested her head on his shoulder and batted her eyelids at him. "She is my guest and we must make her feel welcome."

Mendez smirked, kissing his daughter's forehead and smiling across at her. "Of course, my angel."

He looked to the driver and clicked his fingers, pointing at the bags. "We'll put her in the guest room next to Quella's."

"Ooo, they are adjoining." Quella gave me an excited smile before turning with her father and entering the house.

I shuffled behind them, smiling at the house staff and pulling off masks like my life depended on it, which it actually kind of did.

"Rosa!" Quella squealed, letting go of her father and running into the chubby arms of a short Mexican woman. She grabbed the slight girl to her and squeezed and kissed her cheeks until she wiggled out of her grasp.

"Mi querubín. Estás en casa, estás en casa! Esta casa esta tan sola sin ti. No lo puedo creer que estés aquí viéndote mas hermosa que nunca. ¿Cómo voy a dejarte ir otra vez?"

"Ah, yes, Rosa, our little angel is home and has grown even more beautiful while she was away." Mendez smiled as the woman pulled Quella in for another embrace, and then he turned to me.

I met his gaze confidently in spite of the fact it made me want to melt into the floor. If I wanted him to buy into who I was pretending to be, I had to act like it.

His masked face was quite pleasant, his smile soft and welcoming. I snatched his mask away and saw it again, drinking in that dark malice. It took every ounce of courage I possessed to smile sweetly at him. I was about to open my mouth and thank him for having me when another man appeared behind him.

He was tall and handsome with jet-blue eyes and a perfectly manicured goatee. His nose was sharp, his dark eyebrows dipping inward as he caught sight of me.

Mendez leaned back and whispered something to him. The man looked me over one more time and nodded.

Terror sputtered through me as I ripped off his mask. He had a smug smile on his face like somehow the idea of catching me out would make his day. Who the hell was this guy? I scrambled for information I'd read in the Mendez file. He did look familiar. I could picture an image, slightly blurry. He was wearing shades and a business suit, walking behind Mendez, but who...

"Miguel." Quella was now free of the short woman's arms and gazing at the man with a soft smile. Her mask slipped free as she stepped toward him and I saw it all. Her gushy smile, the enamored glint in her eye. This must have been the love she was talking about.

"*Señorita.*" He took her hand and gently kissed her knuckles, making her swoon.

No one else saw this, of course. Mendez was smart enough to realize Quella liked Miguel, but he had no idea to the extent.

I whipped the tall man's mask off, expecting to see a secret. These two were probably planning on sneaking off together sometime during the weekend for a little tryst above ground.

But I didn't see that at all.

It was an effort to keep my lips together as Miguel's flirtatious expression became one of disgust. He had no interest in Quella Mendez. He was putting on a show, purely for her benefit...and maybe that of his boss?

Wait. Miguel...head of security. He was Mendez's right-hand man. That was why he was always in the photos.

What was the bet Mendez whispered at him to look into my background, check me out? Man, I hoped Kaplan had done her job and kept my past clean. The last thing I wanted them digging up was my involvement with the Pali High cheating ring and the UCLA underground gambling/drug fiasco.

The back of my neck prickled as Quella dragged Miguel toward me.

"Meet my friend, Caitlyn."

I smiled, thrusting out my hand and wanting to get this over with. He grasped my fingers. His hand was strong and I was sure he could snap my bones if he wanted to. I forced myself not to swallow as I greeted him.

"*Hola.*" His smirk was back, dark and calculating. I shoved his mask back on and caught the cool, formal exterior he presented. "Welcome to Casa Mendez, Miss Davis."

It looked like he'd already gotten started on that security check, because no one else in this room had told him my surname.

I swallowed then. I couldn't help it. He wanted me to know he didn't trust me. He wanted me to know that he would be keeping a very close eye on me.

My fingers crunched as he gave them a final squeeze. I captured my hand back, giving it a gentle rub before being ushered upstairs to get freshened up for dinner.

I glanced over my shoulder as I ascended after Quella, fear ripping through me. The two men were staring after me, their unmasked expressions enough to give me nightmares.

thirty-four

caitlyn

I wanted to stay in the bathroom for the rest of the night, but I couldn't. Quella was knocking at the door, telling me dinner would be served in ten minutes. Glancing at my watch, I frowned. It was twenty past nine already. How did people eat this late?

I felt sick. The idea of actually eating was incomprehensible to me. Terror-filled nerves were feeding on my stomach lining, gnawing away at my insides. I was sure any food I did eat would run straight through me.

"Caity, are you nearly ready?"

"Yes," I called, pinging back my shoulders and straightening my blue button-down shirt. "Confidence," I whispered into the mirror. "You are not afraid of these guys, because you don't know them as anything other than Quella's family."

I gave myself a few more reminders before flinging the door open and letting Quella take my hand. We skipped down the stairs together, walking down an open corridor lined with multiple archways. They looked out over a picturesque garden, another water fountain working its magic in the corner.

The dining room was in a small atrium. I gazed at the tiled ceiling, a beautiful mosaic of aquatic life. It would be like eating in the ocean. The effect was enhanced by the blue lights shining up from the ground, lighting the plants around us with a soft, magical glow.

I took my place opposite Quella and thanked the waiter as he pushed in my chair. I gave him a kind smile, wondering how much he knew about what went on in this house.

My brain had been ticking over since arriving, wondering where Mendez's office was situated and how the hell I was going to get into it.

There were enough staff in this house to run a hotel. Meek bodies in starched uniforms scurried about constantly. I wouldn't be surprised if my bed was turned down when I got to it tonight.

The first course was laid out in front of me: a crab salad served on rings of toasted baguette. It was garnished with some kind of herb and looked so beautiful I almost didn't want to eat it.

Quella clasped her hands together and bowed her head. I quickly followed suit as Mendez said some kind of prayer in Spanish.

I opened my eyes when he was finished and found him gazing at me. He pointed at my plate and smiled. "*Cóme-Cóme!*"

"That means you can eat now." Quella winked at me before picking up her cutlery.

I kept my eye on her throughout the meal, trying to copy her ladylike eating habits and wondering what had happened to them back at UCLA.

The meal was quiet and reserved, the conversation focused on school. I jittered my way through class explanations and the papers I was enjoying the most. Mendez really grilled me, obviously trying to figure out everything he could about his daughter's roommate.

For one second, I had the fear that maybe he could read faces like I could, because he didn't seem to be buying into a word of mine. His skeptical gaze nailed me to my chair, making me want to crawl beneath the table.

Thankfully, I didn't disintegrate and when dessert was finally served I was able to relax for a moment.

Mendez turned his attention to Quella, mentioning some family members in Palm Springs who were unable to join us for Thanksgiving dinner.

Quella groaned. "I was looking forward to seeing them."

"I know, my sweet, but work has been very busy for me and I need to be here. I have some business associates visiting tomorrow and I have to be prepared for my meeting."

"For Thanksgiving?"

Mendez's smile was broad and friendly. "It will not interfere. We will have a lovely midday meal and then you can watch football with Rosa. You love that tradition."

Quella frowned.

"*Mija.*" His deep voice soothed. "My plan was to meet you in Palm Springs, but there was a sudden change and I could not stand the thought of waiting until Christmas." He gently touched her cheek and she forgave him with an instant smile. "It is probably a good thing you have your friend here to keep you company. She can watch the football with you while I talk boring business."

My insides curled as I imagined what type of business he was planning. I had to figure out how it all worked. If he did have the girls, was he hiding them here? Or did he only hold meetings here and the girls were stashed somewhere else? I had no idea where we were, but I had a gut feeling we were close to the border...certainly made smuggling humans a whole lot easier.

The thought was so unnerving I fumbled my teaspoon as I lifted it off the table. I gave them a sheepish grin before dipping it into the dessert.

I popped the spoon into my mouth, the delicate mousse making my senses break into a happy dance. I wanted to let out a sweet moan and tell them what I thought, but I couldn't make my voice work. Something in the corner of the room had caught my eye. I'd seen a flash of it earlier in the meal but brushed it off, too busy trying to answer questions.

Now that the heat was off me, I had the time to look and oh, man, what did I see?

Miguel was standing in the corner of the room, his eyes scanning the area like the good security guard he was. The only thing to break his attention was the appearance of the young waiter who had been looking after us. Each time he came into the room, Miguel's unmasked face would light with a smile, his gaze traveling over the young man.

Okay, so Mr. Head Security was gay, that was clear to see, but it wasn't just lust that made his eyes light each time the man of his affection walked into the room. Miguel seemed genuinely in love with him.

I scraped the remaining mousse out of my bowl, sitting back to let the waiter collect it from me. This time when I smiled at him, I whipped off his mask. He seemed sweet, genuine, nothing much to hide. As he took my empty dish, his gaze flickered to Miguel, and a warm smile quivered over his lips only shifting to a scared frown when he turned to see Mendez's impatient glare.

Interesting.

So maybe Miguel had a boyfriend Mendez didn't approve of...or maybe didn't know about?

Yeah, that was it. There was no way Miguel would be putting his flirt on with Quella if Mendez knew the truth. His fake charm was probably a cover to hide the truth from everyone.

I flicked my gaze back to Miguel, his unmasked face darkening with a vicious glare as he eyed Mendez. His expression softened slightly as the waiter walked past him. He tracked the young man until he was out of sight. His attention then returned back to the room. He gave a big, exasperated eye-roll. I frowned until I realized I was studying his unmasked expression. Putting it back into place, I realized that he was smiling kindly at Quella, a playful mischief lurking in his eyes. He winked at her and her cheeks turned pink.

I tore her mask free. She looked like a gushy-tween at a pop concert, but lurking beneath her giddy gaze was that *I want it* look I'd seen so many times before. She snuck a quick glance at her father who was chatting on the phone.

When did that ring?

Man, I needed to up my game and focus!

Happy that he was distracted, she turned back to

Miguel and ran her tongue over her upper lip. I nearly choked on my saliva.

Miguel arched his right eyebrow, but beneath his mask I could see his repulsion.

"Miguel, my father is taking too long. Would you mind escorting us back to our rooms?" Her attempt at a smoldering smile was almost pathetic. She really was just an innocent rich kid trying to play a grown-up's game. I figured she and Miguel had never gotten it on or anything, and he was just playing along to keep her happy. I hoped when she did find the courage to make her move, he would let her down gently.

I rose from the table and followed Quella.

My mind went into business mode again. I scanned my surroundings, looking for hidden doorways or corridors that might lead me to a gold mine.

"Can I have a tour before bed?"

The two in front of me jerked to a stop and turned to face me.

I smiled. "This house is so amazing and beautiful. I was wondering what the rest of it looked like."

Miguel gave me a tight smile. "Perhaps tomorrow."

"No, why wait. Let us do it now. The house is so magical at night." Quella grabbed my wrist. "Come, let me show you."

Miguel shot me a molten glare as we dashed past him. I picked up my pace, skipping after Quella as she led me on a tour throughout the house, which included two living areas, a formal lounge housing a shiny grand piano, an entertainment theater, plus a lush garden that was even bigger than the entrance way. I'd never been in a place like it, and thankfully I didn't have to hide my awe.

Miguel kept up his banter with the rich daughter throughout the tour, growing more agitated with her as the minutes ticked by. It worked in my favor. He was expending so much energy entertaining her that I was able to look around each room closely, studying doorways. I walked toward a few and was stopped short.

"Where are you going?"

I turned innocently each time. "Are we not going this way? I thought this led to a new room."

"No." Miguel's head shake was tight and minimal, his unmasked expression steaming. "Some rooms are private...for business. Mr. Mendez would not appreciate you going into them."

"Oh, I'm sorry." I hurried away from them, biting back my smile both times.

I made a mental note of each place, making sure I paid careful attention as we walked away. It looked like I had my sneaking around work cut out for me.

"Quella, it is really very late. You should head to bed." Miguel tried again to end the tour.

The girl beside me blushed, her eyes dancing with delight at Miguel saying the word *bed*.

Even I couldn't suppress my eye-roll over that one. Miguel tipped his head with a charming smile, but his expression was adamant.

"Oh, fine." Quella stamped her foot with a cheeky grin. "But we must go via the pool. It is so beautiful with the lights."

Grabbing my hand, she dragged me down the tiled hallway and skipped down the circular stairwell before Miguel could protest.

"Wow." I grinned.

She was right—the pool area was incredible. Blue light shone up from the base, giving the water a mysterious, enchanting quality, but the coolest thing was the waterfall that cascaded from the top floor, over two tiers and falling into the massive pool.

The large, circular area looked like it belonged in a high-class resort, with huge windows making up the outer wall. I walked past the deck chairs and stood against the glass, gazing out at the night sky. I realized that this underground mansion was actually carved into the side of a mountain. We were up really high and although I couldn't see the view due to the darkness, I could sense a long drop beneath me. I made a mental note to make sure I returned there in the morning.

"The pool is heated, so we can swim all year round. Not that it gets that cold here." Quella crossed her arms and shrugged.

"Where is here?" I glanced over my shoulder.

"Okay, you have seen the pool. It is time for bed, girls." Miguel flicked his head toward the stairwell.

Quella moaned but did as she was told, making her

way to the stairwell. I shuffled after her, my eyes darting to each doorway.

There were two, one a stone arch and the other a square, wooden door.

I sensed Miguel watching me and turned to look at him, flinching as I took in his hard glare.

He pointed at the archway. "The sauna and bathroom."

I nodded and forced a tight smile, noticing he said nothing about the other door. His mask was already off, making his dark eyes so much more sinister. I flicked a quick look at the wooden door.

"Curiosity killed the cat, Miss Davis."

My lips parted, unable to hide my fear until Quella started giggling.

"Do not listen to him." She slapped his arm and I threw his mask on in time to see a light, mischievous smile. "My father used to say that all the time to try and stop me from looking through doorways, but we have nothing to hide here." She smiled.

I grinned, but kept my eyes on Miguel. An anxious wave crested over his unmasked expression.

"That other door is only the maintenance room, and if you value your life, you will not go into it." She shook her head.

"Why not?"

"Juan, the maintenance man, is so fussy and mean. We are never allowed to touch his things. I tried to sneak a look once and Miguel nearly chopped my hand off." She lightly slapped his chest with the back of her hand.

He smiled at her. "I was only trying to protect you from a greater threat."

They chuckled together, but I didn't see their laughter or smiles.

All I saw was the lie.

A second flash of panic skittered over Miguel's face. It was quickly overrun by a penetrating gaze that held enough threat to make me nearly pee my pants.

That room had nothing to do with Juan or maintenance.

I swallowed down my next few "innocent" questions and walked after Quella.

Miguel waited for me to pass him before we all ascended the stairs. I could feel him tearing strips off my back as he walked behind me. My heart beat erratically and I forced a quiet breath though my nose.

There were now three doors to look behind, but I knew which one to start with.

The very idea of sneaking down there once everyone was asleep terrified me.

But I had to.

If I wanted to save those girls...if I wanted to get my boyfriend back, I had to get over myself and trust that somewhere nearby, the FBI were waiting to save my ass.

thirty-five

eric

I made it down to San Diego around seven, but I went to the beach first. I don't know how long I sat there with my toes buried in the cold sand, my gaze locked on the dark horizon. The cool air nipped at my skin, sinking into my core, but I remained a statue, unable to think or move.

I didn't know what snapped me out of it. Part of me

felt like I could stay all night, but common sense pushed me toward Gramps's house.

Banging on the door with my fist, I checked my watch and saw it was ten. I was pretty sure the man would still be up; the guy seemed to exist on minimal sleep.

After a little shuffling from the other side, the door swung open and Gramps stood there in his PJ pants and a T-shirt.

"What in heck's name are you doing knocking on my door at this hour?"

"I need to stay." I shifted sideways to step into the house, dumping my bag in the middle of the floor.

"What's going on, son?"

"I don't want to talk about it." I sniffed and rubbed my nose with the back of my hand before looking at him. "I'm going to bed."

"Now, wait one second. You ain't welcome in that bed until you tell me what's going on. Is everything okay with Shayna?"

"Mom's fine." I kicked at the floorboards, slightly ashamed that this was the first thought I'd given her in the last few days. Damn, I'd have to remember to call and let her know I wouldn't be over for the football game like I'd planned.

I grimaced.

"O-kay." Gramps crossed his arms, his large eyes narrowing to tiny slits. "How's Caity?"

I swallowed, but it did nothing to remove the lump

from my throat.

"Where is she tonight?"

I shrugged and shook my head.

"Talk to me, boy."

My lips pressed into a tight line, my jaw clenching. Finally, I muttered, "She broke up with me."

"Why?"

Unable to stand still a second longer, my arms lifted into the air and a loud expletive shot from my mouth. "How the hell should I know? It's always the same! People just take off without any kind of explanation! Kenneth! Brayden! Richard!" I listed Mom's slew of boyfriends, the ones who'd actually stuck around long enough to become important to me. "I don't know why they can't tough it out. Are we so unlovable? Is that what it is? I know Mom can be a pain in the ass sometimes, but she's really not that bad. And what the fuck is wrong with me?"

Gramps stood strong against my rant, a solid lighthouse in the midst of my raging storm. His expression remained bland and unreadable as I shouted at him.

"Why, Gramps? Why didn't he stay?" My voice broke, tears blurring my vision. I dug my fingers into my eyes, hating that it was all surfacing. I should have been crying over Caity, not whining about my loser father.

I sucked in a sharp sniff, lashing at the one tear that managed to break free.

"It doesn't matter." I snatched my bag off the floor.

"He's gone. Caity's gone. That's just the way it is."

Gramps let out a soft sigh. "For what it's worth, I love you, son."

"Yeah, well, you're the only one."

He didn't argue my final statement, probably knowing it would do no good. Instead, he let me walk out of the room without saying another word.

I slammed my bedroom door shut and slumped onto the bed, the child inside of me weeping.

I could hear the Dodgers game going on behind me, the yell of the crowd as runs were scored and bases were stolen. I'd stood with my hands in my pockets, shuffling my feet, kicking at the concrete as I waited...and waited.

People passed me, a couple of the older parents stopping to ask if I was okay.

"My dad's coming. He'll be here in just a sec." They all smiled at me, satisfied with my enthusiastic answer.

I'd said it for four hours straight, my enthusiasm not wavering until the crowd began to dribble out of the stadium.

The game was over, and somehow I knew.

There'd be no more waiting. There'd be no more let-downs.

Dad wasn't coming ever again, because I wasn't going to let him hurt me anymore.

I ran my hands through my hair and banged my head

against the wall.

Watching Caity run away shot me back to that moment in time faster than I thought it could.

She didn't want me...and I had to live with that, because I wasn't going to let her hurt me the way Dad had. I couldn't let her rejection destroy me. I had to man up and move on.

With a heavy sigh, I laid down, bunching the pillow beneath my head.

I wondered where she was right then. Probably hanging out with Quella's family, getting drunk and dancing the night away.

I didn't get it.

I didn't get how Quella sucked her in so easily.

I didn't get the sudden change of heart.

Trying to figure out her reason would probably send me over the edge, so I squeezed my eyes shut and forced the image of her beautiful face away...those eyes, that smile, the delicate curve of her chin.

I couldn't think of those things anymore. I was single now. My own man. She didn't want me to take care of her. She wanted me to leave her alone and that was what I had to do.

thirty-six

caitlyn

The house was eerily quiet. I clutched the door handle to my guest room, breathing in slowly as I turned it. The click sounded deafening. I flinched, crouched against the door, waiting for Miguel or Diego to spring from the shadows and haul me into one of his 'private' rooms for questioning.

At least I'd see what was behind those doors.

I snapped my eyes shut at the thought. There were better ways to find out.

Quietly sucking in a breath, I crept out of the room. It was two-thirty in the morning; the house had been silent for the last hour. It took forever for Quella to leave my room. She'd lain on my bed chatting away like a magpie until I'd pretended to drift off to sleep. She'd finally gotten the hint and left. As soon as the adjoining door shut, my eyes snapped open and I clutched the sheets to my chest, waiting for an opportunity.

The cool tiles were cold on my bare feet. I descended the first curved set of stairs toward the entranceway. To my right was the corridor that led to the first private room off the second living area. It was closer, and I could sneak in and out then move on, but the one that piqued my interest earlier was that wooden door by the pool. I could tell Miguel wanted me to steer clear of all three, but it was that flash of panic on his face that made me turn left toward the pool area.

I paused in the hallway, listening for any noises, but all I could hear was the soft cascading water. Pressing my body against the wall and feeling like a novice spy, I crept toward the sound.

I reached the pool stairs quicker than I thought I would. Glancing over my shoulder, I felt the wall and used it as a guide to descend the stairs without falling on my ass.

The black cellphone in my back pocket dug into my butt as I stopped by the pool and squashed myself into a shadow. I thought I'd heard something.

My breathing was unsteady as I waited out the noise, but it never came again. I'd called Kaplan from my bathroom a few hours earlier while I was pretending to take a shower. It was Rhodes who answered. I'd rattled off my plan and he told me to be careful. They were waiting for my call.

I gripped the wall, hoping to make it out of the 'maintenance' room in time.

Sneaking around the pool, I headed for the door. It was locked. Rhodes told me it probably would be. Taking his advice, I felt around the door, reaching on my tiptoes above the frame before crouching down and scouring the wall. Panic sizzled through me. Nothing. My movements became frantic as my fingers skimmed every dark surface around the doorway.

I was about to give in and call Rhodes. Maybe he'd have another idea.

My fingers were so shaky when I pulled out the phone, it slipped out of my grasp and skidded across the tiles.

"Shit!" I whispered, scrambling after it. "Please don't be broken."

My nose wrinkled as I dove after it. With the serious lack of light, it was impossible to see anything. I slapped the cold corner it had slid into and finally found it. It was wedged underneath a crack of some kind. With a little difficulty, I pulled it free and heard a soft tink.

I froze.

What was that?

My hand launched back into the space, scraping my knuckles on the rough wall.

"Ouch." I ignored the sting and dug my fingers into the space, the very tips brushing a flat, metal object. "Oh, thank you, God," I breathed, wrestling it out of the space and sliding it toward me.

With my shaking fingers it was a challenge collecting it off the slippery tiles, but I finally snatched it into my hand and squeezed tight. The phone in my other hand had a large crack running across the screen. I held my breath and turned it back on, nearly crying with relief when the screen lit up.

Carefully sliding it back into my pocket, I moved to the door and jiggled the key into place.

The deadbolt was a little stiff, but it eventually shifted. Once again, the door sounded loud and obnoxious in the quiet space. I winced, hurrying to shut it behind me.

Leaning against the wood, I gulped in some air and tried to regulate my heartbeat. With the key safely in my pocket, I pulled my phone free and turned on the flashlight app. It was a closed room and I felt safe using it.

I squinted against the instant light, blinking rapidly as my eyes adjusted. A few moments later, I was able to see clearly and wasn't surprised that there was absolutely no maintenance equipment in the closet. In fact, it was nothing but an empty room. I frowned, disheartened that my suspicions had been wrong.

But, no, wait.

I had seen the look on Miguel's face. He did not want me in this room.

Stepping forward, I ran my fingers along the empty walls. There was a power box on the left and empty shelves on the right. The wall in front of me was plain. I ran my hand over the smooth surface until my fingers hit the joint and I felt the whisper of air.

"Hmmm." Running my fingers all the way to the bottom, I shone my flashlight on the bottom edge and saw a definite gap. This wasn't a wall; it was a door.

I shoved my shoulder into it, trying to budge it free, but it wouldn't give. Stepping back, I searched the room, looking for any kind of switch. My eyes landed on the power box. I flicked back the green casing and took in all the switches.

"Great, which one?" I sighed, going on tiptoes to get a better look. The labels read:

Lights 1.

Lights 2.

Waterfall lights.

Deck lights.

Pool heater.

Pump

I skimmed the writing until I reached the end of the second row. That one didn't have a label.

Biting on my lip, I cautiously reached for it.

It was a risk. For all I knew, it could set off some kind

of disco party or fireworks display in the pool area. That would get security running. My mind scrambled for a quick escape plan—run out, hide in the sauna.

It wasn't world-class, but it was enough to give me the courage to place my finger on the black switch.

I squeezed my eyes shut and flicked it. A grumble sounded to my right and I opened my eyes to see the door shunt open.

"Yes!" I whispered, slapping the green box shut and squeezing through the space. I checked the wall to make sure there was an out switch. I noticed a red button. Satisfied, I closed the heavy door with my butt and shone the flashlight around me.

It was a passageway. The walls were rough, as if someone had carved out the tunnel with a pickaxe. I placed my hand on it to steady myself and shuffled into the darkness.

After only a few steps it turned into a narrow staircase.

Oh, man, what was down there?

I had visions of it opening into a medieval torture chamber or something, because that was exactly what it felt like. Punchy breaths tore out of my mouth as I took one stair at a time. Wanting to keep my entrance as clandestine as possible, I flicked off my light and fumbled my way down.

The stairwell was tight and curved in a spiral. I could tell I was getting near the end, because a soft glow lit the bottom stairs. I paused, my body going into silent protest.

Move, Caity! I argued back.

Biting the inside of my cheek, I forced my limbs to obey. When I reached the bottom step, I couldn't help an audible gasp. The sight before me broke my heart and made instant tears pop onto my lashes.

In the middle of the dirt-floor, circular room was a single bulb with a string switch. It was the silent soldier watching over its prisoners. I blinked at my tears, taking in the cell doors with an aching heart. Thick metal bars crisscrossed over the doorways, behind them were a tangle of skinny limbs and slumped figures.

I stepped into the room, running to the first cage. The two girls inside were huddled together on the floor, their locks of greasy hair straggly and lifeless. Their skinny arms were wrapped around one another as if trying to draw what strength and comfort they could. Their clothes were dirty and torn and I could see a large bruise on one face and thick finger marks on her arm. She must have struggled.

"Who are you?" A small voice from the other side of the room caught my attention.

I flinched, spinning at the sound. Scuffling over to her, I crouched down to look her in the eye.

They were large, brown, and I knew them.

"Angela?"

Her bony fingers gripped the cage bars. "How do you know my name?"

"Your family's looking for you."

Her lips wobbled, fat tears popping out of her eyes as she sucked in a ragged breath. Her fingers trembled and she covered her mouth. "Help me," she whispered.

"We're going to. It's okay." My voice grew with strength. I poked my hand through the bars, grasping her fingers and giving them a gentle squeeze. "I'm working with the FBI and we're going to get you out of here."

"There is no way out," came a wooden voice from the next cage. "Unless you're sold."

I shuffled over to see who was talking, but I didn't recognize her. She looked to be about thirteen or fourteen. Her large, green eyes looked too big for her pale face. Her blonde hair was matted and dirty.

"No one's going to sell you."

"Yes, they will. Two were taken a couple of days ago, dragged out, screaming for their mothers." Her voice wobbled.

I clutched the bars. "Who?"

"Rowena and Melanie," Angela said. "They don't use our names, though. We're just a number."

"How does it work?" The question tasted vile in my mouth.

"We're cleaned up and put into nice clothes, our hair and makeup done, slinky dresses that show off our bodies." Angela's eyes were large and lifeless, her tone robotic.

"They take us through a tunnel." A skinny finger poked out from the cage. I turned to follow the direction and saw a heavy metal door in the corner of the room. I moved toward it.

"Don't!" one girl softly called.

I stopped and looked over my shoulder.

"They come through that way."

Heeding her warning, I moved back to crouch next to the girls.

"Where does the tunnel lead?"

"To this room with tinted windows and bright lights," the girl two along from me pitched in.

It was Janey...the Lacey look-a-like. I closed my eyes, thinking about her parents' reaction when they found out their only child was alive.

"We have to stand there and..." her voice pitched, "and then your number gets called and you're taken into a room where the buyer can decide if he wants you."

"Who are the buyers?"

"Rich, fat men with soulless eyes," Angela spat.

I felt sick. Acid burned my throat and I pinched my nose, squeezing my eyes shut to ward off the nausea.

"If you don't make a sale, you're thrown back in here until the next time."

"I want to go home." Janey leaned her head against the bars and started weeping, her sobs sounding pitiful in the dank room.

"I'm going to get you there. I promise." I stood, turning a slow circle and looking into each cage. All the girls were awake, their skinny faces peering through the bars. I counted eight.

"How many have been sold so far?"

"Ten or twelve?" one girl guessed.

"But...we only know of twelve girls. No other kidnappings have been reported."

"Not all of us have families to report it."

I glanced at the girl next to Angela, the one I didn't recognize.

I squatted down beside her cage. "I'm getting you out and I'm gonna find you somewhere safe to live."

She didn't believe me. I peeled off her mask and saw the resignation. She was going to be sold to some sick bastard who would use and abuse her until every ounce of innocence had been stripped from her soul.

"I know you don't believe me right now, but I will make it happen. The FBI is waiting for my call and they're gonna bust in here and save you guys."

Angela let out a laughing sob, desperately wanting to buy into my speech.

I whipped out my cellphone, thinking there was no time like the present. I was about to speed dial Kaplan when I noticed I had zero reception. I held it up with a frown, swearing softly to myself.

"I have to go and make this call."

A girl behind me whimpered.

"It's all right. This will all be over soon."

I backed out of the room, watching the girls carefully. I saw flickers of hope on some faces while others were blank slates, fear and abuse wiping them of all emotion. A protective shell had gone up around them in an attempt to keep them safe.

My heel hit the first step and I steadied myself against the wall.

"If anyone comes in here, don't tell them you've seen me, okay?" They all nodded. "I'll be back soon."

thirty-seven

caitlyn

I bolted up the stairs two at a time, only tripping once. I was out of breath by the time I made it to the top. Seeing those pitiful girls in their wretched state had injected my body with renewed vigor. I checked the time on my watch, just after three a.m. I couldn't wait to tell Kaplan to get her ass in here right now.

Pressing the red button, I shuffled back into the

"maintenance" room and then eased out of that door. Checking all was clear, I locked the door behind me and returned the key. It was probably unnecessary caution, but I did it anyway.

I scurried into the pool area, looking for somewhere safe to make the call. It felt weird to think that any minute now, federal agents would be swarming in, guns at the ready. I couldn't believe I'd found the girls so quickly. At this rate, I'd win my man back before the turkey was served.

Standing by the glass, I looked over my shoulder, up at the dark stairwell. It felt so open and exposed to make the call from there. I checked my reception; I had a few more bars, but it wasn't full. I didn't want anything to disrupt this call. It was the most important one I'd ever make.

As I eased around the pool, I caught a glimpse of something outside. Squinting my eyes, I padded toward it, spotting a small decking area. My eyes shot around each surface, looking for a door. It took me a minute to realize that one of the glass windows was actually a very narrow sliding door. I turned the latch and slid it open, easing out onto the small space. The fresh air was cool on my face, but it smelled good. The mountain air was so clean and inviting.

I breathed it in and contacted Kaplan.

She answered after two rings.

"Did you find anything?"

"I found the girls."

"You what?"

"The girls. They're here."

"He's keeping them in his house?"

"They're downstairs in like a dungeon. You have to come and get them out."

"How many?"

I licked my lip. "Eight. They said ten or twelve have already been sold."

My quiet response was met with a heart-wrenching silence. Unnerved, I quickly filled the space, telling Kaplan what the girls had told me.

"And I think they'll be paraded around again tomorrow night. Mendez said he has a business meeting in the evening. I can only assume he has a new set of buyers coming in. He said it was a last-minute change, which is why Quella's been brought here instead of going to Palm Springs."

"Okay, good. That's good. So, we'll move tomorrow night then."

"What? No, you have to come and get them now." The cool breeze kissed my skin and I shivered, rubbing my arms.

"It's a waste if we don't catch the buyers at the same time. Now tell me the logistics of the house."

I clenched my jaw, hating the idea of those poor girls spending a second longer in those dank cells.

"Blondie, you still there?"

I huffed out a sigh and went on to explain exactly how I'd gotten into the room and that I had no idea what was behind the black door.

"Okay, well, I have someone trying to track down the plans for the house. Now that we know the location, we might have more luck. I'll get the team prepped. Do you know what time the meeting is?"

"Not specifically, just in the afternoon or evening."

"See if you can find out. We have the house surrounded on all sides, from a distance admittedly. His security is pretty damn tight, but we have been monitoring incoming and outgoing traffic. As soon as we see the buyers arrive, we'll move in."

It felt good to know they were close enough to monitor traffic. The isolation of this mission didn't feel quite so debilitating. "You can't let those girls be taken."

"They won't be. Trust us. Mendez and his dirty little business associates are going down tomorrow night; I can assure you of that."

"Thank you."

"Go get some sleep. You still have to play innocent tomorrow and I want as many details as you can get me."

"Yes, ma'am."

"Hang tight, Caitlyn. In less than twenty-four hours, you're going to be free."

"Promise?"

Kaplan snickered and hung up.

I lowered the phone and ran my thumb over the large crack in the screen. I missed Eric. It was an insane time to think of him, but I couldn't help it. Gazing up at the star-filled sky, I thought about where he might be. Hopefully tucked up in his bed, unable to sleep as he worried about me. I hated to put him through that, but I was where I was supposed to be.

I was given this gift for a reason and this time around, that reason was pretty damn good.

Squeezing the phone in my hand, I slid it back into my pocket and turned back for the "maintenance" room. I wanted to tell the girls what the plan was, ease their fears before they were yanked into that God-forsaken room again.

I sniffed in one last taste of fresh air before squeezing back into the pool area.

"That was an interesting late-night phone call you were making."

I gasped, my heart exploding as a strong hand clamped around my arm, dragging me away from the pool and any chance of warning the girls.

thirty-eight

caitlyn

His fingers were sharp and hard, digging into my arm until I thought my muscles might pop.

"Please, Miguel," I whispered.

He ignored me, hauling me up the stairs and throwing me into a small room off the hallway. I landed on the bed and spun around to face him.

He loomed over me. The menacing glint in his eye

told me he was about to have a little fun.

That was obviously how they controlled the girls, an over-powering threat that weakened them with terror.

I couldn't let that happen. Those girls were counting on me not to lose it.

"Who were you talking to?" he barked.

I peeled his mask free, soaking in his expression. There was no way he planned to rape me. I wasn't his type. It was a comfort not to fear his persona, like so many girls probably did.

I shifted on the bed, hanging my feet over the edge and gripping the mattress. "I was trying to call my boyfriend."

An explosion of pain burst across my cheek as he backhanded me.

"Ah!" I grabbed at it, the stinging pain radiating across my entire face. I hadn't even seen it coming.

"Do not lie to me." He crouched down, getting in my space and grabbing a fistful of my hair. I whimpered as he yanked my head up to face him. "I know how to break people." The back of his finger whispered softly over my aching cheek. "Do not make me spoil this beautiful face."

"You don't think I'm beautiful."

"Don't I?" He shoved me back onto the bed, slipping off his jacket.

My mind scrambled for the right words. I made sure his mask stayed off as he pulled his shirt free and slowly undid his belt. He was just delaying things. Making me think he was going to abuse me when he had no intention.

I glanced at his beefy hands. In thinking that, there was nothing stopping him from using those hulking fists.

"Tell me what I need to know." He leaned over me, grabbing a handful of my shirt, his silent glare threatening to rip it off.

"You're not going to do that."

His eyes narrowed.

So I kept going. "I mean you could, if you wanted to, but you don't want to. You don't find me attractive. You're just trying to scare me with the idea that you do."

The corner of his eye twitched, his skin paling. Stepping back, he yanked my shirt, bringing me with him.

"You are a good liar."

"I'm not lying." I swallowed. "I saw you looking at that waiter. You're in love with him."

His brow creased, his hand balling into a fist.

I held up my hands. "No, please, wait! No one else knows. It's just me." I patted my chest. "I have a gift. I see things no one else can. That's why I had to check out that room. Your face told me. You were worried about the idea of me going in there."

"I gave nothing away."

"Not to any normal person, but I'm different."

"You a witch?"

I shook my head. "I can just see...behind people's

masks. I know what they're feeling and I can always tell if they're lying."

He looked skeptical.

"Like right now, you don't know whether to believe me or not, but a small part of you can't help it."

I kept staring at him, ripping off layers and reading whatever I could.

"You don't like your boss, but you stay because of that waiter. You love him. You'll do anything to protect him." My lips parted. "You feel guilty that he's here. Is he a slave?"

His eyes grew wide and he let go of my shirt as if he no longer wanted to touch me.

"You're scared. You're scared that I can see the truth, but you don't have to be. I won't tell anyone. I can see that my life depends on that."

Whipping a gun from his back pocket, he pressed it against my forehead.

My voice quaked, my words spurting out of me in a quick torrent. "I'm telling you the truth. I won't say a word, I swear."

"Who's coming for the girls?"

The hard metal on my temple made me spill. "The FBI. They've been investigating the missing girls and one of the agents, the one I work for, suspected Mendez. Quella was my in."

"You are too young to be an undercover agent."

"I know. I'm not even getting paid. No one knows I'm here except her and her team."

"Mendez will kill you."

"Only if you tell him." I looked up, trying to ignore the gun in my peripherals. "These girls should not be enslaved like this. They don't have anyone to protect them. They're being sold and abused. Imagine what would have happened if you hadn't managed to save your love. Where would he be right now?"

Miguel blanched and pushed the gun a little harder into my skin. I kept my eyes on him, whipping off masks as fast as I could. There was that guilt again, the disgust in helping Mendez run his business, the fear at losing the man he loved.

"Please, don't kill me. Help me. Help me with these girls."

It was the wrong thing to say.

I should have stayed on point and kept talking about the waiter, but the words came out and I couldn't take them back. A hard edge morphed his humanity into something dark and sinister.

"They are not my problem. If I help you, Mendez will kill me." His fingers danced over the gun. "But if I kill you, or better yet drag you to him and reveal your treachery then he will reward me nicely."

Money.

Miguel loved money. No, wait. He needed money.

A hungry, desperate spark traveled across his face and he snatched my arm, yanking me off the bed. "Come."

I dug my heels into the floor. "No, please! I can

reward you even better. I can get the money you need."

He stopped, glaring down at me. "How do you know I need money?"

"It's a guess. You said reward and I saw it on your face, a spark of desperation and the hope of freedom. Are you in debt?"

His eyes flashed with a warning.

"How much? I mean, who do you owe it to?"

The muscle in his jaw clenched tight. He was ashamed of his debt, like he should never have let it happen.

My mind scrambled to decipher what it could mean, my own desperation making the task a challenging one.

He humphed and continued to drag me toward the door.

"Listen, I've told you what I can do. I can spot lies, read emotions. Those skills can be really helpful. Like...like...in poker! I never lose! I could win you money."

That made him flinch.

"Yeah." I nodded. "I really kick butt, because I can see what everyone is feeling about their hand, so it makes it easy to call the bluff and play smart, you know? I could—I could win you some money and you could pay off your debt."

The shift in his expression was encouraging. My stuttering heart slowed just a little.

"Do you—do you like poker?"

His lips twitched with a smirk. "You can win at

poker?"

"Every time."

With narrowed eyes, he wrenched my arm, pulling me out of the room and down the hallway.

"I need you to prove it." He pushed me into a large kitchen area. A wooden table sat in the corner, surrounded by staff. They were still in their white uniforms.

They all stiffened when he approached the table and yanked out a chair. It scraped against the tiles.

He plonked me down. I winced as my butt smacked into the hard wood.

"Deal her in."

The staff all eyed each other. I gave them a quivering smile.

"Do it!"

I jerked at his shout. He pulled out some money and threw it in front of me.

"Quadruple it," he whispered in my ear.

Picking up the twenty-dollar bills, I counted out five and felt like throwing up. "I don't know if I can—"

He squeezed my shoulder, hard. I winced and shut up, peeking at the two cards in front of me.

It was Texas Hold 'Em again. I memorized my cards then looked around the table. They were all really nervous having Miguel sit in and it was overtaking my ability to read their hands.

"Dude," I muttered. "What the hell did I ever do to you?" I gave the dealer the finger and it broke the tension. The men chuckled while Miguel crossed his arms, his eyes tightening with an advisory glare. I tried to ignore it and get on with proving my worth...and hopefully saving my ass.

With the tension snapped, faces began to relax and I was able to see a little better. I lost the first round intentionally, wanting the boys to think I was a little dumb. They were still confused as to why Miguel even wanted me to play, but they quickly cottoned on by the third round. Ten rounds later and I had more than quadrupled Miguel's pot. The rest of the staff sat in stunned silence, confusion marring their tired features.

Miguel pulled me from my chair, extracting his gun at the same time.

"Not a word about her to anyone." He aimed the gun at each poker player until their heads started bobbing erratically.

"*Si, señor*," was muttered by all before he pulled me away.

I handed him his money. His right eyebrow arched, a smug smile pulling at his lips. I didn't know what the hell Quella saw in this jerk.

He hauled me upstairs to my room, shoving me inside. Roughly spinning me around, he yanked the phone out of my pocket. My eyes bulged wide. He smirked at my fear, his intense glare making me shrink away from him. Unsure what to do, I slid beneath the sheets in my clothes, hoping he'd take the hint and leave.

"Tomorrow, when Quella is watching football with Rosa, you are to tell her you feel sick. Come up here to lie down. There will be a dress waiting for you. Make yourself look rich and pretty."

Dread sucked the moisture from my mouth. "Why?" I croaked.

"Because you are going to help me pay off my debt and then make me a rich man."

"And if I refuse?"

He shrugged. "I'll take you to Mendez instead. You're a little old, but I'm sure he could find a buyer for you...or kill you."

I bit my lip and laid my head on the pillow, pulling the sheets up around my shoulder.

With a snicker, he left the room. My eyes burned as I squeezed them shut, wishing Kaplan had said she'd come that night. Damn those stupid buyers! Why did she need them anyway!

My heart ticked inside me, like a time bomb waiting to explode. I had to get some sleep. It was after four, and I still had a harrowing day to survive before Kaplan came to save my ass. Tears slipped from my eyes. I chewed at my lip, praying I could handle whatever shit was thrown my way in the morning.

thirty-nine

eric

"Get up." Gramps kicked my bed, making it shudder.

I groaned and pulled the sheet over my head. "Let me sleep. It's not even morning yet."

"It's past nine o'clock. That's enough moping; now get your butt out of bed. We got some talkin' to do."

I flicked the sheet down and threw him an evil glare.

He met it head-on with two raised eyebrows and his *don't mess with me* face. I rolled my eyes and sat up, leaning over the bed and pressing my fingers into my eyes.

My head felt like sawdust, my mouth dry and gluggy. It had been a crappy night's sleep and facing a new day was damn depressing.

Gramps slapped me on the shoulder.

"Up you get, boy. There's coffee waitin' for ya in the kitchen."

I slumped after him, rubbing the back of my neck and rolling out my shoulders.

The smell of brewing coffee tantalized my taste buds and I eagerly grabbed a mug. Gramps gave it to me black, just the way he liked it, and we sat down at the table together.

"Talk."

"I did," I mumbled. "Last night."

"But your rationale was unsound, illogical." He rubbed his bald head. "Caity is in love with you; I saw it when she was here. She wouldn't just walk away for no good reason."

"She did, Gramps." I slapped the table. "And she didn't just walk, she frickin' ran, okay? She. Does. Not. Want. Me."

Gramps's wide lips pursed before he shook his head. "I ain't buyin' it."

I let out a disgusted huff.

"And you're a fool to believe her so easily. There has

got to be a better explanation for this."

"Well, whatever it is, she sure as hell doesn't want to tell me."

Gramps gave me a hard look. "You're probably not in a frame of mind to hear it anyway." He took a loud slurp of coffee, eyeing me over the rim of his mug. "You know what you need?"

I shrugged.

"To burn off some of that anger. Let's go." He stood up, slapping me on the shoulder again.

"Where are we going?"

"For a run." A slow smile stretched across his face and my heart sank.

It wouldn't be just any run. It would be a Marine boot camp *he's trying to kill me* run. I sighed, knowing there was no way out of it. Pushing myself up, I grabbed a banana from the fruit bowl and went to get changed.

He drove me out to Cleveland National Forest, which was about an hour and a half away. I munched on my banana and the granola bar he shoved under my nose. We didn't talk much. I slid on my shades and rested my foot up on the dashboard while Gramps drove. There was no music, no chatter, but it wasn't an awkward silence either. The only thing to taint it was my raging emotions. I kept them under wraps, letting them simmer and burn until I thought my insides might combust.

Closing my eyes, I tried to make up for the sleep I had lost the night before, but it didn't work. Every time my lids shut, I either saw Caity running or a young kid waiting outside a baseball stadium. It was torture.

Eventually I gave up, sitting forward in my seat and distracting myself with the scenery.

By the time we pulled into the park, my nerves were vibrating with a deep-seated angst I couldn't shake. Although the run would probably kill me, I felt like shouting to the sky, "Bring it on!"

Gramps slammed the door shut and locked the car, looking over at me.

"You ready?"

"Yeah." I nodded.

"Let's go."

For an old guy, Gramps was a freaking machine. He jogged ahead of me, starting out at an easy pace I knew he could maintain for miles. I loped after him, feeling good for the first thirty minutes and then the weariness of lost sleep kicked in. I began to stagger and stumble. Sweat ran into my eyes as we negotiated the rocky trail. Gramps, of course, had to choose the steepest, narrowest trail for us to take.

In the end, I gave in and started walking. It was damn humiliating, but my burning lungs and spaghetti legs gave me no choice.

Gramps paused and looked down at me. His chest was heaving, too, but he was still standing.

I squinted up at him, lashing at the sweat running down my neck.

"You done already?" He grinned.

I glared at him.

"Come on, son, we're gonna make it to the top. I don't care if you have to crawl there."

A low growl reverberated in my throat and I marched past him. He chuckled softly behind me and let me take the lead. We hiked the rest of the way, scrambling up precarious rocks near the end. We finally reached the pinnacle and were rewarded with a glorious view. I drank in the valley below us, and I could do nothing but marvel. The earth was beautiful. The air was clean. Being in a place like this revived the soul. Gramps had done the right thing in bringing me out here.

My breathing was still labored. I sucked in the air, trying to regulate my heartbeat. Gramps sat down next to me and pulled a water bottle from his backpack. He chucked it to me.

"Happy Thanksgiving."

I snorted out a dry laugh before slugging back a gallon. Tossing it to him, I finally found my regular rhythm again.

"Ready to talk yet?"

"I guess." I slumped down on the rock beside him and pressed my elbows into my knees; my skin was so sweaty they nearly slipped off.

I tucked a loose lock of hair behind my ear, squeezing the band holding my stubby ponytail. Caity loved it when I tied my hair back. Too bad she wasn't there to see it.

Damn, she'd love this place.

My face scrunched as the raging emotions tried to take me out. "It hurts, Gramps."

"I know," he said softly. "But it still don't feel right. When we get back, you need to head to L.A., find your girl and fix this thing."

"How am I supposed to do that when she doesn't even want to talk to me?"

Gramps shrugged. "Find a way."

"How? How do you make someone love you? You can't do that! You don't think I tried?" I stood up, pacing away from him. "I was everything she needed me to be...at least I thought I was." I threw my hands in the air.

"You still are. I don't think this has anything to do with you."

"It's like Dad all over again," I muttered, kicking the dirt.

"Boy, you have to let that go."

I whipped around to face him. "He abandoned me. He up and left. I don't know how the hell you've forgiven him so easily. That loser left us! He didn't give a shit. He just fucking disappeared."

"Watch your mouth!" Gramps shook his head, anger coursing over his face. His lips pressed into a firm line, twitching a few times before he finally looked at me and said, "Your father may have made many stupid decisions in his life, but he deserves a little respect. He loves his family. He loves you."

"Yeah, right." I swung my leg back and booted a

large stone. It scuttled across the ground and smacked into the boulder Gramps was sitting on.

He shot from his spot, marching toward me and getting right in my face. I wanted to step away from him but he wouldn't let me, grabbing my shirt and holding me in place.

"Boy, don't make me slap some sense into you. You think your father ran away out of selfish pride? There's always more to the story. You don't hurt the ones you love without a really good reason."

My breath evaporated, my eyes searching his. "What are you not telling me?"

He sighed, letting me go and pacing away. He gazed out at the distance, rubbing his head. "Your father cared about you and he left to keep you safe...and he stayed away to save your life."

I wanted to ask more, demand why he hadn't told me this before, pepper him for details, but I couldn't, because one thought came screaming through my brain so fast it nearly blinded me.

Caity.

The most self-sacrificing person I knew.

She'd give up anything to keep me safe...including me.

Breaths punched out of my chest. I squeezed my eyes shut, hating myself.

Why the hell hadn't I thought of that before? Too caught up moping like a spoiled five-year-old, I'd totally missed the fact that Caity was no doubt messed up in some kind of trouble.

What had she seen?

What was she doing in order to keep her friends safe?

She hadn't told any of us. She broke her promise not to lie to me, but she must have had a good reason.

I pictured her face; it swam through my mind, flashing me images of her from the moment I first saw her to the day she ran away. Her blue eyes shone, her cute smile was always given like a special gift just for me. I felt her in my arms again, the look in her eye after we'd made love, the way she ran her fingers through my hair...and then that sudden change. I forced myself to relive that moment she ran away, and suddenly that look of malaise I thought I'd seen turned into something different. She hadn't been annoyed about me trying to win her back. Damn it! She'd been scared.

I had to call her. I had to make sure she was okay. I patted my running shorts, realizing I didn't bring my phone with me. Where the hell was it?

"Shit! My car!"

"What, son?" Gramps spun to face me.

"I gotta get back."

"What's going on?"

"Caity. You're right, she wouldn't just leave me for no good reason, and her whole needing space bullshit was just that...bullshit."

"What do you think's going on?"

"I don't know, but it must be something pretty huge

if she was willing to hurt me like that."

"I told you it wasn't her style." His lips tipped with a small grin.

I stopped and pointed at him. "Can we talk about Dad later?"

"You go get your girl back first. Then we can talk for as long as you like."

I squeezed his shoulder. "Thanks, Gramps."

He nodded, knowing how much I meant it.

There were no words after that, we just turned on our heels and sped back to the car as fast as we could. With each step and slide down that hill, my turmoil grew.

Caity was in trouble.

I could feel it.

And I had to get to her.

forty

caitlyn

Thanksgiving lunch was impossible to eat. I nibbled at my turkey and played with my sweet potatoes. I managed half of my pumpkin pie before placing the silver fork down on my plate.

"You are not hungry today?" Mendez eyed me carefully.

I gave him a closed-mouth smile and patted my

stomach. "I'm not feeling very well."

It was an easy lie to buy into. My skin was no doubt sallow, my eyes felt dull. I'd put makeup on that morning to try and hide my fear, but it hadn't really worked. I felt sick, down to my very core. Kaplan and her men couldn't get there fast enough and I still had the ordeal with Miguel to endure. I had no idea what I was expected to do. I assumed he wanted me to use my eyesight to win him more money at poker.

I cleared my throat. "I don't mean to be rude, but would it be okay if I went to lie down?"

"But you'll miss the football." Quella pouted.

"I'm sorry." My smile was tight as she reminded me once again how immature and self-absorbed she was.

She huffed, giving a little shrug and looking away from me. She was still pissed with her father's change of plans; I didn't have to read her to see that.

Mendez gave me a kind smile. "You go and rest. I will send up someone to check on you soon."

"No, that's okay." I waved my hand in the air. "I just need to sleep."

His mask slipped and I noticed his eyes narrow. He was trying to figure out if I was lying or not. I forced a shaky smile—not hard to do in my current state—and left the room. Miguel was at the door, his intense stare searing through me as I walked past him.

My feet were filled with lead, making it difficult to ascend the stairs. I clutched the marble railing, trying to stay calm and not let my imagination destroy all common sense. I had absolutely no one to help me. Miguel had stolen any chance of communication with my rescuers. The only hope I could cling to was the fact they'd be busting into the house later in the day.

I closed my eyes, praying Mendez's meeting was sooner rather than later.

By the time I reached my room, I genuinely felt like throwing up. Bile surged up my throat when I entered and saw the gold sequined dress lying on the bed. On the floor was a pair of stiletto heels. Miguel obviously didn't know me that well if he thought I could pull this off.

I was so dead.

My lips quivered as I neared the bed, my body fighting me each step of the way. I slowly stripped off my clothes, dropping them on the floor. Collecting up the shiny dress, I stepped into it and pulled it over my hips. It was a snug fit; I had to lose my bra and struggled to get the zipper done up. Walking to the mirror, I examined myself. I looked like a freaking James Bond bimbo. I slid my hand down the skin-tight dress. It hugged my curves until just below my hips then opened up into a slight flare. The material draped on the floor at my feet. I poked my leg out of the high split and grimaced. It was ridiculous. I needed a name like Pussy Galore wearing this stupid thing.

Running my fingers through my hair, I piled it high and looked both ways in the mirror. If I was going to pull this off, I had better go the whole way. I stepped into the bathroom and opened up my makeup kit, applying another layer of foundation and fattening up my eyelashes with some more mascara. I pinned my hair up, letting a few loose curls roam free and put on the sparkling jewelry Miguel left for me.

I had to say, by the time I was done, I looked pretty glamorous.

My lips quirked with a small grin.

The shoes were the next challenge. I slipped them on and teetered around the room, getting in as much practice as I could before someone knocked on my door.

"Who is it?"

"Miguel."

I tottered over and let him in. He closed the door behind him and eyed me up and down.

"I suppose that will have to do." He nodded.

Snatching my arm, he pulled me toward the adjoining door and through Quella's room. In the back corner, attached to the wall, was a full-length mirror. Miguel pulled it away to reveal a narrow doorway.

I frowned and Miguel looked smug as he yanked me into the passageway. Stopping to open up the flashlight app on his phone, he led us down a set of narrow stairs into what looked like a panic room.

"Mendez and his paranoia," Miguel muttered a quick explanation.

I stood in the middle of the padded room while he moved to the heavy, black door on the other side and punched in a code. It grumbled open to reveal a much larger passageway. This one was more like the tunnel leading down to the girls, with the roughly hacked walls and dank oppression.

He grabbed my arm again and pulled me along until we reached a garage. Two black cars that looked like the kind royalty were transported in sat side by side. Miguel shoved me toward one of them.

"Get in." He unhooked the key from the wall and beeped it open for me.

I slid into the passenger seat and settled myself into the plush leather.

A garage door whirred up and Miguel reversed onto a large, round disc, which spun the car around by ninety degrees. We then entered a dark, narrow tunnel. About five minutes later, we popped out into the sunshine and Miguel accelerated down a dirt road. I looked out the back window, trying to figure out where we had exited the house from, but all I could see was a rocky wall that looked like the side of a mountain.

"It's the east exit. The tunnel pops out two miles from the house, so we use this when we want to sneak away."

I swallowed, shuffling back around to face out the front. "Which one did Quella and I come in the other day?"

"The west."

"Are there any others?"

"The buyers come in through the south." Miguel

kept his eyes on the road, missing the shudder running down my spine.

"What time are they coming today?"

He glanced at me. "Even if I tell you, you will have no way of contacting your outside party."

"They said they're watching the traffic anyway." I winced, wishing I'd kept my mouth shut.

I still didn't trust him. The man had eyes like a snake, deceptive and unpredictable. I could read him, but I couldn't see into my future. We may have a deal going on, but I had no guarantee he wouldn't turn on me at any moment. There was a pretty damn good chance he'd spill the beans to Mendez as soon as I'd done whatever he wanted me to.

I had to try, though.

I wasn't ready to die.

I cleared my throat, staving off another spine tingle. "So, where are we going?"

"There is a private casino about twenty miles from here. It is for select members only." His eyebrow arched. "You are accompanying me as my date to a very important poker game."

I eyed him carefully, letting his mask fall away. He was nervous about this one, but also angry?

"Are we playing the man you are indebted to?"

He lips twitched. "No. We are playing the man who *put* me in debt. I am going to win back every penny I owe, get Gomez off my back...and then make a profit." He gripped the wheel, his expression hardening with molten rage.

I had no idea who Gomez was. He hadn't mentioned the name before and I could only assume he was the man Miguel owed wads of cash to.

"Where did you get the money to play this game?"

His anger landed straight on me, making me shrink against the car door. "Mendez is funding it."

"Does he know that he is?"

Miguel's jaw clenched. "The money will be returned before he even notices it's gone."

Oh, man, this just kept getting worse. I closed my eyes and swallowed back my nausea.

"So, um…" I cleared my throat. "How am I supposed to help you win this money?"

A slow, creepy-looking grin eased the right side of his mouth up.

"What? If I'm not playing, how am I supposed to help you?"

"You have eyes, and you are my lucky charm. You will never leave my side and will constantly be touching me, kissing my cheek and telling me exactly what I need to know without saying a word."

I swallowed.

"You pay off my debt and make me a profit, then we will return to the house and Mendez will know nothing. I will disappear before the raid and we will both get what we want."

"What about your boyfriend?"

His jaw clenched. "He will be safe. The kitchen staff

know nothing of Mendez's underground affairs."

I threaded my fingers together. "So, what kind of silent code am I giving you?"

"I was thinking a shoulder squeeze could mean the player opposite me has a good hand. Playing with my hair could tell me the person to my right has a good hand, that type of thing."

We spent the rest of the journey devising a code that would be subtle, yet effective. I hoped I could remember it all. We pulled through a plush set of gates into what looked like a resort. It was in the middle of nowhere, like an oasis in the desert.

I got out of the car as gracefully as I could, squeezing the valet's hand in order not to topple over in my heels. Miguel put on a tender smile and presented his arm to me. I placed my hand in the crook of his elbow and walked beside him.

We were led through the fancy lobby and down a red carpet hallway. As we neared the intricate double doors, Miguel pressed his lips to my ear.

"Remember, we are in love. You are my new catch and I cannot get enough of you."

He wrapped his arm around my waist and squeezed me too him, kissing my cheek at the opportune moment. The doors swung open and everyone in the room saw us entering. It was an effort not to push the large man off me, but my life depended on playing this right, and so I gave 'my man' a sultry smile. Thinking fashion model, I swayed my hips and tried not to fall over in my ridiculous heels.

"Mr. Vera, welcome back." A short man with dark, threadbare hair, who was trying to pull off an Armani suit, approached us.

Miguel grasped his bejeweled fingers and gave them a squeeze. "Thank you for inviting me."

"Well, I was surprised to get your call this morning, but the opportunity to take even more of your money was too good to pass up." He chuckled.

Miguel laughed, but beneath his mask he was throwing the stout man a murderous glare.

"And who is this?" The man eyed me greedily, his dark eyes sparking with something that made my insides turn.

"This is Carlotta."

I extended my hand with a demure smile and let him kiss my knuckles.

"So young and beautiful."

"Thank you." I only managed to whisper the words. Trying to keep his mask in place was an effort; the guy's creepiness made my skin crawl. I looked away from him, finding minimal refuge in Miguel's fake smile. I kept his mask on, needing to pretend that someone in this room actually cared about my well-being...that just one person was going to protect me from the circling sharks.

Every man in this room was an arrogant prick; it didn't take long to figure that out. They all sat around the table, some with their bellies pressing into the padded leather edge. Two were smoking cigars, another was sipping on what I assumed was brandy. There was only one other girl in the room, and she dangled off Mr. Armani Suit like a diamond earring. Her look was vacant and behind her mask I could see a bored, rich lover that was only sticking around for the expensive wardrobe and fine cuisine.

I placed my hand on Miguel's shoulder as the first hand was dealt. He was tense beneath my touch, his need to win so potent I could practically smell it. I rubbed my hand over his back, trying to calm him down. I needed him to win just as badly.

He collected his cards and I eyed them. Thank God he had a good hand.

The man left of the dealer threw in the small blind, followed by the man next to him, who tossed in the big blind. Everyone else then matched the bet, which meant every player thought they had a chance at winning this round. It was an effort to keep my expression neutral when I noticed they were playing with $1,000 chips. I pressed my lips together and scanned the five faces around the table, squeezing Miguel's shoulder to let him know Mr. Armani, sitting across from us, had a good hand, too.

No one else seemed too big a threat, but the flop was yet to be dealt.

I watched the dealer set aside the first card then deal the first three community cards face-up. All eyes shot to them and I saw a shift in the player sitting to the right of Miguel. I ran my finger up the right side of his neck, kneading my thumb below his right ear, like we'd discussed. He kept his poker face on as the next round of betting continued.

As the turn card and finally the river card were dealt, I kept up my subtle antics, warning Miguel of any dangerous players...and it worked like a charm. Miguel won the round easily. It helped that he'd started with two aces in his hand. He'd won with a three of a kind.

His smile of glee as he stacked up his chips was almost sickening.

His pleasure was in no way making me feel better. I could taste his desperate greed and hunger, and it scared me.

I was obviously an asset to him; what if he changed his mind and wouldn't let me go?

It was tempting to let him lose, but then he'd feed me to the lions back at Quella's house. I had to win him this game.

My nerves grew tighter with each passing round. I thought they'd actually snap when he lost the fourth round. His unmasked glare felt like a bullet. I leaned forward with a demure smile and pecked his cheek.

"Losing one round makes it more plausible." I hid my error with the whispered lie. "Don't worry; you'll walk out of here a wealthy man."

He grinned at that, rubbing my arm and kissing the inside of my wrist.

The move made me think of Eric.

A deep yearning I'd been trying to ignore bubbled

inside me. I wanted him to burst in that door and rescue me.

I peered over my shoulder, looking at the double doors, waiting for them to be thrown open. But it was a dream. The only way I was getting out of there was by staying focused.

The next few rounds went smoothly. Miguel's chips were piling up quickly.

"You are having a lucky day, Vera." Mr. Armani puffed on his cigar.

Miguel smirked at him.

"Maybe she is your lucky charm." He pointed at me and his mask slipped. I looked away from his lusty eyes, seeking solace in Miguel once again.

I didn't get it. His mask had disintegrated, too, and although he was probably smiling at me tenderly, all I could see was his gloating triumph.

Forcing a simpering smile, I rubbed his shoulders and gave myself a quick break, scanning the rest of the ornate room. The artwork looked expensive, the decor filled with artifacts that no doubt belonged in a museum. I was gazing at a Samurai sword hanging against the wall when I spotted him. He was a tall man, with narrow eyes and a sharp nose. He looked young, like maybe only a few years older than me.

His suit was tailored and fitted his muscular frame perfectly. I could tell he was strong. His very presence oozed assurance...the kind ninjas walked around with.

He caught me staring at him and shifted further into

the shadows. I had no idea who he was, maybe a security guard?

Miguel's hand wiggled beneath the split in my leg and he pinched the back of my knee, forcing my attention back to the game. It really hurt, but I hid it like a pro, managing to win him the round in the nick of time.

His hard glare told me not to make it that close again. I blinked at him, a subtle way of nodding, but he didn't notice; his gaze was on the man in the shadows. Stretching his neck, Miguel adjusted his tie and took the dealer's button with a small smile. The chances of him winning the round were that much better. The dealer's button was always a clear advantage, because it meant he could bet last, although with me by his side, he probably didn't need that advantage.

As I predicted, he won, forcing Mr. Armani out of the game. The short, rotund man swore like a losing school kid and left in a dark huff. He shouldered his way past Shadow Man and that was when I noticed him staring at me. Because of the distance and the lack of light, I couldn't really read him, but the hairs on the back of my neck prickled.

I turned away but could still feel his eyes on me, like they were drilling a tunnel between my ears. I didn't know why he'd become so fascinated with me, but I couldn't help wondering if he'd spotted our cheating code.

forty-one

eric

The drive back was torture. I pushed Gramps's car to the limit, speeding back to Black Beach with all the finesse of a roadrunner. Gramps was not impressed, but he kept his lips clamped together and let me get it out of my system, yet again proving why he was the best man in the world. I loved the fact he knew when to challenge and when to keep his mouth shut.

We swerved onto his street, screeching to a halt outside the house. I jumped out and raced to my Jeep, swearing loudly when I realized I didn't have my keys.

"Here you go." Gramps threw them to me from the front porch. I caught them and shoved them into the lock, wrestling the door open and throwing aside the towels on the back seat. My phone clunked to the floor and I snatched it up, turning it on and hoping it still had enough battery power.

Gramps stood beside me, his hand lightly resting on my shoulder.

The screen lit up and I breathed a sigh of relief as I found my girl's number.

"Just be patient with her. Remember, she's trying to protect you."

I gave my grandfather a soft smile, impulsively wrapping my arms around him. "Thanks, Gramps."

"I love you, son. I'm always here to help you. Whatever you need."

"Yeah, yeah, I know."

We thumped each other on the back and pulled apart. "I'm gonna go inside. You come in and tell me what she said, and we can head up to L.A. as soon as you're ready."

"You're gonna come with me?"

He grinned. "Just you try and stop me, boy." With a quick wink, he left me by the car.

I shook my head with a wry smile, grateful for his rock-solid support.

Pulling in a breath, I swallowed back my nerves and pressed Caity's name. Her phone went straight to voice mail. I huffed, wishing she didn't turn the damn thing off so much.

"Hey, Caity, it's me. I—" Squeezing my eyes shut, I rubbed the back of my neck.

Patience. Understanding.

I forced my tone to be soft and gentle. "I'm still not sure exactly what's going on, but I'm convinced you're hiding something from me...possibly to keep me safe? I love you for that, babe, but I'm worried about you. Please, please call me when you get this."

I hung up the phone, doubt hitting me for a moment.

What if I wasn't right? What if she genuinely wanted to leave me?

"Eric, shut the hell up," I muttered to myself, noticing I had a few text messages. They were all from Scott.

Call me.

Dude, where are you? Call me!

I've left you a message. Check it then CALL ME BACK!

Frowning, I dialed my voice mail. The usual robot answered, telling me I was indeed calling voice mail.

Message received at 4.35pm on Wednesday, November 25th

Then Scott started talking.

Hey, man. I'm guessing you've taken off. I don't know where you are, but can you call me back? I bumped into Caity this afternoon and she gave me a note for you. I haven't read it or anything, but something's up, man. She was really jittery and I think she's in some kind of trouble. Anyway, I just thought you should know. Call me as soon as you get this, okay?

It was an effort not to crush the phone in my hand. I ran back into the house, bringing up Scott's number as I went. Walking through the front door, I found it and was about press the green dial button when I stopped in my tracks.

Gramps was standing in the middle of the living room, his hands raised, a murderous look on his face. Two thugs in business suits stood in front of him, guns aimed at his chest.

Shock froze me.

"Eric Shore?" The broad man with a voice like gravel smirked at me.

I swallowed, my traitorous head bobbing automatically.

"Lucian Marchant would like a word with you."

"Who?"

"Eric, RUN!" Gramps thundered at me, lunging toward the men. I flinched, my eyes bulging as he tore at the shorter threat. His feral yell was loud and intimidating, throwing the man off-guard for a second.

A gunshot exploded.

"Gramps, no!" I threw myself into the fray, leaping over the couch and rocketing a punch at the taller man. I caught his chin and he stumbled back. With a steely front kick, I knocked the gun from his hand and prepared for battle. Gramps was still rolling on the floor with the other guy. I didn't know if the bullet had hit him or not, but I had to eliminate this guy before I could find out.

I raised my fists and bobbed on my feet, eyeing the guy carefully. He lashed out, his metallic gaze a malicious threat. I met it head-on, blocking his attack and firing one of my own. At first I thought we were pretty evenly matched—we weren't really able to touch each other too much—but it soon became clear that he was the more experienced fighter. His strength wore me down quickly, his lightning moves catching me off-guard. I stumbled back, crashing into the wall. The stepladder leaning against it crashed down beside me and I tripped over it.

Spinning around, I blocked the next punch and used a swift kick to inflict a little damage, lowering the guy to the floor. He stumbled over me, but it wasn't enough to stop his left hook. It caught me by surprise, spinning stars in front of my vision. I blinked, trying to ignore the pain rocketing down my jaw.

I balled my hand into a fist and moved to retaliate, but he got me again. My arms flopped as my head reeled and then his fingers were around my throat.

I kicked and bucked, pulling at his arms and pushing at his chin. He held fast, my vision blackening at the edges.

I was vaguely aware of the tussling still going on in the lounge. Gramps was putting up a tough fight.

"Gramps," I croaked.

My arms were weakening, losing their effectiveness against my attacker. I turned my head to look for anything that could save me when a dinner plate came flying across the room, followed swiftly by another. Both struck my attacker in the temple.

He jerked on top of me, his fingers going slack as he fought the daze.

With a loud roar, I shoved him off me and scrambled to my feet.

Another gunshot echoed through the lounge and my world tipped sideways as Gramps jerked, falling against the table. He gripped the wood but didn't have the strength to hold on. His sharp gaze caught me, widening with a moment of fear before he fell.

"Gramps!" I wailed.

Two more shots were fired. His foot twitched as the bullets entered his body and a rage unlike any I had felt before coursed through me.

With a banshee cry I tore at the man, ready to rip him in half. He aimed his gun at me and a shot rang out again.

I expected it to hurt more.

Novelists described it as a burning pain, a searing through the flesh, but I felt nothing. Another shot rang out and it was only then I noticed the man's head jolt. It tipped back and he flopped to the floor like a rag doll.

I spun back to see who'd shot him. Surely not his partner.

Over my shoulder, the tall man was rising to his feet. He smirked at me, his blood-coated teeth flashing through his smile. With a deep chuckle he raised his gun, but before he could even fire, a bullet whizzed past me, entering the center of his forehead.

He crumpled to the ground and I whipped back to find the last person I expected to see standing in Gramps's doorway.

His expression was grave, a mixture of regret and agony. Eyeing the dead bodies in the room, he shoved the gun into the back of his jeans and finally looked across at me.

"Hey, buddy."

"Dad?"

forty-two

caitlyn

The game came to an end after another hour of play. By then, my head was screaming, my feet were aching and all I wanted to do was get the hell out of there.

We walked toward the double doors, Miguel's hand on my back.

"Mr. Vera."

It was Shadow Man. I knew it before I turned, the

goosebumps rising on my skin telling me so.

Miguel spun on his heel. He was in a smug mood, giddy with triumph over his one hundred and eighty-six thousand dollar win. I had no idea how much he owed Gomez or what he borrowed off Mendez, but I could sense that Miguel was walking away with a healthy profit. He tipped his head at the man, his right eyebrow arching.

"We need to talk...in private." The man's sharp gaze hit me. I shrunk back from it, too afraid to whip off his mask in case I saw an exaggerated version of his unsettling expression.

Fear skittered across Miguel's unmasked face. I fingered the diamonds around my wrist, trying to hide my disquiet. Gazing down at me, Miguel flicked his head. "Go wait in the car."

I had no choice but to obey. The double doors closed behind me and all I could do was limp my way to the Mercedes. The valet opened my door with a kind smile and I slid into the car, slipping off my shoes and bending down to rub my protesting toes.

It felt like forever, waiting in torturous cluelessness.

What had Shadow Man wanted?

Why had Miguel looked so nervous?

Had we been busted? Was some thug about to stomp out of the casino and rip me from the car?

By the time Miguel appeared, my imagination had turned me into a quivering mess.

Popping his briefcase full of cash in the backseat, he

slammed his door and we pulled out of the resort.

"Was everything okay?"

"Just business," Miguel mumbled, his eyes on the road. I could only see his profile, but his tight expression was thunderous.

I licked my lower lip. "For a moment there, I thought we might have been caught."

His lips were tight as they rose into a half-smile. "No. We were fine."

An eerie silence descended and I was left to stew in it for the duration of the trip back. It seemed weird that I was actually looking forward to returning to Casa Evil Pit, but I was. I couldn't wait to get out of the revealing dress and heavy jewelry. I wanted to hop into a hot bath, put my sweats on and just pretend like it was a normal Thanksgiving. I wasn't wearing a watch, but I could tell by the sky that we were nearing dusk.

My family would all be sitting on the couches in the living room, their bellies stuffed, watching the game. I should have been with them, or better yet, in Eric's arms, somewhere warm and private where we could make up for lost time.

I'd only been holding him less than two weeks ago, but it felt like forever.

We drove through the tunnel and into the garage. I snatched my shoes out of the car before being dragged back up the stairs. Miguel made me wait in the darkness while he checked the room for an all-clear. Moments later, he pulled me inside and we hustled through

Quella's room.

The briefcase in Miguel's hand dropped to the floor as we entered my room. I gazed past his arm and gasped.

Mendez was standing by my window. He was now in a business suit and looked ready for his important meeting.

Good. It meant the nightmare was nearly over...but that didn't stop the terror hammering inside of me.

"Not so sick after all, I see." Mendez turned and walked toward me, slow painful steps that had my heart leaping into my throat.

I stayed silent.

I had no defense for my lie.

His eyes shifted to the briefcase on the floor. "Gambling again, Miguel." He rubbed his fingers together. "I guess I cannot tell you how to spend your money, but I can tell you this." His voice shifted from warmth to ice. "I do not mind you having your fun, dressing up whatever dolls you need to and parading them around, but you keep your hands off Quella's friends."

Miguel looked at me, putting on a show by studying me with a lust-filled gaze. Even though it was fake I felt completely violated. I rubbed my hand over my arm and squeezed my elbow.

"What if they come onto me?" Miguel's voice was even, but I could see the contempt. He hated his boss far more than I thought he did.

Mendez smirked. "You are a handsome man. I know you don't have a problem finding available women. You can pick and choose whoever you like." An unspoken message traveled between them and I had to assume he was talking about the merchandise he had locked up downstairs. Thank God they would be out of his snare soon.

"But you do not touch her," Mendez finished.

With a flick of his head, he dismissed Miguel. His head of security straightened his jacket and collected his briefcase with the dignity of a king. I watched him leave the room, silently begging for him not to leave me alone. He opened the door and turned to look at me, a wave of pity cresting over his features. My heart began to gallop, nearly exploding when his phone rang. The unexpected noise made me flinch. He pulled the device from his inner jacket pocket and gazed at the screen, his eyes flicking to mine before he slipped out the door.

Snake eyes.

My innards trembled. I had no idea what his final gaze meant, but the disquiet within me grew to a rumbling shout of warning. Unfortunately there was no time to worry about it, because my greatest threat remained with me in the room.

I turned to face the viper. I'd never felt more alone in my entire life.

Mendez's lips twitched as he studied me.

"Nice dress." The back of his finger trailed softly down my arm.

My heart spasmed as he stepped around me, his finger traveling over the exposed skin at my back.

"It used to belong to my wife, you know."

I swallowed, tears burning my eyes.

He stopped in front of me, his expression turning stone cold before he raised his hand in a flash and cracked it across my cheek.

I stumbled back, clutching at my face.

"She was a slut, too." He grabbed my arm, pulling me against him. "And I had to teach her some very tough lessons."

He grabbed my face, his thumb and forefinger digging into my cheeks.

"My daughter trusts you, but I do not think she should. I will not allow her to associate with liars and whores."

Breaths shot through my nostrils, puffing onto his hand. His gaze grew even more malignant, the next layer of his mask disintegrating and showing me the delight he'd take in punishing me.

Fear was pulsing through me in such violent waves I thought I might pass out.

There was no escape from this.

There was no Kaplan.

No Rhodes.

No Eric.

forty-three

eric

"What the hell are you doing here?" My jaw was clenched so tight I thought my teeth might fracture.

Seeing my father standing there after all this time made me sick.

"Saving your life."

My brow furrowed. I hated that I owed him that. I hated that I looked like him. I hated that I was his son.

Gramps had been my real father.

My eyes flicked to the table, my body convulsing as I took in his lifeless legs. Falling to my knees, I crawled over to him. His torso was coated in blood, his lips parted, his vacant eyes gazing at the ceiling. Shuffling my arm beneath him, I lifted his body against me.

"Gramps." I choked out the words, pressing my lips against his smooth head and feeling the wail travel up my body. It exploded out of me, a loud anguished roar that made my muscles tremble. The sound melted away to be replaced with a desolate whine.

My fingers dug into his shoulders, clutching him to me as tears singed my eyes. I squeezed them shut, sobs shaking my entire body. I held them in, my anguish vibrating through my muscles in silence.

This couldn't be real. He couldn't be gone.

"Son, we have to keep moving. It's not safe here." Dad's voice cracked as he crouched down in front of me, gently wriggling Gramps out of my grasp. I would have fought him if I hadn't been shaking so badly.

Dad laid his father on the floor. Sorrow washed over his expression as he carefully closed his father's eyes.

"I'm sorry I didn't get here sooner, Pop." His lips wobbled. "I'm sorry."

I wanted to push him away. He had no right to speak to Gramps that way.

Get here sooner? Where the hell had he been all these years?

I looked over at the two dead bodies.

"Who are they?" My whisper was metallic.

"My past." Dad's voice came out rough and gravely. "I've tried to avoid this happening for the last eight years, but it's catching up with me. I'm sorry." He stood tall and brushed a hand over his face. "Grab your stuff, just the essentials. We need to keep moving."

My glare was black and menacing as I slowly rose to face him. "What the hell is going on?"

"I don't have time to explain right now." Dad raised his hands. "But you have to come with me."

"I'm not going anywhere with you." I stepped away from him. "I've gotta go get Caity."

I'd just lost the most important man in my life; I wasn't about to lose the most important woman.

Charging into my room, I whipped off my bloodstained shirt and dropped it on the floor. My eyes burned. That was Gramps's blood.

Sucking in a breath, I forced myself to turn away and snatch yesterday's shirt off the end of my bed. Yanking it on, I grabbed my wallet and the rest of my gear.

Dad stayed hot on my heels.

"Don't be an idiot. Eric! You think these are the only two? There'll be more men out to get you."

"Why?" I wrenched my bag out from under the bed and scowled at him.

He gripped the doorframe, his head drooping with a heavy sigh. "Because I was a foolish man and I stole from the wrong guy...and now that they know you exist, they're gonna make you pay for it."

My jaw worked to the side as I tried to absorb his words.

I wanted to launch into a diatribe about what a fucking loser he was, but I didn't want to waste the time. I made a move to shove past him, but he blocked my way.

"Please, you have to come with me. Let me hide you. Keep you safe."

"I'm not running away. My only concern now is Caity. She needs me, and I'm not going to abandon her just to save my own ass." I shoved his shoulder but he sprung back, grabbing my shirt.

His sharp, angular features grew hard. "You think that's what I did?"

"I don't give a shit why you left." I tried to wriggle free of his grasp but he fought me, clinging tight. Using my shoulder, I shoved him back against the wall.

The air was knocked from his lungs and I took advantage of his weakened state, driving my fist into his cheek. His head spun back, blood spurting from his nose as he crumpled to the floor.

Leaping over him, I raced out of the house, not even sparing a final look at Gramps. I had to get Caity. That could be my only focus or I'd combust, burn up in a fiery hell of knowledge.

My life was splintering around me and the only thing I had left was my girl.

Revving the engine, I spun my jeep out of the driveway and sped to L.A.

forty-four

caitlyn

A malicious smile curved the edges of Mendez's lips. He still held my face, making my teeth cut into my cheeks. I blinked, desperately trying to figure a way out. His face was giving me nothing. There was no goodness to play on, there was no shred of anything I could appease to make him think twice about this.

Maybe Quella.

He had a soft spot for her.

My mind groped for something to say.

He let me go, shoving me away from him before back-handing me. I fell to the floor, sobs quivering my belly. I felt like I was starring in a Spanish soap opera, except this time there would be no ad break to end the drama.

I kept my eyes on the ground, waiting for whatever would come next.

What did he plan to do with me?

Unlike Miguel, this guy was straight; I could tell by the way he eyed me as I walked into his house that first day.

Pressing my lips together, I tried to ease the shakes as he dug his fingers into my armpit and pulled me back to my feet. His hand was hard as he brushed the hair off my face, running his fingers down my neck and giving it a rough squeeze.

"I'm going to—"

There was a quick rap at the door.

"*Quel!*" he barked.

"*Lo siento, Señor, pero sus asociados han llegado,*" came a nervous reply.

I had no idea what she said, but he let me go. Stepping back, Mendez straightened his suit, adjusting his tie and stretching his neck before looking at me.

"We'll finish this later." He pointed at me. "Do not leave this room."

He walked to the door and yelled something in

Spanish. A few moments later, one of his guards appeared.

"*Asegúrese de que ella se queda aquí.*"

The guard nodded at him and eyed me curiously before closing the door. He obviously knew better than to question his boss...whatever the hell his boss had said. I was guessing it was something along the lines of *don't let her leave or I'll kick your ass.*

The silence left in the room was deafening; the only thing to break it was the flick of a lock on the adjoining room door. I raced toward it, tugging desperately, but it wouldn't budge.

My legs buckled. I crumpled to the floor, tears shaking my body. Gripping the carpet, I let out a soft moaning wail, panic stealing any sense of calm from me. My mind felt like hot mush, my thoughts floating in a black sea.

I had no idea what horrors awaited me or what Mendez might do when he got back from his meeting.

My head popped up.

His meeting.

Was that now? Was that what that lady had said?

Wait, *asociados.* Did that mean associates? As in business associates!

Hope spurted through me.

I scrambled to the bedroom door, clawing the carpet as I crawled. My dress caught on my knee, ripping the split. I tugged it free and bundled it against my belly, blundering to my feet. Pressing my ear against the wood, I waited—listening, hoping.

My breaths were erratic, punching out of me, begging my deliverance to come at any moment.

It started with a loud bang, a thud of a door and officers yelling.

"FBI, freeze!"

A sobbing laugh spurted out of my mouth.

Gunfire quickly followed and the screams of confused staff rang through the house. I yanked on the door trying to pull it open, but it was locked, as well.

"Shit." I knelt in front of it, calling into the keyhole. "Please, let me out!" I pressed my ear against the wood again, then bent down to look under the door. "Is anybody there?"

There were no shadows; the guard must have left. I plopped onto my butt and spun around, leaning my head against the wood. I supposed I was safest in here anyway. The FBI would surely sweep the house and they'd find me.

Thank God it was over.

Hopefully they'd find the girls quickly and get them out of the terrifying fray.

The muffled shouts of FBI agents continued to swarm throughout the house. Machine gunfire punctuated the calls, a new wave of panic traveling through the house as Mendez's men fought back.

My heart beat erratically, breaths shooting out of my nose.

And then it went silent.

I held my breath, praying no agents were injured in the short battle. Pressing my ear to the door, I strained to hear what was going on, but I couldn't make out anything distinct, the muted noises blending into one messy sound.

There was a thud against the wood and I scrambled away from it.

Yes! The calvary!

It was over. I could go home.

Standing back, I blinked at tears of relief until the door flew open...and all hope failed me.

forty-five

caitlyn

My chest heaved as I took in the sight of Miguel, his broad frame filing the doorway. He stood there smirking at me; his intense gaze could strip paint. Mask or not, his expression was the same: he wanted me. I could only guess what for. All I knew with definite certainty was that he had absolutely no intention of handing me over to the FBI.

I whimpered, spinning for the adjoining door. Wrapping my hands around the handle, I shook it violently and banged the wood.

"Help me!" I screamed.

My cries were silenced swiftly. His strong hand wrapped around my mouth, squeezing me into submission as a cold, metal edge caressed my neck. It felt like a knife, a big sharp one that could slit my throat in a second.

"Do not make another sound."

My head bobbed and I let him shuffle me back toward the main bedroom door. Peeking out into the hallway, he began running us along the corridor when the sound of scurrying feet started up the stairs.

"I want each room checked and cleared!"

Rhodes!

My eyes grew wide with elation. He was coming. He'd find me.

Miguel quickly backtracked, ducking into Quella's room and heading for the mirrored closet. I tried to struggle before he dragged me in there and closed the wall behind us, but the point of his knife made my body acquiesce. The sharp sting was only a small taste of what he'd do to me if I screwed this up for him.

Scuffling feet entered the room. Miguel went still, pulling me against him and digging the knife a little further into my skin.

The instinct to stay alive beat through me, slamming into my aching head.

A trickle of blood oozed down my neck. It tickled as it trailed over my skin, but I dared not move. Biting my lips together, I stayed statue-still as the men swept the room.

I figured Miguel was waiting for them to leave before making his way down the stairs. He didn't want to make any noise behind the wall and alert anyone. If I did, he'd slit my throat before they could even get to me. At least if I stayed with him, there might be a chance of escape. Kaplan said the house was surrounded; they could pick us up in Miguel's getaway car.

"Clear!"

"Clear!"

"Good, check the next room."

Tears popped onto my lashes as I heard Rhodes's voice.

A cellphone rang. Miguel tensed, his arm around my torso squeezing hard. He was growing impatient.

"Yeah, Rhodes....uh-huh...Excellent." I heard the smile in his voice. "They found the girls."

I closed my eyes. In spite of my current status, relief flooded through me.

They were safe.

My mission was complete.

"Copy that," Rhodes said. "I'll keep searching up here for any other occupants."

Please find me! Search a little harder!

Someone stepped into the room. "Both rooms clear, sir."

"Okay." Rhodes sounded hesitant. "Any sign of Caitlyn Davis yet?"

My chest heaved and the urge to scream was nearly too strong to resist. The knife dug in so hard, I flinched. A whimper sounded in my throat and Miguel's hand came back over my mouth.

"I will kill you," he breathed into my ear.

"....Quella Mendez is already with the men downstairs."

"Does she know anything?"

"No, sir. She said her friend was sick and went upstairs to lie down."

"Well, she must be up here somewhere then. We'll sweep the rest of the rooms and if we can't find her, bring Quella up here for questioning. I'm not leaving without Davis."

"Yes, sir."

We waited out the shuffling feet and remained still even after the room was silent. Miguel must have been counting or something, because I heard him finally mutter, "*Cien*" before yanking me down the stairs.

He set a quick pace and I ended up tripping down the last few stairs and twisting my ankle. He had no patience, throwing me roughly over his shoulder. I beat his back and screamed while I got the chance, but he took the blows without flinching.

No one came running down the stairs to find me; my cacophony went unnoticed and was rapidly silenced when he dumped me into the trunk of a car.

"No, wait!"

The lid slammed shut and I was shrouded in darkness. The engine rumbled to life and the car screamed out of the garage. I was knocked around, whacking the back of my head before being thrown forward and jamming my fingers as I tried to stop myself from smashing into the hard edging.

I whimpered and cried, terror eating away at the air in my lungs. As we sped to who knew where, my body was tossed and thrown about like a Raggedy Ann doll. I wasn't measuring the time, but it felt like we sped along for nearly an hour. I waited desperately for the car to stop, for some kind of roadblock to discover me.

As soon as the car slowed and pulled to the side, I began my scream-fest. "Let me out! Someone help me!"

The trunk popped open. The sky was a dusky blue, the sun setting in the distance.

"Shut up!" Miguel slapped me.

I bit the edge of my cheek, tasting blood. I was tempted to spit it at him, but another face appeared.

Shadow Man.

He gazed down at me, his expression hard and stony.

I tried to pull his mask free but before I could, his hand reached toward me. There was a white cloth in it. I struggled away, slapping at him, Miguel caught my wrists and wrenched them clear.

Holding the top of my head steady, Shadow Man

pressed the cloth over my mouth and nose until my violent struggling turned to slop. My arms went limp, my head lolling to the side, and the world around me fuzzed.

"She's worth at least a hundred thousand. My debt is now clear."

The distorted voice crackled in my ear and then faded into silence, oblivion capturing me in a cruel hold.

forty-six

eric

I made it back to L.A. by nightfall. Pulling into my driveway, I shoved up the hand brake and leapt from the car, nearly leaving my keys in the ignition. I wrenched them free and dove up the stairs, wrestling the front door open.

"Scott!"

I'd tried calling him every fifteen minutes on the way

up, but his phone was off.

"Scott, you home?" I strode down to his room, flinging the door open.

Piper gasped, clutching a sheet across her naked body. "What the hell, Eric! Don't you knock?"

"Sorry," I muttered, looking at the floor. "Where's Scott?"

"Here." I spun around and saw him standing behind me. A towel was wrapped around his waist and his hair was wet and spiky.

"I've been trying to call you," I snapped, frustration and embarrassment making my voice sharp.

"Oh, yeah, sorry, Piper and I were..." He pointed through the doorway, trailing off as he caught his fiancee's pointed expression. He cleared his throat. "You got my message?"

"Yeah," I breathed. "That's why I'm here. Where is she?"

"I don't know." Scott winced, looking a little sick over the whole thing. "She said she was going out of town with Quella, right? But she didn't tell me where." He flicked his thumb down the hallway, indicating my room. "She left you a note."

I busted past him, lunging into my room and snatching the note off my bed.

Tearing into it, I quickly scanned the words and plonked onto the mattress.

Sorry to put you through this, but I'm working an

undercover job and this is the only way to keep you safe.

I'll explain everything when I get back. Please trust me.

Living without you is a foreign concept to me. I could never break your heart.

I love you so completely.

Your girl-next-door forever xx C

I pressed my elbows into my knees, relief raining over me, big fat droplets filled with hope. She still loved me. She did want me and what we had wasn't over.

I scrunched the note in my hand, wondering what the hell she'd gotten herself into and if I could stand to just sit around and wait for her to come back.

Scott appeared in my doorway. "What'd it say?"

I held it out to him and he pressed it against his now-clothed chest to straighten it out. Lifting it up to the light, he read it. "Aw, shit."

"I know. I don't know who dragged her into it, but when I find out, I'm gonna kill them."

"What's going on?" Piper's head popped over Scott's shoulder. He held out the note to her and she quickly scanned it, her mouth dropping open. "That's why." She gasped. "That's why she was acting so weird. Why she didn't want to move in with us. It all makes sense now. I knew she wanted to!" Piper covered her mouth, pinching her nose and shaking her head. "Who could be controlling her decision? Why would she have to stay in the dorms?"

We all jerked still at the same moment, looking at each other before saying in unison, "Quella."

"Damn it." I reached for my phone. "Does anyone have her number?"

Scott and Piper both shook their heads.

I swore loudly, tempted to throw the phone across the room. "Well, who else! Why the hell would Quella be a person of interest and who would be interested in her?"

"Undercover operation, it'll either be the police or the FBI." Scott crossed his arms.

"Yeah, but they can't employ Caity..." I swallowed, dread building in my system. "Can they?"

"They can blackmail her, though," Scott said softly, waving Caity's note in the air. "The only way to keep you safe?" He read Caity's words aloud.

"Shit!" I wracked my hands through my hair.

"But who would—"

"Kaplan!" I spat.

"Oh shit, that's got to be." Piper seethed. "She's the only one ballsy and bitchy enough to pull Caity into one of her schemes."

"She couldn't possibly." Scott shook his head. "The FBI has protocols they have to follow."

"Oh, come on, protocols?" Piper scoffed. "Like all the ones she followed when she sent Caity into Cameron's house? If any agent is going to ignore the rules, it's Kaplan! I highly doubt her superiors knew a college freshman was involved in that sting operation; her ass would have been fired in a second. It didn't matter what we said in our exit interviews, she covered it up for sure."

"Do we even know if she still works for the FBI?" Scott's nose wrinkled.

"We know it's her." Piper threw her hands in the air. "You can't tell me she's not involved with this; my gut is screaming that she is!"

Scott scratched his hair, tipping his head with a look that told his girlfriend she was probably right. "What I don't get is...why Caity? Why use her again? I mean, I understand why they did last time, because of her connection with Cameron, but this time around, they could have picked any girl from the dorms. Heck, a young, trained agent could pull this gig off easily. Why pick an amateur sophomore?"

With a heavy sigh, I drooped my head. I figured it was time to tell them.

I hadn't uttered this secret to a soul.

It had been Caity's to keep, but she wasn't there to stop me, and if it could help me find her, then it was worth it. I pressed my elbows into my knees and muttered, "You guys remember the first time you met Caity?"

"Yeah, for that lunch thing." Scott nodded. "She was having trouble with the Donovan brothers."

"Do you guys remember what we told you?"

Piper gasped again. "I'd completely forgotten about

that!"

"What?" Scott glanced at his girl.

"She can read people, right? Like, has really phenomenal observation skills or something?"

"It's more than that." I shook my head. "It's like a freaking super power and Kaplan's using it." My voice quivered with rage as I looked at my friends. "Caity can read people. She knows how they're feeling, and if they're lying. She can read emotions and say all the right things to get them talking...and Kaplan knows this." My jaw clenched tight. I closed my eyes and threaded my fingers together, squeezing until I thought my bones might crack. "She's using my girl and she's put her in danger, I just know it." My eyes popped open.

"So, what do we do?" Piper crossed her arms.

I stood from my bed, running my hands through my hair again. "We're gonna find Caity, and we're gonna pull her out of this before something bad happens to her."

"What if something already has?" Piper whispered.

Tears stung my eyes as I looked at my friends, desperation clawing at me. My insides felt shredded, raw, incapable...but I couldn't give in.

"I have to find her." My voice wobbled. "I have to bring her home. I don't care what it costs me, but I am not resting until she is back in my arms."

TO BE CONTINUED...

****

Can Eric stay out of danger long enough to find Caity and save her?

Keep reading to find out what happens in the explosive conclusion—Poker Face (Masks #4)

dear reader...

The ending of this book is a nail biter. Thankfully, Poker Face is already available, so you don't have to wait to find out what's going to happen.

The one hope in this dire situation is that Caity and Eric's love for each other is stronger than ever. And they're going to need every ounce of their strength and determination as they fight this final battle.

Caity and Eric are about to come face-to-face with an evil darker than anything they've encountered before.

Caity has been sold to a wealthy casino owner, and Eric is being tracked by a man who wants to make his father suffer.

Can they find each other and disappear before it's too late?

Find out in the gripping conclusion to The Masks Series.

xx
Melissa

acknowledgements

Once again, I have a long list of people I want to thank for their contribution to this story.

Margery - the original publisher and editor. Thanks for being so great to work with.

Emily - your cover is beautiful!! Nailed it!

Cassie and Rae - thank you SO much for your feedback. Cassie - you always have the best insights and Rae - your knowledge of Spanish was so brilliant.

Lindsey, Karen, Kristin & Marcia - thanks for being the final eyes on this project.

Rachael - thank you is never a sufficient word to express how grateful I am for all you do.

Songbirds & Playmakers - I love hanging out with you guys!! Thanks for your enthusiasm and awesomeness.

My readers - what would I do without you? Thank you so, so much.

My dear friends and family - thank you for always

believing in me and giving me the right pep-talks on the days it gets too hard. I love you for everything you pour into my life.

My Lord and Saviour - thank you for giving up everything to rescue me, for never turning your back on me and showing me what real, unconditional love looks like. I love you with all my heart.